P9-BZX-924

GIRL
MINUS
X

ALSO BY ANNE STONE

jacks: a gothic gospel
Hush
Delible

A Buckrider Book

This is a work of fiction. All characters, organizations, places and events portrayed are either products of the author's imagination or are used fictitiously. Any resemblance to actual persons, living or dead; events or locales is entirely coincidental.

Buckrider Books is an imprint of Wolsak and Wynn Publishers.

Cover design: Michel Vrana
Interior design: Jennifer Rawlinson
Cover image: Tocarciuc Dumitru / istockphoto.com
Author photograph: Hiromi Goto
Typeset in Cambria and Virgo 01
Printed by Rapido Books, Montreal, Canada
Printed on certified 100% post-consumer Rolland Enviro Paper.

10 9 8 7 6 5 4 3 2 1

The publisher gratefully acknowledges the support of the BC Arts Council, the Ontario Arts Council, the Canada Council for the Arts and the Government of Canada.

Buckrider Books
280 James Street North
Hamilton, ON
Canada L8R 2L3

Library and Archives Canada Cataloguing in Publication

Title: Girl minus X / by Anne Stone.
Names: Stone, Anne, 1969- author.
Identifiers: Canadiana 20200172387 | ISBN 9781989496114 (softcover)
Classification: LCC PS8587.T659 G75 2020 | DDC C813/.54—dc23

For Wayde & Senna (my loves).

PART ONE

| CHAPTER 0 = X + 1

Dany can just make out the ruined rails of the roller coaster, its black bones rising into the sky. She knows better than to be here. Knows to leave well enough alone. Knows the smart thing to do is turn her back and say goodbye. She knows all of this, but it's not so easy letting go of those you love. So Dany takes one step and then another, huffing her way up the hill, as her kid sister falls behind.

When they crest the hill, she sees the whole of the prison. The old racetrack is girded by fences, each topped with razor wire. Where once were horses, she sees infected. Where once were grooms, she sees prisoners in orange jumpsuits. And watching over all of them, inside and out, military guards.

Below them, scattered across the face of the hill, a dozen little groups. The families of the women they've locked up inside. Some cluster around foam coolers, some sit on what scant grass can be found and some, she can tell, have given up on the visit. Laid out on old blankets, their faces are tuned to the clouds. Some, like her, have one eye on the prison-hospice. Dany is scanning the compound when the kid's tiny hand slips into hers. Tugs once, twice.

"Give me a sec," she tells Mac. Dany wants to see Aunt Norah, but there's no sign of their aunt. Not yet. But there, just inside the fence, Dany spots a chicken coop. Beside the coop, a half dozen birds are stacked in tiny cages. Stunned and ragged, the birds shift on bony feet. In one of the cages, a bird lays dead. Its legs jut out, stiff as Popsicle sticks.

There's an old and stunted apple tree at the bottom of the hill. But it's not nearly tall enough, and besides, it's too far from the fence. But there, beyond the apple tree, she sees an enormous maple with leaves the size of dishrags. The maple is close to the fence, and a few of its branches arch up and over the barbed wire. Her eyes follow the largest branch, trace a path over the razor wire, make the ten-foot drop to the chicken coop's roof.

Again with the tugging, but Dany is looking at the racecourse – an oval track dotted with a hundred of the infected. More virals than she's ever seen together in one place.

Stick thin legs. Sallow skin. A strange human herd.

Only *herd* isn't the right word. Together like this, the infected don't move like any group of animals Dany's ever seen. They don't move like a crowd of people, either. Each viral's path is erratic. When she traces pathways over the track, she sees dark particles in a stirred glass. Atoms in Brownian motion. And then a picture of the virals lives in her mental album, too, for always, added to all of everything she's ever seen in the world.

At the centre of the field, a few virals stand with faces tipped to the sun, stumbling in slow circles. She takes in each of their faces, but none is familiar, or else all of them are, with that strange, waxen skin. On each yellow jacket a little metal clasp flashes when the viral hits six o'clock. Round and round they go, slowly spinning tops.

The virus, she knows, has left its mark on the brains of the infected. At this stage, the grey matter is riddled with tiny holes. The hypothalamus has shrivelled up like an old pea. And the cortex and medial temporal lobe are pitted with deep, unforgiving lesions. The virus causes all kinds of psychiatric symptoms. But that's not what gets to Dany. What gets to her is this: Once the disease has gone this far, the infected forget. They forget just about everything. They forget to even care. They forget friends and loved ones. They forget how to act. How to be. They forget *who* to be. Looking out over the prison-hospice, Dany knows that the virals she sees are literally dying. But at this stage, people say, death hardly makes a difference.

And maybe one day none of this will matter. To anyone.

Maybe one day, if the virus infects enough people, they'll just run out of fence. If that day comes, the whole world will be a hospice. Maybe then, places like this will be reserved for the uninfected, the few who can't help but remember – themselves, the past, all the rest of what once was. Maybe one day it'll be Dany inside the fence.

The kid gives Dany's hand another yank. Only this time, the kid tugs so hard she nearly takes Dany's hand off at the root.

"Hey," Dany says. But looking down, she sees her sister's brown eyes, huge with need. Hungry. That's what the kid is. That's what they both are. Pretty much all the time, these days. "Lunch?" Dany asks with a yawn.

For a bright penny of a second, Dany thinks she's actually done it, that the kid is going to answer. For a moment, Mac's big brown eyes fix on Dany. Like a goldfish, that little mouth opens. But with a final yank, the kid lets go and stomps off towards the apple tree.

| | |

They picnic under the apple tree, in spite of the mud, in spite of the smell. This close to the fence, the smell of shit and bleach is overpowering. By the time Dany has taken her first bite, her kid sister, sandwich in pocket, has abandoned their muddy blanket.

The kid monkeys her way halfway up the trunk and clings to it, looking down at Dany. Blinking expectantly. Slowly, Dany rises and makes her way to the trunk, giving the kid a leg up. Mac settles herself in a nook, pulls her glass-eyed doll out of her backpack. The kid takes tiny bites of her sandwich, offers it to the doll, the two small figures framed by a clutch of scrawny buds. She looks sort of peaceful up there, in that gnarled old knot of a tree. Nesting there, among the apple buds, the kid almost looks safe. But then, kids fall out of trees all the time. Break arms. Dislocate elbows. An unlucky kid might even crack a skull.

The letter the prison sent Dany said this would be a picnic.

But there are no birds or dragonflies. No pond for her sister to skip stones into. Just a balding hill, with more bare spots than grass. And spread out across the rounded side of the hill, a dozen tiny groups – families, friends, the people who belong to the women locked up with the infected inside. All around the hill, swirling and settling on each of their skins, the sounds and smells of dying virals.

Only it isn't virals dying inside of the hospice, not really. It's people. Isn't it?

Maybe not legally, not anymore, but Dany knows it.

They're people still.

| | |

On the highway, eighteen-wheelers kick up clouds of dust and ash-laden smoke drifts out of the prison-hospice. Soon, every last bit of her is covered in a film of grit. The stench of the place licks at Dany's clothes and seeps into her bread sandwich. Still, she's hungry, and she isn't going to let a little soot get in the way.

As she eats, Dany watches the yard.

On the other side of the fence, pair by pair, a group of prisoners gather up. It's not possible to pick her aunt out of the bunch. Not at this distance. Not when all of their faces are grey with sweat and ash.

As she waits, Dany digs into her backpack, pulls out a pair of books.

The first is a primer on security systems and cryptography. The other, a coil-bound photocopy of a prison guard manual, courtesy of Antoine. Between each page she reads, Dany scans the compound. Finally, it's her aunt's name in the guard's mouth. Finally, her aunt Norah is standing on the other side of the fence and there's a spot for Dany and the kid, down by the red rope, just opening up.

"Hey, Mac," Dany shouts and, without waiting, makes her way down.

| | |

There, on the other side of that red rope, past the scrabble of bare dirt that is the no-go zone, past the chain-link fence, stands Aunt Norah and another prisoner, the two chained at the wrist. Dany takes in her aunt's orange jumpsuit. The suit is covered in filth, and the ankles and cuffs are practically black. On her chained wrist, the fabric is threadbare and worn. Slowly, the chain is wearing holes into the suit. Into their lives. Into everything.

The rope might only put a few extra feet between Dany and her aunt, but that little whisper of distance changes everything. The red rope puts an end to quiet talk. Outlaws affection. Next to the highway, like this, Dany will have to yell just to be heard.

But what Dany has come to say can't be shouted.

Some words can't be said that loud. Some words can barely be said out loud at all. Dany studies the vacant-eyed guards, there, at either end of the red rope like a pair of stupid bookends. But one look and she knows. The guards they've posted out here might be bored out of their skulls, but they're taking it in. They're listening, hard.

When Dany finally looks at Norah's face, her aunt is looking past Dany, searching the hillside. "Where's Mac," Norah asks, but her voice is barely audible over the traffic. "Where is she?" she calls. Louder this time.

Dany nods back at the apple tree and, glancing down at her aunt's mud-caked boots, she takes in that chain. The chain will be a problem. A three-foot-long problem, to be exact; one that binds Norah to the gap-toothed redhead beside her. Dany adds one three-foot-long metal chain to her mental list.

The prisoner with the bottle-red hair, meanwhile, is making herself heard too. And beside Dany – so close that when the wind shifts, she can smell her – a musty old woman is cussing. Working herself up. Words hurtle through the air all around Dany. And beneath it all, like a river, she hears the muttering of the infected and the low groans of passing trucks.

"Dany," her aunt is saying. "Hey, honey, look at me. Focus."

Dany's eyes find the red rope. The fence. The outline of her aunt behind it.

"Where's your papa?"

Dany frowns.

She doesn't know why Norah cares about Antoine so much. After all, everything is Antoine's fault. Pretty much everything that's ever gone wrong for Dany can be traced back to Antoine, one way or another. If Norah hadn't gotten involved with Antoine, her aunt would still be at home. Still cleaning houses. They'd be hungry, sure, they'd be having a hard time making one end meet the other, but they'd be together. Now, thanks to Antoine, Dany and her aunt are screwed. "I'm an orphan," she says with a shrug.

"Jesus," her aunt says. "Can you let it go?" Norah shakes her head and takes a deep breath. When she tries again, she clasps the fence, as if she needs something to hold her up. "Look, where's Antoine?" she asks.

But Dany shrugs the question off.

She has so much to tell her aunt. There's so much to work out between them. She glances at the closest guard. Focuses on his heavy black boots. But she can feel it. A pair of cold blue eyes shift in their sockets, take her in. Dany draws in a quick breath, glances back at her aunt.

"Talk to me," her aunt is saying. "Where are you staying?"

Dany shrugs again. "Home," she says.

"Antoine's farm. You two are at the farm?"

Dany shakes her head, no. Shrugs.

And everything falls to pieces. Because there, in the yard, just behind her aunt, the world has gone topsy-turvy. A fight has broken out. Or worse. Dany nods her chin at the ruckus just behind Norah.

Norah turns, and her whole body tenses up. Because there, in the prison yard behind her aunt, the group of waiting prisoners has parted – moving back in a loose circle – drawing an anxious ring around a pair of prisoners. At first, Dany thinks the woman has been hurt and that's why she's screaming. Screaming and tugging at her chain. But when Dany traces the chain to the other end, she sees the real problem.

There, lying on the ground, a prisoner is face down in the muck. Her face half buried in the foul stuff. Her head is wildly thrashing. Above her, the other prisoner is yanking on the chain that binds them – trying to get away. She yanks so hard that the prone woman's arm pops right out of its socket.

All around them, the world has gone quiet.

And in that quiet, Dany hears the sound of bone, dislodged. Hears sinew, tearing. An echo of it there, in her head. For always. And ever.

Norah takes one step back. And another. Presses her back against the fence, dividing her jumpsuit into small orange diamonds. But Aunt Norah has hit the hard limit of her world. There's nowhere for her to go.

Dany takes in the prisoner, face down in the yard, thrashing. She knows what an epileptic seizure looks like. But this is no ordinary seizure – no, this is something worse. Dany studies the prone prisoner, there, convulsing in the muck. Jasper, her biology mentor at the lab, would see it too. One look and he'd see it. This woman is sick. Something has shorted the circuits in her brain. Dany tries to get a look at the prisoner's eyes, her pupils, but, with all that thrashing, it's impossible. As she watches, she feels her little sister's hand glide into hers. Feels tiny fingers gripping her own, falling slack, gripping again, as the kid's huge eyes take all of it in.

A shrill alarm splits the air and, for a long beat, Dany forgets all about her mentor.

Forgets the woman, seizing up in the muck.

Forgets her aunt, back pressed to the fence.

Forgets everything, except that tiny hand in hers.

| | |

For a long time, the air screams, and when the screaming stops, when all is quiet, Dany's ears ring with an echo of the alarm.

Before her, the rope trembles. The guards, on either end, have unclasped the hooks. As she watches, the red rope drops to the ground, lifeless, a skinned snake. Dany grips her sister's tiny hand, grips it hard.

The closest guard turns on Dany and the kid, taking the two of them in. His hand hovers over his baton before settling on his belt buckle. He leans in. "Go on," he tells her. "Get out of here."

Dany grabs up her backpack and takes hold of her sister's hand. But the kid's feet are planted in the earth. "We've got to go," Dany tells her. "Now." But the kid just stands there, staring past the fence, at the outline of her aunt.

Dany follows Mac's gaze, takes one last look.

She gets it, she does. Her little sister wants their aunt to face them, to acknowledge them one last time. To hold up a single hand. To wave. To let them know she'll be okay. But the guard shifts his hand, takes hold of his baton.

"Move," Dany hisses. She tugs on that little arm and the kid stumbles forward a step. And then Mac just stands there, again, staring up at Dany out of bottomless eyes.

"Aunt Norah will be okay," Dany tells her. "She can handle herself."

The guard steps forward, eyes on Dany.

"We're going," Dany says and pulls. But the kid is a square wheel, so Dany has no choice. She drags her sister away. Time and again, the kid squirms from her grip and, turning back, fixes big eyes on the yard. Another need as insistent as hunger has taken hold.

"She'll be okay, I swear."

The kid looks up, searches Dany's face.

"I swear," Dany whispers. "I've got a plan. I promise. I will get Norah out."

| | |

Back at home, Mac goes for the Scrabble box. The kid gives the box a shake and stares up at her sister.

But Dany looks from the game to their ancient answering machine. The dusty black box is analogue. Inside, there is a tiny compartment to hold a little tape cassette. The thing belonged to Antoine – who is seriously paranoid about digital technology. On the black box, a little light blinks red.

Dany knows it will be bad news – because it's always bad news – but she hits the button anyway. On the inside of her chest, there's this tiny whisper of hope that refuses to die. The little whisper is telling her that maybe Eva called. Maybe Eva is on her way over.

But the first message is from the phone company. Not only are landlines being permanently phased out, but their bill is past due. Dany hits the button again, and the tape skips forward. The machine blips and there, from that dusty plastic box, comes the voice of a tired old man.

"Danielle, mon chou, it's me, it's papa," the voice on the machine says. The kid sets down the Scrabble box and stares, head cocked.

Dany frowns.

"You're mad. I understand." Antoine sighs, and for a beat, there is the sound of his tired breaths. "Can you tell Mac there's going to be chicks?" he tries. "Four, five days more, I think. Maybe she wants to come see the baby chickens hatch. Maybe you both want to come and see. I've fixed up rooms for both of you. You know that I –"

Dany hits the button and the machine shuts off. But too late. The kid is looking up at her, eyes bright. She's heard it all. With a sigh, Dany reaches for the phone. "I'll call, I'll call," she tells Mac. "Stupid chickens."

But the kid is grinning.

Dany picks up the phone and frowns. Taps on the little button. But when she holds the receiver to her ear, there's no dial tone. No nothing. Just a dead hunk of plastic. Because they've finally done it. Cut the landline off.

She holds the telephone out to her little sister and shrugs.

| CHAPTER 0 = X + 2

She doesn't know if it's the failed visit, Antoine's call or the dead telephone. Maybe it's the long session of failed Scrabble, in which the kid breaks all of Dany's simple words into random bits of sound. What is *mo* and *cu* and *ga* supposed to mean, anyway? She doesn't know what does it – but that night, sleep takes a long, long time to come.

For what feels like a hundred years, Dany lays there, staring at the popcorn ceiling over their bed. She thinks about their file, sitting on a desk at the ministry. At some point, somebody will figure out that they're on their own. And then there's the rent she can't pay. She pictures the chickens at the prison-hospice, the ones who woke one day in a cage inside of a jail. She thinks of the rats at the lab, the half-empty shelves at the food bank and the prisoner who went down, thrashing. Her arm half out of its socket. As Dany stares at the little spikes of stucco, her mind is an unhappy Ping-Pong ball, and the little stucco spikes are like needles in her eyes.

A second later, an hour later, a million years gone – Dany doesn't know – but she's up with a start, clawing at the twisted comforter. Her heart skitters and skips, and her breaths come in tiny gasps. Dawn is bleeding through the threadbare sheet they use as a curtain.

But she is here, Dany tells herself. She is here, and here is home.

Dany tears the coverlet off her arms, freeing herself. But for a long time, she looks at that sun-faded sheet. Traces each stain and tear. Wrapping her arms around her chest, she breathes, and the fingers of her nightmare slowly loosen their grip.

Still, the feeling of the dream is slow to die.

Dany takes in her small room, in all its solid reality.

She makes herself look at her dresser, take in each chip in the paint. *Two, three, five.* She makes herself look at the wall beside her bed, smudged with dozens of tiny Mac-size handprints. *Seventeen, nineteen, twenty-three.* And all the while, she runs her primes. *Forty-seven, fifty-three, fifty-nine.* But best of all, for grounding, are those tiny feet, ice-cold and insistent, the ones digging into her side.

Best of all, always and forever, is Mac.

Dany cups her sister's little feet in her hands. She huffs, warming Mac's frozen toes. A moment later, the kid twitches awake. She sits straight up, clutching at her doll, and blinks at Dany out of sleep-drunk eyes.

"School day," Dany tells her, and Mac shuts her eyes. Falling back against the pillow, the kid pulls the comforter over her head.

"No way, not today," Dany says. "I've got lab." She tugs at the thick blanket, but her sister grips the thing in her little fists. "Look, get up now and I'll taxi you in to breakfast."

The cover slides down and Mac's wide-awake eyes blink out at her.

Dany's been played.

| | |

Without her aunt to help, mornings are a bit much for Dany. There's the hassle of getting the kid into clothes, there's the worry of breakfast. This morning, Dany shakes the last of the powdered milk into a glass of water, stirs and pours the translucent liquid into a bowl of sugar puffs. When the kid looks at the milk, eyebrows raised, Dany shrugs and tells her it's skim.

Finally, they're both ready to go.

Mac has her sneakers on, the ragged laces tied off in knots, and all Dany needs to do is get the nose plug on the kid. But it's the same every day. A monumental struggle. Some mornings, the kid hides her face in her hands. Some mornings, she stares at Dany's nose, a look of utter betrayal on her face. Today, as soon as Dany's back is turned, the kid vanishes into the closet – and when Dany opens the door, Mac is buried under the pile of old coats.

Dany shakes her head. You'd think, with the fuss Mac made, that Dany was trying to shove the plug *up* her nose.

"Look, I know it bugs you," Dany tells the squirming coat pile. "And I know it pinches, but it has to, if it's going to work." Dany gets it. She knows why Mac is upset. Mac's the only kid who goes to kindergarten with a nose plug on. Some of the kids wear N95 masks and some show up in old dust masks. A few have homemade cotton jobs. And at least a quarter of the kids wear nothing at all. Dany's seen it all, but she knows science and what's more, she knows kids. The plug will work better on a five-year-old than any oversize mask.

"You know why it's important," she tells the kid. "I told you how the virus works." Dany pauses, and looks at the plug. "Besides, this isn't an ordinary nose plug. It's magic."

The coat pile shifts.

"Did I ever tell you about the girl who could breathe underwater? She gave me this plug, so I could breathe underwater, like her." Dany rests her hand on an old coat, tells it the whole story. How, a long time ago, there were things called swimming pools. How pools were pretty much like bath tubs, abandoned by giants. How a single swimming pool could hold all of the kids at Mac's school and more. How sometimes, if you were very lucky, in the deep end, you might find a little mermaid, who'd slipped in among the human children.

The coat pile shifts again and this time Dany can see a dark pair of eyes peering out at her.

"Back then," Dany tells her, "everyone wanted one of these." Dany holds the plug up, examining it like a pearl. "This one was hers," Dany says softly. "And it's special. Really special. You know what, I bet it still works."

Dany starts to put it on her own nose. From the coat pile, a tiny hand reaches out and takes the plug from her.

| | |

But the hassles don't end with the nose plug.

Because across the hall, outside of Kuzmenko's unit, she sees the same garbage bag as she saw the day before. The air in the hall stinks. Dany shakes her head and grabs the bag. And worse, when they head into the stairwell, the only light bulb has been smashed to bits. Frowning, Dany abandons the garbage bag on the landing.

She pulls out her stainless steel water bottle, grips it by the neck. The bottle is full and the weight of it feels good in her hand. If someone bothers them, a full water bottle will crack a skull. Theoretically.

"Keep close," she tells her kid sister, and Mac does.

The kid doesn't like the dark, but Dany knows better. You don't have to worry about the dark. Worry about the people who use the dark. Her whole life is a dark stairwell. One misstep, a bit of bad luck, and it's all over for them.

She isn't worried about the sixteen-year-old boy on the third floor, the one who probably smashed the light bulb in the first place. He lives with his cousin, a parole officer with two pit bulls, and she worries less about him than the clothes he steals from the laundry room. Some days he steals underwear, some days he smashes light bulbs and some days he scatters thumbtacks in the hall. *That boy is the Eastside weather*, her aunt used to say, but that was a long time ago. And then there are the street kids he runs with, a pack of hairless wolves. Eyes as cold as stones. Dany wonders if her own eyes look like dead rocks, too, after the places she's been.

But the worst of all is the Ministry of Child Services and all the places they can put you in. Because to get in trouble is to risk being sent back. And no matter what happens, she can *never* go back there again.

| | |

When the two reach the bottom landing, Dany cracks open the door and peers out.

There, in the blinding light of the alleyway, she sees her.

A kid. A little kid who's somehow fallen down next to the dumpster.

Dany takes a couple of steps towards the girl before she realizes how perfectly still she is. Too still. And then she sees it. The girl is made of plastic. The doll's matted hair, like Mac's, sticks up at all angles.

Only the doll's not a doll. She's a message. A message aimed directly at Dany. Someone wants to tell her something. Needs to tell her something. So, no, she doesn't even notice that Mac isn't holding her hand anymore. All she sees is the doll and then the woman, the one wheeling her shopping cart around the dumpster. And before she knows what's happening, the kid has bolted.

Her little sister runs fast, but Dany – seeing the woman's face – is, for a long beat, held in place by those eyes. Then Dany, too, breaks away, long loping strides. She scoops the kid up into her arms just before Mac hits the street. A car horn blares, her heart pounds and the kid reels.

Her kid sister is trembling, her little arms shaking.

Still, Dany can't help it. She turns back.

Behind them, the woman has wheeled her shopping cart up to the dumpster. In the cart, there are picture frames, bits of bric-a-brac. The debris of a broken life. The woman plucks up the doll from the trash and settles it in the front seat of her cart, stiff legs poking through the bars like a taxidermied child. Dany takes in the cart – sees the doll, surrounded by half-familiar odds and ends. She's seen the woman around before. Too many times to be by chance. But today, for the first time, she notices the picture. The framed photograph in the woman's cart. But it hurts to look at it, and she wants to turn away.

Is the woman infected? Dany can't say. But there aren't any obvious signs. If this woman is infected, over time, the virus will colonize her brain. And day by day, the light in her will dim, consciousness will dim, until the day comes that someone glances at her in passing and sees that there is no pilot light left. No one on the inside of those eyes. They'll call her in to the medicos.

She won't have much of a life.

There are outbreaks of typhus on the streets, and lately, Dany's been hearing about a new strain of cholera. Most people give no thought to the street people they see. But Dany does. Every time she sees this woman, she asks herself who she is, if she has family. And even if she hadn't seen the photograph in her cart, Dany would know the answer. This woman had a family. This woman had kids. *Has* kids. Two of them. Girls.

In her arms, Mac is trembling.

Dany holds her sister tight. Slowly, she raises her eyes to take in the woman's face.

The woman's staring back at her and, for an instant, Dany could swear it was there. A flicker of recognition. There, in the woman's eyes.

But when Dany looks again, two empty dark pools stare back at her.

Maybe the woman is slipping away. Maybe she is losing the last of herself. Maybe it's the virus. Maybe it's a more ordinary kind of loss. In a way, it doesn't much matter. All Dany knows is that looking into the woman's eyes is like looking into a black hole, where the future is void. Looking at her, Dany too is sliding into a dark nothing. Not even the terminal cases, out at the hospice, scare Dany. Not like this. The woman is a glass with a crack, slowly draining down.

"Go home," she whispers. Only, when her mouth forms the words, Dany feels a crack open up inside of her, too. The kind of crack all kinds of things can leak out of.

Mac slips from her arms, turns to clutch at her, shaking her. The kid wants Dany to move.

And all at once, Dany breaks away.

She turns from the woman and takes her kid sister in. Feels the warmth of the kid's hands on her arm, sees her panic. Lets Mac fill all of her mind.

"You and me, we're okay," she tells her. "We're okay."

Taking her little sister by the hand, Dany turns her back on the woman. And together, they walk away.

| | |

At the elementary school, security is just finishing up. Dany watches the guards hustle the last few addicts and homeless from the school doorway and waits, as janitorial sprays the steps down with disinfectant.

If Dany's mentor at the lab is right, among the street people, impossible to detect at the early stages, are infected. How many, no one can say. But if Jasper's right, the virus is responsible for more than the upswing in viral encephalitis cases. The virus is responsible for the huge increase in psychiatric cases and homeless, too.

Some people watch birds, ticking off exotic names in little red books.

Dany watches the virus. Looking for patterns in the noise.

Only now, because of what Jasper's taught her, Dany watches everyone.

| | |

There are maybe a dozen kids in Mac's kindergarten class. Most people home-school little kids – because nobody wants to send small children to a public school, not now. They're too small to take basic precautions. Mac's classmates are the kids with no other option.

Miss Papadopoulos spots them in the doorway, raises an eyebrow, and Dany sees it too: the tangle of Mac's hair, the kid's dirty fingernails. The teacher nods at the sink.

Dany takes the kid over and carefully washes Mac's hands up to the elbow. She runs her fingers through Mac's wild hair, but the kid shrugs her off and heads to the cubbies. Together, they settle Mac's glass-eyed doll in the little wooden box.

Dany bends down, putting herself level with her sister's eyes. "I'll be here for you at three," she says and swipes again at Mac's frizzy locks.

Mac dodges her. When her little sister straightens up again, her gaze is focused on some distant universe, a speck of a place, thousands of light years past Dany's shoulder.

"I love you times a million," Dany says. "Times a googolplex." She kisses one finger and touches the tip of the kid's nose. Smiles. But that look, that thousand-mile stare, it just makes Dany sad, impossibly sad.

Then she sees it: the worst of her morning is yet to come. Because there, at the door to the classroom, Mac's teacher is waiting to have a word.

On her way out, Dany stops by the door and frowns at the scuffed tile floor.

"Your sister took the motor to pieces last week," Miss P is saying, "the one that ran the filter of our fish tank." And Dany can't help it, she grins. "Killing half the salmon fry," Miss P finishes, and Dany's smile dies.

When she glances up, the teacher's lips are pressed in a thin line of disapproval. Dany tries to find an answer to that tight frown, but all she's got is a shrug. "Did you look it up?" she finally asks. "The thing I told you about."

"Einstein syndrome," the teacher says and sighs. "Just tell your aunt to call me."

| | |

Dany scuff-walks the tiled hallway, eyes cast down.

But the worry follows after her. Trails her through two bus transfers, stalks her on the long walk across campus. By the time she lets herself into the university lab, she can feel the whole of child services half a breath behind. She feels the beginning of it, too – a truly awful headache. All of the forces in the world have lined up like dominoes, poised to come crashing down on their heads.

She knows what causes the headaches. Stress.

Dany tells herself not to worry. Because she doesn't need to worry.

Eva says that they both have it made.

At the beginning of the year, Dany placed first on the district tests for math and the biological sciences. Eva came in second. That's how they got their places at the BioGENEius project – at the university lab. Two days each week Dany's at the lab and the rest of the time she's in special classes at the micro-school.

"We'll definitely get full scholarships," Eva always says. Not that Eva needs one. Besides, on her bad days, like today, Dany can't see how university is possible. Even with funding. The promise feels surreal. Like a tornado's promise to deliver her to the Land of Oz. What's she supposed to do with her little sister? Put her in a bicycle basket? Cart her along to physics lectures?

No. It'll never happen. Besides, Dany doesn't need university. What she needs is to adopt Mac. What she needs is to *be* eighteen.

Dany doesn't need a scholarship. What she really needs is a lifetime supply of cheese and noodles and a time machine.

| CHAPTER 0 = X + 3

Dany cards her way into the lab. On her mind: the prison-hospice, her aunt, the Ministry of Child Services, the empty cupboards in her kitchen, the two months of rent past due, the poetry exam in English Studies on Friday, the food bank closing early today and worse, the oral presentation she has to give tomorrow, with Liz Greene, in spite of the fact that Dany does not *ever* open her mouth in class . . .

Dany lays her forehead against the cold locker door, lets the cool seep into her brain. Screwed. With her aunt locked up, that's what she is. Entirely, endlessly, screwed. For half a second she thinks of Antoine – *Papa,* he called himself. Anger tightens her chest and Dany shuts the thought down right there.

She runs through her padlock combo, *eighteen, twenty-nine, forty-seven,* shoves her bag in and twirling the lock shut, heads into the lab.

| | |

Dany passes a dozen researchers without so much as a nod. She makes a beeline for Jasper. As usual, his keyboard looks like it's about to be buried under an avalanche of research papers and old candy wrappers.

Under the fluorescent lights, she makes out the peppering of grey in his tightly coiled black hair. Then, glancing down, she sees the biologist's hands, curled like crabs on the keyboard. His fingers dance over the keys.

Here, at this desk, everyone but Jasper fades like background noise.

In Dany's book, Jasper is okay.

Jasper is the one who taught her how to hold a test tube properly. Now, she can grip the tube and remove its cap with the fingers of the same hand. He lent her a book about Harry Harlow and monkeys and wire-and-cloth mothers – about trauma and the human brain. And just last week, he showed her how to do Yates's correction. Now her P values are tighter than her high school math teacher's.

At the BioGENEius lab, variables don't lurk in stairwells. Here, variables are neatly contained in equations and controlled. At least, all except for the virus – which nothing can contain or control.

Jasper nods at a pair of take-away cups, but doesn't raise his eyes from the screen.

"Thanks," Dany says and takes a sip. A half a beat later, she's swearing. A mouthful of sugary tea sprays across the papers on his desk. Still, Dany can't help but smile. "You want some tea with your sugar?" she asks him.

Jasper absently dabs at the papers with a tissue. "What can I say? Sweet tooth." He glances at her. "Yours is the other one."

Dany turns the other cup, sees her initials and takes a sip. Synth, black, just the way she likes it. Dany glances at her mentor. But today, Jasper looks different. Stress lines have settled in by the corners of his mouth. Finally, Jasper pushes his chair back from the computer. As he faces her full on, she drops her gaze.

"I've got good news and bad," he tells her. "Start with the good?"

Jasper tries to catch her eye, but Dany takes in his shoes – those old beaten sneakers he wears, day after day, and that never look like they'll last out the hour. His shoes put the faint scent of gym locker in the air. That and Lysol.

"Well, take a look," he says, nodding at his computer screen.

Dany glances again at the screen, but what she sees is a lonely planet, suspended in a strange liquid. Only, no, this is no planet...

"So, that's it?"

"Well, this," Jasper says, "is in its own way both good news and bad."

"The virus is good news?" Dany asks.

"No, not exactly," Jasper says. "We isolated this from an outbreak at the hospice. So, what you're seeing is a mutation in the virus, a new strain. Maybe we'll be the ones to name it."

Dany's heart skips a beat and she turns to the screen once more. But the thing is tiny. A little bumpy sphere, like a meteor or a rocky moon. Jasper gives over the keyboard and Dany adjusts the image. For a second, it's almost as if she is looking at an ovum, a human egg. Dany glances from his screen to the wet lab. There, in a glove box, she can see the digital microscope he's hooked up. Still, the whole thing makes her nervous. As if the *idea* of the virus is enough to infect her.

"It's hard to imagine," she says. "I mean, how such a tiny creature can... unmake a person, like, unmake a world."

But Jasper corrects her. While some argue that a virus is alive, Jasper believes that a virus is a thing, no different from a chair or rock or soup ladle. "A virus," Jasper tells her, "is just a bunch of molecules – that's it. It's about as capable of acting on the world as a wooden leg. I know some scientists argue differently but –"

"Aren't we just bunches of molecules, too?" she asks.

"Think of it this way. Unlike us, a virus is at the complete mercy of its environment."

As far as that goes, Dany and the virus have something in common.

Dany adjusts the focus, makes the virus grow so large that it takes up most of the screen. As the image sharpens, the scope's focus finds the sweet spot and she gets her first real look at the thing. Binding proteins blossom like tiny mushrooms on its surface. Dany feels odd. She lays her hands flat against the desk to steady her gaze. A strange vertigo overtakes her. She isn't afraid of falling, exactly, but afraid that something in her *wants* to fall. Looking at the virus, she is Alice, peering down a rabbit hole. The virus sings, *You're late for tea.*

"Viruses are amazing," Jasper says. "Tiny microscopic miracles." And he tells her that the human placenta evolved from a virus. "Imagine that, the placenta, a two-pound viral envelope."

"Um, yeah, I'd rather not," Dany says, and flicks her gaze from the microscope feed to his shirt, the one peeking out from the folds of his lab coat. *IX IN AI*, she reads, but his coat obscures the rest of it.

"Don't get me wrong. The brain is amazing, too," Jasper tells her. "All of it, imagine – all feelings, all trauma, all memory – the work of tiny electric pulses. All of you, heart and soul, just a bunch of flickering light bulbs. Amazing, right?"

Dany doesn't need to look at the feed to see it. Her mind has taken a perfect, precise photograph. As she looks at Jasper's hands, she calls up the image of the broken light bulb in the stairwell. She sees the prison's red rope, like a skinned snake. But then her mind leaps to this new thing, this new idea about the brain.

"I sing the body electric," Dany says. A line from the poem she is supposed to write about in her English Studies exam on Friday. Does it help to know this thing about the brain? Does it? Does it help to know that all of her bad memories are just a bunch of electrical pulses? That all of her memories, like her night terrors, are really just flickering light bulbs?

Yeah, no, it doesn't.

She tunes out Jasper then. Peering at the computer, she nods in understanding. There, in the perfectly detailed image, she finds the knowledge she's come here for. Each person's mind possesses an off switch, a fatal breaker. A *just-in-case*. And this virus – which has as much right to call itself a creature as she does – knows the trick of it. "So, can I go into the hospice?" Dany asks, her eyes on the virus. "Like, to be part of the field study with you?"

She's been working up to this question for weeks. But yesterday, when she saw the sick prisoner at the hospice, the question became urgent. She *has* to get in. She has to. Soon.

The study will take her *inside* of the prison-hospice. Jasper doesn't know about her aunt, imprisoned there. So he has no reason to say no. If she gets in, she can find a way to talk to Aunt Norah. Together, they can make a plan.

But Jasper only sighs.

She feels his eyes on her. Though her eyes are on his lab coat, she can see the subtle shake of his head. "I don't think it's a good idea, not under the best of conditions," he tells her. "Sure, it's a hospice, but it's a *prison*-hospice, Dany." He shakes his head and stress lines reappear around his mouth.

Still, that isn't a no.

But Jasper pauses, looks at her.

She senses it, there's something more – something he doesn't want to tell her. Dany narrows her eyes and looks at the research papers strewn on the desk, sips at her synthetic coffee. "I can handle jail," she says with a shrug. This won't be her first prison visit. Not by a long shot. She's grown up visiting prisons – Antoine's made sure of that. "I'm cleared," she tells him. "I got myself put on the visitor list."

Jasper turns to her sharply, and Dany studies the stubble on his chin.

She shrugs again. "It's just paperwork."

"Look, even if Isobel did say yes," he says and holds up a hand, "which she won't, the prison admin would never allow it – not now. There's an outbreak at the hospice. It hasn't affected the patients, the ones who have the original strain, but it's been burning through the staff. It's too dangerous. So, no. Not now."

Dany looks at Jasper, the tiny frown lines around his mouth. He looks . . . more than worried. He looks afraid. And that makes Dany afraid, too. She doesn't want to think about her aunt being stuck in a place so dangerous that Jasper is scared to go there. Dany pictures the prisoner she saw the day before, the one thrashing on the ground. Infected. The prone prisoner was infected with the new strain.

Version 2.0.

"Okay," Dany says slowly, her mind ticking over. "I can't come with you. But I can ask questions, right? I can read field reports?"

Jasper nods.

"So, is this the bad news?" she asks. Dany takes in Jasper's mouth. The tight lines. On his forehead, a little vein throbs.

"Not quite," Jasper says. His seat rotates, and he takes Dany in. "There's been a small change with the timing of your experiment," he tells her. "We've had to reschedule."

"You promised," she says flatly. "Today. We're going to do it today."

Jasper holds up his hands. "It's just temporary. That's all. Just a small delay. We'll be moving the new virus over to the BSL-4 lab soon, really soon. That virus needs to be in a better wet lab. Honestly, if we'd had any idea, we'd have never brought the sample here . . . But until then? I'm sorry, no wet lab access."

She looks from that throbbing vein to the virus. It's easier to hear him when she's looking away from him, focusing on a screen.

"We'll still practise," Jasper tells her. "We'll get you in the blue suit and do a dry run. We can use the rat house."

"So," she says, "no wet lab, no hospice. But even if I can't go in, I can ask questions, right?"

Jasper, with a look of relief, nods.

But his relief first fades and then dies as Dany's questions – more or less a bazillion of them – unfurl in his general direction.

| | |

Dany stares at Jasper's teacup. Barely touched, his tea is an ice-cold supersaturate. Add a grain of sugar, and the crystals will drop out of liquid form, leaving a heap of sweet at the bottom of his cup. When she asks him about the yellow plague jackets, her eyes are on that cold, sugar-soaked tea.

Yesterday, at the so-called picnic, Dany saw the terminal cases wearing their yellow jackets – but she caught sight of something more. A glint of metal. The image came back to her the night before. The little metal hinge flashed in her dream.

"What's the metal thingie, on the jackets?" she asks.

Jasper pauses, halfway out of his chair. Turns to take her in. Something in her tone has caught him, because Jasper sits back down. She can feel his eyes on her, taking her in. Jasper is thoughtful that way. He takes the time to be aware of the effect his words have on a person, because you never know who the person next to you has lost or how.

"The plague jackets are devilishly clever," he tells her. "They lock in place."

They are alone right then. Dany doesn't think he'd ask otherwise.

"This isn't about my field study, is it?"

Dany frowns and, looking at his fingers, shakes her head once. "Just tell me how the lock works," she tells him. "I need to understand." At this point, she doesn't expect anything from him. She can feel it, desperation, the one chance she has to learn about the hospice squandered. If she is ever going to rescue her aunt, she needs to know how the place works. There is a hand around her heart, and the hand is tightening its grip.

"Look," he says. "Maybe I have a key kicking around."

Dany freezes. Even her breathing stops.

As she watches, Jasper opens his drawer and rifles through a decade's worth of crap. Old candy wrappers. Half a dozen paper clips, the wire roughly reshaped as little cats. A spool of twine. As he rummages through the drawer, he tells her all about the jacket. What's more, he tells her what they keep in those shipping containers at the back of the prison-run hospice.

"Ah," he finally says. "Here it is."

He holds a slim hex key in his hand, considering it.

"The yellow jackets have a reinforced band at the waist. They lock," Jasper says. "It's the only way to keep the damn things on them. This, it's just a modified hex key, really."

Dany has seen what the virus does to the human brain.

She pictures the hypothalamus – shrunken and rutted – like a miniature peach pit. All dried up. That little pea-sized part of the brain doesn't seem like much. But it regulates the body's temperature. It regulates hunger and thirst. Late in infection, when that little pea in the brain shrinks up, body temperature goes haywire. After that, the infected shed their clothes where they stand. Hence the yellow plague jackets, which come down just past the hips.

Hence the locks.

But by then, a person isn't a person. Or so they say. At least, a person isn't a person *legally* speaking.

But if you love them, really love them, they have to be a person still. Deep inside. It just stands to reason. But then, that little pea in the brain also regulates feelings. Like how attached a mother is, say, to her children.

Like the hypothalamus, after infection sets in, love shrinks up like a peach pit.

When Dany pictures the woman in the alley, she sees the silhouettes of two kids in a framed picture, there, in her shopping cart, and her heart feels like it is being squeezed. Her heart is inside of a hand, and the hand becomes a fist. But Dany shuts her thinking down right there.

No more pictures. No more thoughts. She narrows to the razor's edge of the present.

To the key.

"Give it here?" Dany asks and holds out her hand, eyes focused on that little knot of muscle, the Adam's apple, that bobs and dances beneath the skin of Jasper's throat.

Jasper looks at her hand, her trembling hand, and tries to catch her eye. A moment later, he frowns. "I can't take you into the hospice," he says. "It's not going to happen."

Dany shrugs, her eyes dipping down to his shoes. "I just want the key."

Still, he doesn't give it over.

He holds onto that key, shaking his head. Already, she can see him doubting the impulse that had him excavate his drawer.

"Please," she says. "Just let me see it."

"Why? What's with you and the key?"

Dany takes a deep breath.

She wants to tell him all of it. She wants to tell Jasper the truth. About her mom. About her aunt. But she can't. The truth is locked up too deep. So deep, maybe, there are no words. So she tells him the other part. She tells him about the nightmare. How this morning she woke up ice cold, covered in sweat. How she dreamed that she was inside of one of those yellow jackets. How, when she tried to take it off, her hands didn't work. How she couldn't get the thing off. That's not all of it. That's not even the worst of it. But somehow, it does the trick. Because a moment later, the key is in her hand, and she is holding the slender thing up to the light.

"Have you had a chance," Jasper asks, glancing at the screen, "to look at that book I gave you?"

Dany looks at Jasper's face.

She finds it easier to look at him when his eyes are on the screen, absorbed by the virus. Harry Harlow and his wire-and-cloth mothers. She's not only read the book, she's named her damned lab rats after the man. Harry and Lolo. But she isn't exactly going to admit that to Jasper. If she tells him she's read the trauma book, he'll want to talk about it. And, yeah, she knows where that conversation is headed. . . .

"Yeah, no," she says and bites her thumbnail.

Jasper looks at her, but Dany shifts her eyes to the spool in his drawer.

"Here, cut me some string," she says, nodding at the spool. "I'm going to wear this key around my neck."

Jasper looks at her – and she knows there is no way. He isn't going to let her keep it. Not in a million years. But then, she shifts her gaze back to him. Raises her eyes. Lets him meet her eyes for a moment. Even though it's too much. Even though it feels like being touched, here, like fingers wetting themselves on her eyeballs. Even though it feels like letting him reach inside of her.

"I just want to be able to sleep," she says and shrugs. And when she can't stand it a second longer, she looks down from Jasper's gaze. Takes a shaky breath.

Jasper blinks, closing his eyes for a long moment. His expression pained.

But she knows. Even before he opens his eyes again, she knows that she'll have that key, have it for always.

| CHAPTER 0 = X + 4

Dany toys with the hex key. The brass cylinder hangs from her neck on a bit of twine. She'll never again be without it. Already, an image is half formed in her mind. Another piece of the plan. She is testing the knot in the twine when Eva trips into the lab, a sandwich in one hand, a hideous orange mug in the other.

"Deej!" she squeaks.

As always, Eva is dressed like a rockabilly science nerd. She wears a lab coat with her initials, EAW, embroidered on the pocket. Eva is grinning madly – her eyes twinkling from the shadows of enormous rolled bangs.

Dany nods at the lunchroom, and Eva grins – but there's at least a dozen people she just has to say hello to on her way through the lab.

Finally, ten minutes later, the two sit down across from each other in the break room.

Dany sniffs the air, takes in the rich plastic smell of Eva's coffee. Even with all the money Eva's family has, they can't get their hands on real coffee more than a couple times a year. One sniff and Dany knows it. The dark liquid in that cup is synth.

"So, you're going in the wet lab today?" Eva asks.

Dany shakes her head. "Nah. Jasper's got some killer virus in there. So, like, you didn't miss anything."

"Ontologically speaking," Eva asks her, tipping her glasses low on her nose, "bigger picture level, is it even possible for me to miss anything? All your rats ever do is squeak and shit."

"What do you want?" Dany asks. "Fireworks? An explosion?"

"Oh my god, yes," she says, her eyes lighting up. "That would be amazing. I may be a scientific agnostic, but exploding rats, that would make me *believe*."

Eva sounds better to Dany, at least, better than Friday night. "So, you okay?" Dany asks, her voice pitched low.

Eva nods then shrugs – the two expressions cancelling each other out. *It is what it is, then*. "Thanks," Eva adds, "for letting me crash the other night."

Dany nods, but she's looking at the lunchroom floor. In the daylight, Eva was bright and fearless and full of words, but at night, you could tell that things at home got to her. On Friday night, she'd slept over, and the two of them had fallen asleep holding hands, Mac snuggled between them.

Eva pushes half her breakfast sandwich over to Dany. "You need to eat real food," she says, nudging the sandwich. "Even just once a week, say. My second cousin would only eat Velveeta cheese on Wonder bread – like that's all he ate, ever. Guess what he got for his nineteenth birthday?"

"A car?"

"Well, yeah, that and a colostomy bag."

"Seriously?" Dany asks, eyes on the sandwich.

Eva nods. "Eat it. Consider it a present, from me."

Dany nudges the sandwich back Eva's way, and takes in her friend's glasses. A little dot of light – almost imperceptible – blinks from the hinge. There, the little spot where temple meets eyeglass frame. "You are not videotaping this conversation," she says to her friend.

"It's my diary," Eva says.

"I don't like cameras," Dany tells her.

Eva touches her ear, and the tiny light goes out.

"You want to see the virus?" Dany asks her. "Jasper put the sample in the wet lab under a digital microscope."

Eva shrugs and rolls her eyes.

In her mind's eye, Dany pictures the virus Jasper showed her. "It looks like a little planet."

"That's more your gig," Eva says. "I'm not into weird *micro*scopic shit. I'm more into, like, weird *macro*scopic shit. You know, life forms . . . of an exceptional nature."

"Yeah, what life form's that?"

But Eva just looks at Dany and sips from her mug, a mysterious little smile on her face.

Dany, only now, gets a really good look at the mug in Eva's hands, the one she's been toying with the whole time. It is hand thrown, the ceramic shell a hideous orange. At first, she thinks it's a monkey, and yes, it is definitely some kind of primate. But as the features slowly resolve, Dany sees that Eva is drinking from the head of a grinning sasquatch.

"Uh, so, what is that?" Dany asks, squinting at the thing. "Your drinking partner?"

"This receptacle," Eva says, taking in the bright orange mug, "is emblematic of my future studies."

Dany eyes the orange monkey.

"And what's that?" Eva asks, nodding at the key.

"Jasper gave it to me," Dany tells her.

Eva must hear something in Dany's voice, because she narrows her eyes and tilts her head. "I didn't think you were . . . that attached to him," she says. "I mean, that attached to anybody." Eva guffaws. "Well, outside of Mac."

Dany stares at her friend for a beat, surprised.

Her hand reaches for the hex key, and she remembers what they said about her in court. A lot of bullshit about survivor's guilt and flattened affect and post-traumatic stress disorder. As if she'd been *post* anything. But then, that was a long time ago. Still, the thought is enough to make her pull at the long sleeves of her shirt self-consciously.

Dany takes a second to find the words. "We're friends?" she asks.

Eva coughs up a laugh and gives Dany the side-eye.

After a pause and only, Dany suspects, because she is staring a hole into Eva's chest, her friend nods, embarrassed. "Don't be a dummy. I know you 'love' me or whatever." Eva puts air quotes around the word. Still, a blush of red butterflies out over Eva's chest and neck, to blossom on her cheeks. In a whisper, she adds, "Vice versa, too, 'kay?"

Dany's heart is beating rabbit-fast. She looks at the floor in the break room.

The floors are unnaturally clean – everywhere in the lab. It is as if, whenever you lift your eyes from the ground, tiny robots scurry out and scour the surface. At her apartment, the floors look nothing like this.

"Yeah, me too," Dany tells the floor.

"No, yeah, I know, DJ. I know."

Dany hears Eva speak, but the words are far away. In her mind's eye, Dany pictures the virus. The one that probably swims in the eyes of the woman who trawls their back alley, her gaze on Dany and Mac.

And suddenly, just like that, the whole world feels unsure.

Topsy-turvy.

Dany's breaths come quicker and her heart stutters out its beat. Because, yes, she sees an image of the virus and then of the woman. There is an image of Miss P and then a dozen angry beige suits – the Ministry of Child Services. Eva's mouth is grinning – but her friend's face grows small and distant, a tiny satellite, a thousand miles away. And then Dany can't see Eva at all, because her head is flooding with pictures.

First, there is an image of the virus – a tiny planet whose surface blooms with mushroom-like buttons. But no sooner does she picture its bumpy surface than it is replaced by an image of Mac. And then Dany sees the hospital and the courtroom and, as the psychiatrist's voice drones on and on, she sees something worse. So much worse. There and then gone. In the flash of emergency lights, she sees children playing a sad and broken game of ring around the rosy. The last image hits her like a body blow, but one of such short duration she can breathe through it, breathe past it.

Dany knows tricks.

She knows how to shut the pictures down. How to turn the inside of her mind as dark as a theatre. How to push her mind down, under conscious thought, where all is dark and dim. No red ropes. No window well. No fire. No words. No Dany, even. A place *beneath* memory. But she hasn't figured out how to stop the pictures. They float up. Snapshots, set down in mind by a painfully precise memory. She doesn't know how to shut off the tiny light bulbs that are her neurons, the *mind* electric. Her brain is alive with flickering pictures. And through her picture-perfect memory the past lives on and on.

Inside the lunchroom, there is a girl. And inside of her head, there are pictures. So, yes, she sees Eva's mouth forming words. The sound is strange, delivered in slow motion. Dany tries to make the pictures stop, but the memories crash into her, a black river of dominoes. The pictures always end the same way – with Mac and her separated.

Dany knows that her breathing is all wrong. This *isn't* how you breathe. Because she isn't breathing, now, she's gasping.

She pulls at the cuffs of her long sleeves – plucks at the worn seams, the hem half undone already. Eva stands, hand outstretched, and the chair, behind her, suspended in a slow topple.

A moment later, her friend is by her side, holding her steady, and Dany, she's looking right at her. Weirdly, she is looking Eva right in the face, but she isn't seeing Eva, not now. Because the pictures are gone and in their place is pain. A throb of pain. An electric pulse of light. Dany folds over, her head hits the table – and her mind explodes. Electric tree roots shoot up into her brain. The pain takes on a colour, a hue. A blue-violet hum. The pain vibrates up, around, to the place where the knives are, just behind her eyes.

Occipital neuralgia, the work farm's nurse said. *Have you fallen down again? Hit your head?*

Stress, the doctor in the burn ward said. *Have you thought about taking up a hobby? Knitting?* But, with a glance at her bandages, he changed his mind. *Well, not now, perhaps. But catch up on your TV.*

Just breathe, her aunt would say.

I'm sorry for what happened to you, I'm so sorry, Aunt Norah would croon, holding Dany's head in her lap, smoothing her hair. *Breathe,* she'd say. *Just breathe. Let it all go and breathe.*

But with her aunt gone, all Dany has are numbers. When things get bad, she recites primes or runs through a Lucas sequence. Today, she does Fibonacci sums.

Zero, one, one. But inside her skin, the nerves are as sharp as piano strings. *Thirteen, twenty-one, thirty-four.* With each sum, she eases knots and unwinds nerves. *Two hundred and thirty-three, three hundred and seventy-seven.* Each number takes on a hue, shivers with shape and colour. She can almost feel her aunt's hands, almost hear her whisper, *Breathe, breathe.* At *twenty-eight thousand, six hundred and fifty-seven* the pain ebbs and dulls.

"You're okay," Eva is saying, rubbing her back. But Eva's voice drifts towards Dany from another galaxy. Still, Dany follows the thread of Eva's voice back to the lunchroom. She takes one deep breath after another. And then she's here again, a girl, sitting at a table.

Red-faced. A total idiot.

"You okay?" Eva asks.

"Yeah," Dany says. Luckily, it's just the two of them in the break room. "Just, I, I had a rough morning. Wasn't time to eat."

"You scared me," Eva says, nudging the sandwich her way.

And then Eva shakes her head and stares pointedly at the wall. There, by the door, a bullet list has been printed out and taped up.

REPORT ALL SIGNS AND SYMPTOMS is written in all caps at the top.

"Don't tell them," Dany begs her friend. "Please. They'll send me home." Dany knows that no one is allowed to come into the lab, not when they are even a little bit sick. But she isn't sick. "I'm just hungry," she says. Really goddamned hungry.

Eva frowns and shakes her head, staring at her. Finally, Dany meets her friend's eyes.

"If you eat half of the sandwich," Eva says, "I won't say a thing."

Dany flicks a glance from the sandwich to the clock. There is time for a bite. One eye on the clock, she scarfs the sandwich down.

| CHAPTER 0 = X + 5

Isobel Lau, the principle investigator at BioGENEius, puts Dany in the positive pressure suit herself. She spends what feels like an hour going over everything, as if Dany is going into a real wet lab. Which she isn't. Finally, when Dany has eyeballed every last square inch of the blue suit, looking for damage or flaws, Isobel nods.

Dany draws in a deep breath. This is it.

She takes one measured step after another, making her way to the rat house. She doesn't walk so much as plant one foot after another on the ground. Not so bad, not once she gets used to the weight. And a person, in Dany's experience, can get used to almost anything.

As she makes her way across the lab, Lauren Ko and a couple of other lab coats stop to watch. "Oh my God, she's so cute," Ko says in a hush. Lauren's lips twitch into a smile, and Dany flicks her gaze from Lauren's upturned mouth to the clock.

There, the bright red second hand is carving away time. Half an hour – that's what the tank gives her. Thirty minutes in the blue suit.

Ahead, Eva, in her headset, is waiting at the rat house door. Dany flicks to a channel only the two of them use. With the ear-buds firmly socketed, she can hear Eva well enough, even over the hiss and click of oxygen intake.

"You should have taken off your shirt," Eva says, a wicked grin on her face. More seriously, she adds, "You must be broiling."

Dany shrugs, but the gesture is lost in the suit. Experience has taught her better. She always keeps her shirt on. *Always*. Besides, Dany likes it inside of the suit. When she's inside of the blue suit, no one can touch her. Inside the suit, Dany's world is carefully regulated. She is an undersea diver inside her second skin. But this skin is better. Thicker, seamless, stronger than hers, a skin that keeps everything at a distance.

For now, Dany's Wistar rats, Harry and Lolo, are caged in the rat house. Even if this is just a stupid high school project, still, one day soon her rats will be moved to the wet lab. There, the virus will be put inside of them. If not this week, then soon – very soon – the disease will kick in. Then one of Dany's little rats will start wandering the alleys behind her apartment building, collecting up bottles and cans, family photos propped up in the child seat of its shopping cart.

She's thinking about her Wistar rats when Eva's voice cuts into the fish tank on her head.

"I wish I lived with you," Eva says, her voice tinny and small.

Dany glances at her friend, surprised.

But already Eva is turning away. Her friend levels her gaze at Jasper, and Dany follows. She takes in his pressure suit, his gloved hands, and switches back to the official communication channel. The door to the rat house opens, and a moment later, Dany lumbers in. Next to her, Jasper begins the long and tedious process of taking baseline measures of her rats – more practice. And, for the first time since early that morning, she gets a good look at her biology mentor.

Dany frowns.

Droplets of perspiration bead his upper lip. With a plastic bubble over his head, yes, like her, he's cooking in the heat of his own breath. But sweat is pouring off him. She can see the condensation forming inside his faceplate.

Jasper Okello is . . . *off*.

Even his voice sounds wrong. His tongue is thick and when he speaks, there is a subtle slur. An effect of the earbuds? The hiss of his air supply? She doesn't think so. No, it's something more.

As Jasper works with the uninfected rats, Dany takes in his hands. She knows his hands. Has watched them day after day. They are deft hands. Quick. But now, she sees a stranger's hands. Thick and clumsy. Dany raises her gloved palm, signals to Eva and flicks back to their private channel. "Something's wrong," she tells Eva.

"Yeah," Eva says with a smirk. "Jasper's drunk." Her eyes fly wide as she says it. Eva cranes into the rat house window, eyes on their mentor. "Seriously? He's shit-faced, right?"

Dany can see what Eva means, Jasper's clumsy hands, the slur in his speech. But Jasper was sober enough that morning.

"No," Dany says. "Not drunk. But I don't know . . ."

"Hold on, DJ," Eva says. "Let me hear what he's saying."

With an audible click, Eva leaves their private channel.

Dany stares at Eva through the glass. But, superimposed, she can see the reflection of her own face. Dany is everywhere. On the surface of her faceplate. In the stainless steel surface of the counters. On the glass between the lab and the rat house. Inside of her, there is a moiling mess of emotions. But the girl on the glass shows nothing. Dany closes her eyes on the girl, and turns back to Jasper.

"Do you want to confirm the numbers?" Jasper asks.

He should be asking.

He might be asking.

But it comes out more like this, "You wanna confum shnumers."

As he speaks, one of his eyes drifts to the right.

Only one.

Outside the rat house, Eva gawps at Jasper, a look of horror on her face. She tears off her headset and Dany can see her mouth moving. Can see her calling out.

On the other side of the glass, they begin to gather.

| | |

Tobias and Isobel arrive first, followed by a half a dozen others. All of them with eyes on Jasper. Dany turns and looks at her mentor.

The swelling in Jasper's brain is so bad that his eyes are being pushed out, the orbs protruding from their sockets. The pupils are large and dark. Over and over, the pupils list to one side, snap back.

"Nystagmus," says Isobel – her voice echoing inside of Dany's headgear.

Tobias nods, his expression grim. But whatever he says is lost on Dany, his voice contained on the other side of the glass.

This is not the regular virus, because it doesn't cause this kind of damage, not this quickly. The virus causes a long slow slide. It takes the you from you bit by little bit. One glance at Jasper and Dany knows, Jasper has the new strain. The hybrid. He's got version 2.0.

And so begins the last hour of her mentor's life – Jasper's real life, the one in which he is more than a collection of mere molecules. More than a chair or rock or soup ladle. More than the sum of the virus's parts. One of the very last hours in which Jasper is Jasper.

Dany takes one heavy step back.

Beside her, Jasper lets out a shuddering moan and bends over, cradling his head in his hands. Jasper rocks on his heels, and then he's seizing up. Once, twice, three times, his head hits the steel counter.

Dany backs up in panic.

But there is nothing to do. Nothing anyone can do. For now, at least, his blue suit is holding. Eva slips back into her headset. "Stay calm," Eva tells her. "Stay still," Eva tells her. "Stay back."

Overlapping Eva's voice, she can hear Isobel and, even more muted, Tobias's voice. But all she can see is Eva. Her friend steps up, lays a gloved hand on the glass window of the rat house. "Eyes on me, DJ."

Her friend's bare palm is flat against the wall of glass.

Dany turns, takes Eva's hand in, fits her own gloved version against it. For a long moment, she meets Eva's eyes. For a space, that's all there is, just the two of them. Two girls, looking into each other's eyes from either side of a plate of glass. Two girls whose minds, momentarily, stretch out into their fingertips.

| CHAPTER 0 = X + 6

Outside of the rat house, in mask and gloves, Tobias takes samples of Dany's bodily fluids. He swabs the inside of her nose and cheek – heat-sealing each sample into a bag.

And after that, what? A vial of tears? But there, try as hard as he wants, if it is tears Tobias is after, he'll be shit out of luck.

Tobias tugs at her sleeve, inching it up.

Dany shrugs him off and bites her lip. "You won't get at any veins there," she tells him. "My thigh works."

Tobias is looking at her, searching her face, but Dany doesn't bother explaining. She aims her gaze at the floor, stands and unbuttons her jeans. Tobias's face flushes, and he shakes his head. Reaching out, he takes her hand and, turning it over, examines the veins there. "Here, this'll do," he tells her.

Dany sits back down on the stool, eyes on the floor tiles.

| | |

Before he died, Einstein believed in a thing called simultaneity.

Dany knows that what she is feeling isn't what Einstein meant, but sometimes, time collapses, rolls up, so that all of her, all of her life, gathers up in a tiny ball. As small as a pinprick. As an injection point. As the little dot of blood there, on the back of her hand, the one left by Tobias's needle.

Even as a child who couldn't read the clock's face, she felt it.

Sometimes, the present is swollen with the past. Time is stuck in a bottleneck. It isn't that she doesn't understand Einstein and Minkowski and physics. She does. It's just hard to account, in any other way, for the persistence of the past. Even now, she can smell it. Smoke in the air. Darling-Holmes. Her past is on fire.

Dany sits on her stool, five feet from the barrier unit.

Where she sits, she can smell the smoke of the fire. Can hear the rattle of a shopping cart. And, if she looks into Jasper's face, she knows she will see the woman from the alley looking back at her.

If this is the price she pays for her picture-perfect memory, it's too much.

Dany wants to throw something at the rat house window. Just to make the present a *thing*. The pictures in her head are too much with her. She can picture the past so clearly, it overwhelms, overtakes the present.

Tobias's voice breaks the picture.

"You're lucky you were in the blue suit," Tobias tells her. "But the MDC will want to do follow up. They'll quarantine the lab."

The MDC. *The Ministry of Disease Control.* Dany frowns and flicks him a glance.

"We'll all be quarantined, for a few hours – at least." Tobias searches her face. A cool look, clinical. It isn't Dany he's taking in – but her pupils. "Don't go anywhere, kid," he tells her, quietly. "Be over soon. This strain is nothing if not fast."

She glances at the clock, but when she turns back, Tobias has already left. As she watches, he makes his way to the rat house.

In that room, somewhere inside of Jasper, swimming in his eyes, is the virus, version 2.0, an improved version of the *primum movens* that opened a hole in her and her sister's lives. A virus that, muttering in a strange tongue, put her and her sister in a cold window well for a long dark night. The virus that gave her up to the legion of beige suits that occupies the Ministry of Child Services. The virus that first built a hundred work farms for the children of virals – and then put her at the worst of them. The virus that put her sister, too young for a work farm, into the foster home that stole her tongue. All of the ruination of their lives, in some way, the work of a bunch of molecules. Like a chair or rock or soup ladle. She needs to look that virus in the face, and yet, she doesn't think she can.

"I know," Eva says. She lays a hand on Dany's shoulder. "It looks a bit bad right now."

"I was thinking about Feynman," Dany says. "You know, path integrals. The quantum amplitude." Dany doesn't know why her voice is so calm, flat even. But she lets it go. In truth, she's pretty sure Feynman felt the same way she does. He probably wrote that theory because he needed to smash a plate glass window – to separate the past from the present with the sound of breaking glass.

Eva frowns and turns away. As Dany watches, her best friend makes her way over to the rat house. Dany trails after her.

Jasper is laid out flat on the floor, his headgear off. In a pressure suit, next to him, someone breathes for Jasper, by way of a black balloon. The MDC is already here, gearing up to go in. Dany tries to stay out of the way, but no matter where she stands, she's always a little bit in somebody's way.

How can it happen, she wonders.

How can it be that one day you are part of a family, have children of your own, ones you love? And the next, you're a stranger to everyone you know. Wheeling the remnants of your life down a back alley. How do you shove your children, on the longest, coldest night of winter, into a window well?

She remembers it, that small hollow in the garden outside of the basement flat. A winter-cold hole in the ground, just outside of their basement apartment's window, about half as deep as a grave, and rimmed by corrugated aluminum. A dank little hole, meant to let a sliver of sunlight into that cave of an apartment.

"You'll be safe here," Dany's mom said, should have said, might have said, but it was hard to make meaning from the slur of words. And then her mother put them in the hole. Where it was cold, so cold. Dany wrapped her little sister up in of her parka, zipping her inside. Even then, the little toddler was shivering against her chest. Her baby sister was scared. If Dany closes her eyes she can still feel her little sister, trembling against her. She can still hear the sound of her mother's voice, obscene in its strangeness. A stranger, not her mother, muttering on the lawn. All around her, in the lab, come reminders. The sound of an MDC cart rolling by, rickety wheels on asphalt. The downcast faces of the scientists and techs, the wardens of the work farm. The taste of the place, pennies and ash. The past doesn't go away, not just because a place burns to the ground. The past sticks around for a good long time after.

Dany walks those last five feet to the rat house, lays both of her hands on the glass.

But what can she say?

Jasper is laid out on the floor, unconscious. A black bag inflates and deflates, as a man's hand makes and unmakes a fist. And all Dany can think to write is *zero.* And if she writes *zero* on the glass once, it'll come out of her a hundred times, *zero, zero, zero, zero, zero*. Zero, for Jasper's life and the future and the woman and the world, all of it. A series of flatlining heartbeats. Tiny broken pulses on the glass.

Next to her, Lauren Ko is crying. Not weeping, just standing there, a bit of water rimming her eyes. Dany can understand that. Of course, some time during her life, that well ran dry. Dany doesn't think she can cry if she wants to. The water table has dropped so low, not one drop of it can make it to the surface.

Lauren turns, touches her shoulder, and Dany can't help it, she flinches.

A small frown flickers across Lauren's mouth and is gone.

Then Lauren Ko turns and pastes a little sticky note to the glass. On it, she's drawn a heart. But the little sticky is facing the wrong way out. Jasper can't read it.

Dany picks up a dry erase marker. She looks at her mentor, lying flat on his back in the rat house, but what she sees is the woman, rolling her cart down the back alley.

Something has left a deep hesitation in her.

And that hesitation, like a sponge, absorbs time. Absorbs possibilities. Until it is too late. And isn't it always already too late? The woman has wheeled her cart past. Dany has left her behind. And besides, isn't it easier not to think about her? Not to ask? Not to know? Not to really know . . .

| | |

Finally, she does it. She writes a message.

It's the kind of stupid message that will get you all of one point in Scrabble.

N=1, she writes. Only she writes it backwards on the glass, for *him* to see.

By it, she means there is nobody in the world like Jasper, that he is a population of one. Jasper Mungunda Okello. Singular and irreplaceable.

Her mentor. Her friend.

Dany taps Eva on the shoulder. All around them, the lab is a chaos of activity. Dany sees their chance and nods at the door. Then, without saying a word, she edges past the ministry people, past the anxious knot of researchers, slips into the hall and is gone.

N=1, she writes, and then quietly, without a word, she slips out of that place. Out of the ruins of yet another life.

| | |

Half a minute later, Dany finds herself staring up into the sunshine of a surreally blue-sky day. Eva is beside her. And, for a long time, the two girls stand, faces angled to the sun.

"It's all part of the bottleneck," Dany says.

"Are we just, like, blowing off quarantine?" Eva asks her.

"Yeah, no, I don't know." Dany shrugs. "Yeah, sort of."

The lab has samples from inside her mouth and nose. Bits of her have been smeared on swabs. Her blood has been drawn up through the needle's tip. Before long, her cells will flow into a centrifuge. Then she'll be in a lot of pieces, in a lot of places, under microscopes and in fluorescent arrays. And her eyes, her eyes took all of it in, and now this moment, like so many others, will always exist, for the duration of her timeline. From now on, a part of her will always be in the lab with Jasper Okello.

| CHAPTER 0 = X + 7

Eva sits down heavily on the concrete steps. She takes a cigarette out of her lab coat pocket – herbal, suffused with synthetic nicotine – and taps it, filter down, against the concrete.

Only Eva doesn't smoke. Not even herbs.

"My dad's probably freaking out right about now," she says. "What, a mile up in the air, without these." Eva grins.

She looks like a female Buddha sitting cross-legged on the step. One hand, palm up, is curled in meditation. The other holds a lit cigarette. Eva drags the ash of her cigarette across the step, honing the ember to a point. The smell of burning cloves envelopes them. Eva doesn't actually inhale from the thing. She just watches it burn down to nothing, like Jasper's life. As Dany watches, a little frown mark forms between Eva's eyebrows.

"Are you actually okay?" Eva asks.

Dany narrows her eyes. The lunchroom. Eva is back to what happened in the lunchroom. "Yeah, no, it was nothing. I'm fine."

"And what does *fine* mean to you?" Eva asks.

Dany shrugs and frowns. She's promised to be open with Eva. She's promised to tell her things. But it's so goddamned hard. "I saw somebody, okay. On the way here. And it just, it was like, everything hit me and I panicked. It just all hit me at once. That was a panic attack. Plus I skipped breakfast. That's what that was."

A silver hybrid pulls up and a man gets out. In his suit and tie, the man looks less like a driver than a businessman, waiting on a lunch date. Dany nods, but the driver doesn't nod back. After all, Dany's not his problem. Eva is.

"Your ride's here," Dany tells her friend.

"Who did you see, DJ?" Eva asks. She doesn't so much as glance at the driver.

"Nobody." Dany frowns and bites her thumbnail. "Somebody. Maybe she was infected, I don't know. But, like, she had this framed picture, of her kids . . . and for a minute, I thought she was somebody. Somebody I knew." Dany's words trail away. She isn't sure about the woman – so she isn't lying. Not exactly. Still, Dany can't shake the feeling that she is keeping something important from Eva. But how can she tell Eva who the woman is when she can't even bear to say the word. Three letters. Three stupid letters.

Five lousy points.

When she pictures the woman with the shopping cart, there are no words.

"I'm sorry," Eva says.

"Not half so sorry as that woman's kids are, wherever they are," Dany says, brushing all of it off, pushing it down, away. She bites at her thumbnail again. Trims the ragged edge with her teeth. "They're probably stuck at one of the work farms."

The driver, meanwhile, is standing perfectly still by the car door. Like some kind of human statue. Like one of those models that play pretend-mannequin in department store windows.

Dany sighs, and holds out her fingers. Eva gives her the cigarette.

Dany examines the stick, takes a drag, then grinds the glowing tip into the concrete. The smell of cloves is gone. Now, the cigarette smells like something burnt and stale. Like her high school guidance counsellor. She holds the foul stub out to Eva.

Eva tosses it over her shoulder and slips the pack into her lab coat. Before long, Dany knows, somebody will pocket the half smoke.

"So, are we doing this?" Eva asks, standing up. "Making our getaway?"

Glancing at the car, Dany shakes her head. "I've got a bus pass."

"Oh my god," Eva says. "What, you're ashamed to be seen with me. Like, god."

Dany looks at the concrete step. But when she glances up, Eva is grinning.

"It's okay, I'm embarrassed for me all the time."

"It's just, I've got a bus pass," Dany says and shrugs.

And all of this time, the driver is just standing there. Silent. On hold. As if his job is to be human muzak.

"Jasper's going to be okay," Eva says. "Punishing yourself by taking public transit is not going to help."

Dany grins. "It is sort of punishing."

Eva backs towards the car, beckoning to her like a cut-rate magician. Then Eva slips inside the car. All Dany can hear is Eva's voice. All she can see is a single beckoning finger.

"Would you like some candy, little girl?"

Dany can't help it. She grins. Because of course she does.

| | |

Dany's mom always drove the same rusty old compact. There were tears in the faux leather seats and even with the windows wide open, always there was the creeping smell of exhaust. When Dany pictures her mom's car, she sees the soft blue glow of her mom's mood ring, slim fingers tapping out time on the steering wheel. She hears a throaty voice, singing. But then, one day, her mom was gone, and things were bad, and by the time they weren't so bad, the car somehow belonged to Aunt Norah.

But Norah never did get her licence, not even for emergencies. So, the junker just sat there in the parking lot under their building, while the battery drained and the tires deflated like old balloons. Finally, Norah sold it for parts.

"The thing isn't insured, anyway," her aunt said.

"Cars are a goddamned hazard," her aunt said.

"Cars, that's where this mess began," her aunt said.

"If people were meant to roll around this earth, they'd have been born with wheels," she said.

"So, you want to take a bus?" Dany asked.

"Watch it, smarty-pants," her aunt snapped, grinning.

By comparison, the car she gets into now – Len Wahl's hybrid – looks like it was just driven off a showroom floor. Probably was. Dany looks around, takes in the pristine interior, but all she can see is her mom's old compact. All she can think of is a mood ring, gone cold and black. Eva turns to her, eyes filled with raw concern. "Jasper?" she asks.

Dany shrugs. The truth is, Dany doesn't know why she is so sorry.

She regrets a lot of things. *Everything*, pretty much. She regrets her aunt being in jail. She regrets Jasper being sick. Sometimes, she even regrets how Mac, her little sister, is stuck with her.

Dany takes a deep breath, pushes the feeling away and shrugs.

"I should feel worse," she tells Eva. "My life is just so screwed, I don't have room to feel bad. Not half as bad as I should."

Who has it in them to feel?

"I'll make up for it," she promises Eva. "After I adopt Mac." Then she sighs, because how? How do you make up for it all? The truth is, her life comes with a bill she can't afford to pay. A bill that just keeps on getting bigger.

| | |

When the car turns onto Hastings, Dany is hungry. The food bank is up this way. She ate half of Eva's sandwich in the morning, but the food has only made her hunger sharpen.

Dany glances at the digital clock on the dash. Yes, there's just enough time.

"Can you drop me up here?" she asks the driver.

A small and silent nod is the only response.

"The big brick one there, just past the lights."

But when the car pulls up in front of the food bank, she sees the closed sign.

Eva looks from the food bank to her friend. She stares for so long, so intently, that Dany knows she's made another stupid mistake.

| | |

Forty minutes later, the driver pulls out of the elementary school parking lot. In the back seat, Mac is prying open one of the small white boxes. Soon, Mac's popped two chicken balls into her mouth. With one in each cheek, the kid looks like a hamster.

"Look at the box," Dany says. "It's got a really smart design."

She reaches for the box, but the kid sees the gist of it. Dumping the chicken balls in her lap, Mac traces the lines with her finger, then pushes and pulls. A moment later, the box is completely flat.

"But can you make a rabbit appear?" asks Eva.

"Or how about a box to, I don't know, hold chicken balls?" Dany asks.

The kid works the pieces back into place, and a beat later Eva is tossing balls of chicken in the air. Dany, horrified, grabs the box to catch them.

Even Mac is laughing – silently, yes, but the grin is on her face, and little breaths of laughter escape from her mouth.

"I owe you for the food," Dany tells her friend, seriously.

"No," Eva says. "No you don't, dummy. It's an early half-birthday present, 'kay. I'll still make you a cake and everything."

Dany stops. "Wait, what's the date?"

"I don't know, math genius, what's the day before the day you were born, give or take six months?"

"Half birthday," Dany repeats. "That's a thing?"

"Yes, that's a thing, DJ. A definite thing."

"Quarter birthdays?"

"No. Not a thing. Err, not yet." Eva smiles, cocks her head, and lifts an eyebrow.

| | |

The driver pulls up outside of Bea's house, next to the squat apartment building Dany and Mac call home. Liz has parked herself on Bea's front stoop, and there are textbooks spread out all around her, four of them open at once. When the car pulls up, Liz yanks off her hoodie and glares.

Definitely pissed.

Her expression cheers up a bit, though, when the driver emerges from the car, just behind Dany, toting a half a dozen boxes of Chinese food.

"I think you just saved my life," Dany says.

"It's pretty much a full-time job," Eva says and laughs. "Look, I'll get up early for class tomorrow." Eva is *always* late for first period, when she doesn't skip it entirely. "I want to be front row centre for the Danielle-Jean show!"

"You won't miss anything if you sleep in," Dany says. "I promise." She draws an X across her chest.

"Call me later," Eva says and hops back into the car. "We need to talk."

Dany nods at her friend's back. They do, they really do. About a lot of things. But as the car pulls away, it hits her. She won't call Eva. Because she can't. With her aunt gone, they've cut off the stupid phone.

| | |

Bea's house is filled with light. Even in April, Bea's Christmas lights are up. Her latest find is a string of vintage chilli peppers, glowing softly red, up there in the maze of twinkle lights that hang from her living room ceiling like an irradiated spider's web.

Today, Mac has squeezed herself halfway behind the huge cabinet radio, to see its inner workings. Bea is describing all the old radio shows she's heard on that thing, while Mac's eyes trace arcane routes through tubes and wires. The radio hums out old acoustic blues and ancient tube lights glow orange.

At Bea's, there's so much light, it's overwhelming.

You have to be pretty lonely, Dany figures, to need so much light and sound. Bea leaves Mac where she is and slips over to the liquor cabinet. She does that every now and again, sneaking little sips. "A bit of sparkle never hurt anyone," Bea says, with a wink Mac's way. "A little nip helps the lights shine."

Mac doesn't so much as notice. But Liz side-eyes Bea. Lifting her hand to her mouth, Liz Greene pretends to guzzle from her thumb.

Dany shakes her head at Liz. But Bea, at least, doesn't seem to care. Finally, when the lights are bright enough for her, Bea slips the unlabelled bottle back into the cabinet.

"You sure you don't care if we study here?" Dany asks the old woman. "Are we in the way?"

"You're getting in it now." The frown on Bea's face edges into a tight smile. "Look, I promised Mac a game of Scrabble."

"If it's okay?" Dany asks.

"If it's okay," Bea repeats, shaking her head. But with Bea, love comes with sharp edges. Bea gives Dany a look and then sets the Scrabble board on the coffee table, and Mac settles in beside her on the couch. Dany takes the two of them in and knows, no, they aren't going anywhere. Not for a good while.

| | |

At the kitchen table, Liz is thumbing through one of Dany's books on the plague. Every few minutes she mutters or shakes her head. Finally, with an Eeyore sigh, Liz sticks a yellow Post-it Note on a woodcut picture of a plague doctor. "I guess this is the best we can do," she says, eyeing the image. "It'd be better if we had real plague masks for the class, like crow doctors. Creepy as fu-fu-fudge?" Liz finds the word just in time.

Looking at Liz's face, Dany can't help it – she snorts. Little bits of fried rice fly out of her mouth and dot the pages of her plague book. Dany plucks up a soggy pea, a few stray grains of rice, pops them back into the spent box.

"But seriously," Liz says quietly, leaning forward. "I'd like to have seen London back then. The bubonic plague, now that was a *real* plague. Not like this virus." She says the word derisively. "Back then, they would've had total anarchy. You know, you could riot and loot. Smash the system. Smash the vending machines."

"In 1665," Dany says dryly, and shakes her head. "We're probably looking at the end of the world right now, and you want free Doritos."

Liz shrugs her off, eyes on the crow doctor. Her expression is intense. It's almost as if Liz is waiting for him to come to life, hand her a sledgehammer.

"Where are we gonna get twenty crow masks, anyway?" Dany asks, ignoring the rest.

"We could make them," Liz says.

"I've got a box of N95 respirators at home. Field models. You know, the disposable ones."

Liz raises an eyebrow and searches Dany's face. "Of course you do," she says, deadpan. Liz shakes her head and, once more, silently communes with the plague doctor.

Dany frowns and picks the last grain of rice out of her copy of Shrewsbury. She reaches for the fried rice container, but Liz is faster. "You need to show a little more respect for your elders," Liz tells her, holding the container just out of Dany's reach.

Liz has all of eleven months on Dany, but she's been holding it over her forever. Well, since kindergarten, when Dany was five and Liz six. Only three kids from their elementary had made it into the micro-school, and until Eva, Liz had been pretty much her only friend there.

As Liz wipes the last traces of salt and soy from the box with her finger, she keeps up a steady stream about old-school apocalypses and their shiny silver linings.

| | |

An hour later, the presentation talk roughed in, Dany sits back. Her belly is still bulging – a strange feeling. She doesn't remember the last time she felt . . . full. Dany is always hungry. Always. Most days, a small monster lives in Dany's belly, one that is all gaping maw and jagged teeth. But tonight, thanks to Eva, they've eaten enough for ten. The little monster in her belly has been neatly anaesthetized.

Bea and Mac are still at their Scrabble game, sitting at the coffee table – and for a little while, Dany watches them. But Mac still hasn't got the gist of the game. Bea sounds out a word, and sets her tiles on the tray. But then Mac leans in, plucks up a couple of tiles and undoes Bea's word. When Bea spells out *mom*, Mac takes away one of the *m*'s, leaving *mo* on the board. And when she sets out the letters for *Bea*, Mac removes the final *a*.

But Beatrice doesn't get mad. She just goes along with Mac, sounding out the new syllables as Mac arranges them on the board.

Dany can't help it. She feels a pang of shame.

Sometimes, Bea is too much. Too nice. People can be too nice, so you kind of feel ashamed. She doesn't mind when Bea is cutting. Because when she's soft, that hurts more. "Mac," Dany calls out. "Will you just try for once?"

But Mac ignores her.

The kid is completely focused on the board. Only she isn't laying out words so much as random letters. Like *bh* and *be*, *mo* and *ta*. Still, some of the time the kid pairs a consonant and a vowel, and that is kind of like language. Well, it's sound. So maybe Mac is learning after all.

"Earth to Dany," Liz says.

Dany frowns at the dark hoodie that shadows Liz's face.

"So, where are we?" Dany asks her friend.

"The Orion arm of the Milky Way," Liz reminds her. "Virgo Supercluster. Circling a sphere of hot plasma. On the verge of a global extinction event."

This Dany knows. "Earth," she answers.

"Glad to have you back." Liz gives her a cockeyed grimace – her idea of a smile. In the seven years she's known Liz, Dany has never seen her in such a good mood. Liz probably lives with a monster in her belly, too. Sometimes, towards the end of the month, when things get bad for Liz too, she sticks around after lunch and together they forage from abandoned cafeteria trays. She and Liz never talk about what they're doing. They just clear tables and stack trays and talk philosophy or whatever. Like it's nothing at all to be discussing the arbitrary axioms Immanuel Kant uses in his ethical system while chewing on somebody's abandoned pizza crust.

"You're happy," Dany says.

"Look, about tomorrow," Liz says and frowns. "About the talking part."

Dany looks down at the table, struggling to put something into words.

"I was wondering, maybe *I* could do the talking," Liz says. "You could just click the pictures and let me be the mouth."

Dany nods, relieved.

Liz flashes a gap-toothed smirk at Dany. "I mean, it's only fair, since you wrote most of the stupid thing. But don't forget the masks."

Dany nods. "Deal."

| | |

Liz supervises while Dany washes up the dinner plates. Mac is sitting at the kitchen table and, behind her, Bea attacks the tangle of Dany's kid sister's hair with a spiky brush. The kid dodges and ducks, but the old woman never once raises her voice.

"Aie, aie, you win," Bea says, setting down the brush. Bea turns hawkish eyes on Dany. "You need to condition her hair," she snaps. "What have you been washing it with?" The old woman's lip curls and she sniffs at a tangled lock.

Dany can feel her face flush red.

Eyes on the collar of Bea's blouse, she answers: "Dish soap. We learned about it in chemistry. There's no difference between dish soap and shampoo." Besides, only dish soap is available at the food bank.

"She's not a dinner plate," Bea snaps. "I'll bathe her properly. Tonight, she can stay with me." Her voice goes soft as she leans in to talk to Mac. "It'll be a slumber party – just us girls."

Dany frowns. "Mac stays with me." The words come out hard. Harder than she means them to. But Bea doesn't look offended.

"You can all stay," Bea says, her tone easy.

Dany shrugs the question over to Liz.

But Liz shakes her head. "No, not me."

Bea gives Dany another sharp look. "Someone needs to properly wash and brush this child's hair."

Dany sighs. There's no arguing with Bea, not when she gets something in her head.

| | |

The kid in the tub, half-bearded with foam, Dany leaves Bea to do her thing. Back in the living room, Liz is already into the liquor cabinet.

"Don't worry. The bottles aren't marked," Liz tells her. "I checked."

Dany rolls her eyes.

Liz shrugs and takes another gulp. Wiping her mouth on her sleeve, she offers the bottle to Dany. "Want some sparkle?" Liz asks, in a fair imitation of Bea.

Dany shakes her head.

"Seriously, though. I think you should be careful," Liz tells her. She screws the cap back on the bottle. "Did you see that set-up she's got out back?"

Of course Dany has. Every day, the old woman puts out kibble for the stray cats and water for the virals. For a moment, she imagines Jasper's voice, reminding her that these are not walking viruses but people. Still, when Dany thinks about the stupid bowls Bea sets out each day, she can only shake her head. "She loves Mac," Dany says finally. Because, really, that's all that matters.

"She's batshit crazy," Liz shoots back. "Mark my words, that woman is going to snap. And when she does, she's going full-on Vesuvius. It will not be pretty."

For a long moment, Dany can feel Liz looking at her face, appraising her.

Finally, Liz puts the bottle back in the liquor cabinet, easing the door to a close. "So, you going to call your aunt?" Liz asks. When she turns to Dany, her eyes narrow. "You know, ask to sleep over?"

A knot tightens in Dany's stomach. She's forgotten about Norah. "Aunt Norah's pulled overtime. She won't miss us."

"I get it," Liz says, scratching her forehead. "I mean, I get why you lie to the school and your landlord. But why lie to me? Why lie to the kid?"

Dany looks at Liz.

The monster is back now; only it doesn't live in her stomach. The monster lives in her heart. The truth is, Dany hasn't lied to the kid, not exactly. She's taken her to the prison-hospice to see her aunt, after all. And everything she's told both Liz and the kid about their aunt is true. Prisoner or not, her aunt does work there. Technically.

"Look, I won't say anything," Liz says with a frown. Her breath is a potent mix of soy sauce, garlic and barrel whiskey. "Forget I brought it up."

"Mac's little," Dany says. "She might . . . say the wrong thing."

Liz guffaws. "The kid's a vault."

"She's just a late talker," Dany tells her.

"Yeah, I know, Einstein blah blah blah. The kid knows her periodic table, that's for sure."

Dany narrows her eyes at her friend.

Liz frowns and glances across the room to the Scrabble board. "Like I said," she tells Dany, "the periodic table."

Dany takes in the Scrabble board – the random letters and broken syllables her kid sister spent so much time on. And for the first time, Dany *sees* it. The Scrabble board *is* the periodic table.

Dany knows the table of elements perfectly.

There is one, after all, tacked to the door of her bedroom. The *mo* isn't a failed attempt to spell *mom*. It stands for *molybdenum*. The *ta* isn't a child's version of *give it here*. No, *ta* stands for *titanium*. In her mind, Dany flips through pictures of Scrabble boards past. The one the kid did last week, last month, last year. Six months now, the kid has been doing this for a full six months – and Dany hasn't once put it together.

The kid is smart. She is so goddamned smart.

"So, where is your aunt?" Liz asks quietly, her eyes still on the board.

"The prison-hospice," Dany says. She's not sure why she tells Liz the truth. Whether it's because her friend has caught her off-guard, or whether Dany is just so grateful to be able to see the Scrabble board for what it is.

Liz doesn't say anything, but her expression says it all. *That's bad. Like really bad.*

"She's not infected," Dany tells her. "Her parole got revoked, that's all. And they haven't even given her a stupid hearing yet. The whole thing's going to get tossed out by the board. So like she's getting out. Soon. It's all a big mistake."

But Liz is looking at her in that strange way again. On her face, the doubt is plain. "I should go," Liz says, tucking her face into her hoodie.

Dany nods, but she's looking at the Scrabble board.

When she looks up, the patio doors stand wide open. And her friend Liz Greene has been swallowed by the night.

| | |

Another few nips at the sparkle and Bea transforms into a sea star, snoring face down on her queen-size bed.

On the fold-out in the living room, Dany and her sister cuddle up with a book. Mac flips through the bug entries in her illustrated encyclopedia until she finds the entry for cockroaches.

"Yeah, oh man, they had fast ones back at . . ." Dany doesn't finish. She doesn't want to talk about that place. She and her sister are here now, together. No matter what, they are going to stay that way. "Did you know cockroaches can eat glue?" she asks the kid.

Mac's fingers underline those very words in sequence.

She can read – Dany is sure of it – though her teacher doesn't seem to think it's possible. Mac's lips move when she reads, but no sound comes out. Still, Dany thinks that this is hopeful. If her lips move, Mac is practising. The muscles of her mouth are getting ready. At some point, the kid will simply open the faucet and the sound will pour out.

Einstein was a late talker. Richard Feynman and Julia Robinson, both mathematical geniuses, were late talkers too. "Look here." Dany points a little lower in the page. "They can eat soap, hair and nylons too. Pretty amazing, eh."

The kid looks up at her big sister. But still, she doesn't speak. Dany is about to kiss the kid when she pictures Jasper and stops herself. Instead, she nuzzles the top of the kid's head with her chin. Her hair smells good now, like the conditioner Bea has doused it with.

"I love you," she tells the kid. "Do you know how much?"

The kid spreads her arms as wide as forever and her eyes, Mac's eyes, are good to look into, and never hurt, and Dany looks into her kid sister's eyes and, inside of her, the sun breaks the dark line of the horizon. Smashes that line to bits. Dazzling.

| CHAPTER 0 = X + 8

The next morning, Dany sits at the very back of the history classroom.

But Liz Greene is nowhere in sight.

Dany stopped off at home for a big box of disposable face masks, N95, and Liz is supposed to be here, drawing black beaks on each of them. Dany glances at the clock, and then to hell with it, the other students can draw their own damn plague masks.

"Draw a beak," she mutters, tossing a mask down in front of one of her classmates. She goes table to table, throwing down masks on each.

By the time class starts, some of the kids have taken out Sharpies and pencil crayons and decorated the thin white face masks. A couple have drawn cartoonish versions of lips. One has etched in a few broken teeth. Eva has pencilled hers with sutures, set in a gruesome approximation of a smile.

But no beaks.

Eva is sitting up at the front today, by way of moral support. Her hair is in a messy bun – all but those signature rolled bangs – and she looks like she is half asleep. In front of her, filled to the brim with black synth, is the hideous orange sasquatch mug.

Dany puts her mask on. She toys with the elastic, eyes on her desk.

When the bell rings, she searches the room, but no Liz.

Her presentation partner – the one she worked with last night, while Bea and Mac played Scrabble; the one who promised to do all of the talking – has not just blown the presentation off, but Dany as well.

Mister Faraday, too, is scanning the faces in the classroom. When he gets to Dany, she glimpses a raised eyebrow. *It is what it is*, his look says.

Dany nods at her desk.

She should have known better than to count on Liz Greene.

| | |

Dany makes her way to the front, swishing the blackout curtains to a close on the way. In the dim light, she clicks on the remote. A figure from an old woodcut appears on the screen – wearing a black cape and a crow mask. She looks down at the notes, difficult to see in the dim light. Then she looks out at the faces in the class, which, by some perverse law of the universe, she can make out perfectly.

Sweat trickles down under her arms.

Finally, she seeks out Eva's form and settles her gaze on the table just in front of her friend. She doesn't think about the twenty history students. She doesn't think about her teacher or his PhD from Cornell. Dany sees objects, not people. The hollow ceramic replica of a human-primate hybrid. The nub of a pencil, indented by human teeth.

"During the Black Plague," Dany says, glancing at a pink eraser, "plague doctors, like this guy, tried to protect themselves. But they didn't know about bacilli they, well, they couldn't know about anything too small to see, like viruses. Or virii. Or whatever."

Eva adjusts the mug in her hands, so that the orange sasquatch winks.

"Sorry," Faraday says. "A little louder if you can."

Dany looks at the knot of Faraday's tie. Then she looks at the cue cards that hold her notes. She doesn't need them, because she knows the words, knows them inside out. She inked each card –

and has a perfect visual memory of each. It's like that with the written word, with books. They stay with her forever, each page indelibly imprints on her brain, to be pulled up before her eyes in an instant. But it doesn't matter if she can picture the cue cards. Because the words will not come out. Words get chewed up in her mouth, and she sounds like an idiot.

She is an idiot.

She belongs at her desk, where she can keep her eyes down, where she can go an entire period without speaking, where, at the back of the room, she can completely avoid all eye contact.

Eva is looking up at her from her seat in the front row. By way of encouragement, she yawns. Next to Eva, a girl is adding scrawls of ink to a page already filled with illegible doodles. Sonja, her name is. Sonja's notes look like they are some kind of cross between a comic book and Linear B. She looks up at Dany and points a finger at her own temple.

"Pkow," she says and falls dead on her desk.

Dany blinks at the corpse for a beat and then looks up at Faraday's hands, clasped in a steeple under his chin.

"I could just give you me and Liz's notes and you could, like, read them later," Dany says quietly. "Or I could show you the pictures."

"You're doing just fine. Take a deep breath, you can do this."

Faraday nods. An expression meant as encouragement forms on his face – but she can tell, Faraday knows it. Dany – the girl whose classroom participation is limited to a series of forced monosyllabic grunts – is leading the discussion for the next twenty-five minutes.

Ergo, they are all in for a world of pain.

| | |

Dany's essays are brilliant. Her presentations? A series of enormous, stinking hellholes into which she drags all who are forced to be witness.

After her first term paper for Mister Faraday – she wrote a treatise on Mary Mallon – he asked her to stay behind after class.

As the others filed out, Dany sat in her seat, twisting a black lock of hair, knees jittering under the desk. She'd been ready for what was coming because it wasn't the first time.

Math and science are easy. But arts courses are different. In arts courses, you have to talk. Dany tries, but in English and history, inevitably, her teachers think she's more idiot than savant. Whenever she hands in the first paper of the semester, the teacher takes one look at her, the girl who can't string together more than three words – at least, not out loud – and then looks down at the essay in front of them. *Where did you buy this?* is the next logical question. So, when Mister Faraday asked her to stay behind, Dany knew exactly what to expect.

"Your essay," Mister Faraday said, swinging his chair around to face her.

She narrowed her eyes and stared a hole into her teacher's neck. *Bring it, Faraday,* she thought. *I know this shit inside out – right down to the peer-reviewed sources and their citations in APA.*

Mister Faraday eyed her contemplatively. "It's good," he said.

Dany looked up in surprise. And even more surprisingly, he smiled.

"You think it's good," she repeated, looking for the flaw. She blew out a breath of air. The fact was, her paper was *more* than good.

Faraday smiled. "Yes," he repeated. "*Good.*" The second time, he emphasized the word, as if he wanted her to reconsider its meaning.

Dany shrugged the word off. *Okay, it's like 'good' or whatever.*

The teacher leaned forward. "If you don't mind," he said, "I'd like to give you a book." This had been even weirder. But yes, he opened his bag and pulled out a first edition, still in its dust jacket. Shrewsbury. *A History of Bubonic Plague in the British Isles.*

Dany stared at the pale green cover.

"It was foundational," he added. "And still a good place to begin."

He fingered the dust jacket for a moment and then offered the book to her.

Dany flipped open the cover and saw the inscription. His thesis supervisor had given the book to him, the day he earned his PhD at Cornell. But below that, scrawled in fresh ink, the book had been rededicated.

To Danielle-Jean Munday, a promising young scholar.

"It's just Dany," she told him. "Thanks," she added roughly. Then, for the first time since entering the micro-school, Dany looked up and met a teacher's eyes. Because he saw something. In her essay, he saw, what? Promise? So, yeah, that one time, she let him look her in the eye – let him glimpse the girl who lived behind a wall of glass.

| CHAPTER 0 = X + 9

The presentation is rough, but she gets through it. Barely. Only, probably, because it is for Faraday. But the presentation isn't all of it. Then comes Q & A.

Still no Liz.

Faraday closes up his notes and makes his way to the front of the class. Dany is stuck front and centre – but, as always, he referees from the podium.

"You know what comes next," Faraday says to her, and then he turns to the class. "Shoot," he tells them.

"Like, literally," Sonja mumbles in the front row.

Dany tries to ignore her, but Sonja's right. Faraday might as well stand her in front of a firing squad.

She knows how Faraday operates Q & As, but wonders if he'll really let the clock run out in silence, the way he says he will. Dany looks at Eva, waiting for her to ask a question. But Eva doesn't move. She may be sitting up, but her eyes are closed, and Dany suspects she's fallen asleep upright in her chair.

Finally, after a small eternity, a kid in the back row half-raises a hand. George. Aside from Dany and Liz Greene, he's the only other kid here from Brit elementary. Dany takes in the lettering on George's shirt, but can't quite make out the quote. Something about an Indigenous multiverse. Then a name printed underneath. Roanhorse.

In third grade, Dany and George had been partnered up in math, deriving pi from rusty old oil drums at the port. Even as a kid, he'd been utterly calm, a kid everybody liked. These days, though, as soon as the bell rang, he'd slide out of the micro-school and back to his old friends in the larger school's gen pop.

"So did the beaks do anything to protect doctors?" George asks. "Or are you thinking there's another reason for them?"

Dany stops to think, because he's right. The beaks do look like respirators.

Sometimes, crow doctors stuffed them with sponges soaked in vinegar or camphor, both of which are antimicrobial. And that's when it happens. Dany is working through all of this out loud when she gets interested in the subject. She forgets about the kids who are whispering. Forgets about Sonja, drawing a picture of Dany's head exploding.

Dany goes over what she knows. How, back then, they thought disease moved in the air. But not like an airborne virus. Because they didn't know about viruses, not yet. But the smell of the disease, the stink of it – that everybody recognized. They called it the scourge. So, in a way, they mistook the smell, the symptom, for the cause.

Dany frowns, deep in thought.

"But then," she says, "you have to ask *who* these doctors were. So, like, the bubonic plague spreads through Europe. Who gets hit hardest? Front line workers. So, what do the surviving doctors do? Run, a lot of them. So we have somebody pictured here, wearing the suit of a plague doctor, but is it a real doctor?" She shrugs. "It doesn't matter. These crows don't doctor. Because there's no cure. So, their job is to identify the sick. You know, like the medicos do with virals. I mean, the infected. Sick people. Whatever. When the pilot light goes out, boom, under the Rodriguez act, people lose basic human rights, and they're rounded up and sent to camps to, to . . . to die."

Now the whole class is awake.

The teacher takes a deep breath. "We're going to confine ourselves," Faraday says, "to today's topic, for now. But Dany has a point, one I want us to come back to. I want us to think about fear and stigma, about naming practices, about our use of language. I want us to ask the hard questions: What do our words carry? What do they allow? It's something we'll return to more than once in this course, as we see how language shapes perception and how perception, in turn, shapes practice. . . . But for now, let's focus on the groundwork. So," he says, bumping a question Dany's way, "were these doctors or bureaucrats? And if these plague doctors could offer no treatment, why did they sort the sick from the well?"

Dany looks from Faraday to Eva's sasquatch mug and thinks about it. Crow doctors didn't help the sick, because that wasn't their job. Their job was to keep the sick away from everyone else. *Without a cure, what else could you do*? And then she knows, all at once she knows – the MDC haven't taken Jasper to treat him, because there is no cure for the virus. And the only treatments they have are failing. Badly.

The Ministry of Disease Control has *contained* him.

In some places, she remembers, they nailed the doors to houses closed, with the sick inside. "Isolation," she says, finally.

"Back then, they might use nails in a door. Now, they use the prison-hospice up by Second Narrows. But it's the same, really. If you're on the wrong side of the line? You've got two choices: you survive or . . . you die."

Dany looks out over the class, finds George. "I mean, what would you do?" she asks, slowly. "Like imagine you've got two kids. One of them has the plague. She'll die no matter what. Do you stick with her, even if it means your other kid will probably catch it and die too? Do you do that, knowing that you can't help? That it may kill all of you?"

Then Dany looks at Eva.

This is the question she's been asking herself. Since yesterday. This question, and a billion variations of it, has risen up in her, again and again, beating under everything.

But right then, Faraday's watch beeps, and she wonders if he's set it off on purpose. "And that's time," Faraday says. "I'll take the hot seat now."

.| | |

For the next thirty minutes, Faraday reminds her of why this is her favourite class. At one point, he even pulls out a replica of a plague doctor's cane. The students use it to listen to each other's heartbeats. The cane is hollow, like a sounding rod. Like a stethoscope. The cane carries the sound of one person's pulse to another person's ear, all while keeping a few feet of distance.

Then, the lights in the classroom flicker.

Dany glances up at the dying fluorescents. But what follows isn't another brownout. What follows is the moment that sets everything in motion. The beginning of the end of the world.

The classroom door opens – and, for a moment, Dany closes her eyes, closes them tight. She senses some change in the air. The hairs on the back of her neck crawl with nervous electricity. She feels it. Danger.

When Dany opens her eyes she searches the classroom for a breach, sure she'll find a long, lazy crack opening under her feet. A chasm for them all to tumble into.

Dany's gut twists. If the kids in the room were dogs, they'd be barking right now, and running in terrified circles. But no, like her, they are all looking stupidly around, as if trying to think of a half-forgotten word, there, on the tip of the tongue.

And then Dany sees her.

In the doorway. A girl, her outline.

Liz.

Liz stands there, framed by the door, and something in Dany's guts are telling her that something is wrong. That everything is wrong. Liz is clutching her backpack, and as she steps into the room, a rock falls out of her bag and clatters to the ground.

"We're glad you could join us," Faraday says.

Liz cocks her head at the teacher and goes still.

Under her desk, Dany's hands are plucking at her shirt sleeves. Over the space of a half dozen heartbeats, Dany has moved from relief – that the ground is solid beneath her feet – to a deep bodily fear. "It's all right," Faraday is saying. "Come in." But it isn't all right.

It will never be all right again.

Liz takes one step, then another.

She presses against the concrete wall, inching along the side of the classroom. And for a second, Dany's fear becomes something else. Because Liz looks like a scared five-year-old. Like a kid in the dark, blind-eyed with fear. Like a kid who is afraid there is a monster in the dark.

And then the pity is gone, and the fear doubles up like a stomach cramp.

She knows where Liz is headed. Her favourite seat at the back of the classroom. The one next to Dany.

Liz drops her bag under Dany's desk – there is the clatter of more rocks – and then she flings herself into the seat. Dany slides a mask over to Liz. Dany doesn't look at her friend, just pushes that mask over the table towards her desk mate.

Liz ignores it.

"Now," says Faraday, "let's close up this talk of plague. We need to discuss the final term papers you're all working so hard on."

| CHAPTER 0 = X + 10

Next to her, Dany can hear Liz muttering. It's no more than a ghostly whisper, the curling edges of her words falling just short of comprehension.

Her classmates aren't looking at the teacher, not anymore.

The entire class, turning in their seats, is looking at Liz Greene.

All around Liz, they're reacting. Like the rings that form on the surface of the water after it has swallowed a stone. Stiffening backs, half-turned faces, and there, in the centre of it all, Liz. She is hunched over the table, pulling at her hair. Sweaty strands hang over her eyes like a ragged curtain. Dany tries to look, to see why Liz is upset. But when she turns Liz's way, her desk mate reacts instantly, turning in her seat, her shoulder shielding her notes.

Liz is scribbling so furiously that her pencil tears the page.

Dany can smell it in the air. Fear. A sour scent, astringent. Like the scent that, in her experience, precedes some small and half-ashamed act of violence. The teacher, up at the front, has abandoned his lecture and picked up his cell. And Dany, she sits very still, looking straight ahead – the only one in the classroom who doesn't have eyes on Liz Greene.

| | |

At the front of the room, Faraday sets his cell phone down.

"We're going to leave the classroom slowly," he says. "Keep calm. Gather up in the hall – they'll come and get you. All except for you, Liz," he says, turning to Dany's desk mate, who doesn't seem to hear. "Paramedics are on their way to help."

Liz Greene is muttering – but it's gibberish, nonsense. As if language can be broken, as if words, like proteins, can be malformed. The disease does this? It does this to language? And what, then, is it doing to her brain?

Liz pulls at the zipper of her hoodie.

No one moves.

On the ground, by Dany's feet, there is Liz's backpack. The pack is open and Dany can make out, just inside, a few stones. Painted stones. A little kitten with human eyes. A frog with purple polka dots. And then, all at once, she sees the stones for what they are – can see the rough brushstrokes of little children. These stones have been taken from the little garden outside of the kindergarten class – where they were set down by the hands of little kids. By Mac. Maybe even, in their day, by Dany and Liz and George.

Dany tries to make sense of it. Why Liz, instead of going to class, would go to the elementary school. Why Liz would come to history class with a bagful of rocks.

In a flash of sudden understanding, she turns and looks at her friend.

This is a bag meant for carrying you under the surface of the water and keeping you there. Liz has gathered up rocks just like that writer – the one from English Studies. A lot of the kids were horrified by the stones Woolf filled her pockets with, the ones meant to weigh her down in the river. But Dany got it. You must know, deep down, that once you are submerged, something in you will kick to stay alive.

The Burrard Inlet is just a ten-minute walk from here.

And Liz, she must know that she'll kick her way to the surface, given a chance. She's filled her bag with rocks so that their sheer weight will cancel the impulse out.

For a moment, just half of a second, Dany feels that same vertiginous pull, the one she felt yesterday, while looking at the virus. Only now, she feels it while looking at Liz Greene.

"Calmly, now, exit the room," Faraday repeats. But no one listens. Finally, raising his voice, he snaps at them: "Go!"

Everyone breaks at once.

Twenty chaotic trajectories – a chaos of elbows and legs tangling as they run for the door. But Dany doesn't move. Because the instant after she turns to look at Liz, Liz turns to look at her.

Dany takes in everything about Liz's eyes: She can see that the orbs of her eyes are too pronounced – as if the brain, swelling in her head, is pressing them out. She can see the way her pupils are enlarged; the way that her eyes are, slowly and inexorably, listing to the right, only to snap back.

Nystagmus.

But the worst thing she sees in Liz Greene's eyes is blame.

Your fault, her eyes say. *Your fault.*

Slowly, Dany moves her gaze to the table. Nothing has prepared her to see Liz like this. Nothing. All around the classroom, there are chairs knocked over, backpacks abandoned. A single sheet of paper floats lazily in the air and lands, feather-quiet, on the ground at Faraday's feet.

"Go," Faraday tells her. "And close the door behind you."

Dany looks at her teacher's brown leather shoes, unable to move. And in the next instant, Faraday is by Dany's side. She feels his hand on her arm, feels him take hold of her elbow, feels him pull her up. She clutches the box of masks to her chest as she stands.

Finally, he gives her a shove, starts her towards the door.

Dany crosses the distance of the classroom. But at the door, she turns back.

Liz must be feverish.

There is a flush to her skin – and she's struggling to take her hoodie off. But she can't get her arms out of the sleeves and so, the sweater hangs behind her, hampering her movement like a pair of cuffs. Dany pictures the hypothalamus, inside Liz's brain, shrivelling up like a peach pit.

Dany feels the door handle pressing into the small of her back.

When her hand grips the knob, she feels relief and, a beat later, shame.

Because somehow, she knows that this is her fault. She doesn't know how, she doesn't know why, but she knows – this is all on her. And she can't *do* anything to help Liz. Can't make her better. Not anymore than she could help Jasper.

Dany pictures Liz as one of the so-called virals. The ones dotting the hospice yard. The ones that the government trucks come for. The ones that are put in yellow jackets and taken to the camps to die. Two days ago, she took Mac up there on the bus, and the two of them sat on a little hill outside the fence of the hospice, and she saw them. A few stood with arms held wide, turning slowly, unseeing eyes turned up towards the sun.

Will they put Liz in a yellow plague jacket? Will they truck her out to the hospice grounds? Will Liz – muscles riddled with tiny spasms, her face a waxen grimace – end her days in the camp? Is Lizzie a viral?

Somehow, the word didn't fit.

The silence breaks, and she hears her friend. Over and over Liz is muttering a word, words. Dany, so adept at finding patterns in noise, is probably the only one who could make out the slur of meaning.

"Fire," Liz is saying, over and over. "I'm on fire."

A paramedic brushes past Dany, and her eyes lock on his respirator mask.

Seeing that mask, all of her body goes still, cold. Then the security guard, bigger and less cautious, knocks Dany into the wall on his way past.

| | |

Dany turns her back on Liz, her hand on the door handle. She is taking her first step through the door when she hears it. What stops her, what turns her back, isn't the suddenness of the noise, but the strangeness. So out of place. Surreal. It is a noise that does not make sense.

It sounds like someone has dropped a melon from two stories up. Or taken a sledgehammer to the head of a sleeping dog. Dany hears the sound and, looking back, sees Liz bringing her forehead down against the desk.

Three solid, bone-bruising blows.

Cursing, the paramedic struggles to pin Liz upright against the chair back. The guard, next to Dany, scowls.

The last Dany sees of Liz is this: her friend from kindergarten is pinned against the chair back, and her nose is bloodied, broken.

Dany grasps her box of N95 masks and, turning her back on Liz Greene, she walks away. She's heard what Liz is whispering, she's seen what is in Liz's eyes.

Liz knows, somehow Liz knows.

The virus, the fire, all of it.

Everything is all Dany's fault.

| CHAPTER ⊙ = X + 11

All around her, wherever she goes, they turn.

They turn, they burn, they die.

Dany learned about pain her final night at Darling-Holmes.

She learned that fire can invent a new category of pain. A pain so sharp, so searing, so bone-deep, the mind is razed clean. Alarms, rattling her brain. Smoke-filled halls, blinding her. The heat and the fire and the fear and the smell of burning hair and flesh. And then Dany isn't Dany. She is her arms, burning. The dead weight she carries. Searing white flame and a mind, brutally wiped clean.

A firefighter found the two of them where she collapsed. There, just past the exit, next to the concrete foundation of the building.

Dany's eyes were open – unlike Zeke's – and a man, a firefighter, tried to scoop up the little boy. He tried to take the little huddled form out of Dany's arms. The pain of Zeke being pulled from her arms was more searing, more intense than anything she'd ever known – right up until the darkness took her.

| | |

When Dany opened her eyes again, she was lying on a gurney.

The fire, a distant glow.

At some point, someone must have separated them, because Zeke was sleeping on the grass. He was so tiny, the smallest kid at the work farm. And maybe that was why he had reminded Dany of Mac. Zeke, who – as best she could – Dany took care of, because she so badly wanted to believe that, in whatever place they'd put her sister, there was someone there likewise looking out for her.

Magic.

Dany believed in magic. Which was stupid. Because magic never worked.

Zeke had been covered in a blanket, but even so, Dany recognized the kid. She knew it was him. The body on the ground was just so small, there was no one else it could be.

She dragged herself over – and the morphine drip twisted and pulled out of her neck. And then she was on the ground, next to Zeke, pulling the blanket back from Zeke's face, because she wanted the little boy to be able to breathe.

There was the ruin of her arms.

There was a burned little boy, and there were her arms.

Zeke's pyjamas had caught fire, they were melted into his skin, and to lay the boy out on the ground, they had to have literally cut him away from Dany. Or cut Dany away from him. It hurt her to even think about.

Dany pulled back the blanket, because she thought that Zeke was sleeping, that Zeke needed to breathe.

And when that blanket came away – what she saw became a picture. And the picture entered Dany's head and made echoes there. Thousands of tiny echoes, as delicate as Zeke's face. Echoes that touched every other memory to come.

But at the time, she didn't understand.

Because when they lifted Dany into the ambulance, the morphine drip reinserted in her neck, her head lolled to one side and she thought, *That's strange*. All the little kids are outside, but it's past curfew, and they're playing a game, the one where you all fall down.

She looked at the kids and thought, *That's really strange.* Not just the curfew part, but the falling down.

Because they'd fallen so neatly. Because they'd made of themselves such a tidy little row.

| | |

Outside of the classroom, Dany counts through it, counts past it.

Into the thousands, into the tens of thousands.

And then she moves on force of will, making herself go through the motions that are necessary. In the parking lot, Dany tosses the box of N95 masks to Eva.

Eva takes one look at Dany, and lets it go. Lets go whatever she was about to say.

Instead, Eva walks up and down the line of students – making sure they all wear masks, handing out new ones to students who have left theirs behind. And that's when the VP chooses his moment to announce his plan for them. The kids, the ones he's lined up in a tidy little row – they are going to take a sponge bath. Like they are kids with sand between their toes. Dany doesn't know whether to laugh or scream. The whole thing is so completely ludicrous.

She wants to tell them, to stop them, but the only word her brain finds is *run*. Run far, run fast, it doesn't matter where. Run, until her mind empties out and there is nothing left, until her thoughts are as empty as wind.

Like Zeke, Liz Greene digs into her heart like a splinter.

| | |

Dany isn't getting in any stupid line.

She stands by the school, leaning her head against the cool brick wall. She knocks her forehead against the brick once, twice, but that only makes her think of Liz.

And with that picture of Liz burning in her brain, Dany turns and strides up to VP Bricker.

The vice principal is rustling through the pages of an old photocopied manual. A couple of admins, next to him – the ones whose job it is to sit around while phones ring and look personally offended when Dany is late – are filling buckets with water and counting out capfuls of bleach. Next to them, leaning on an old car, there is a dog-faced security guard in a bored slump. He probably gets paid to look stupid. And her classmates? They are all standing in a line. To complete the picture, all they need are sheep costumes.

Dany turns on Vice Principal Bricker, her eyes choose a little black button, there, at the top of his shirt. "Are you an idiot?" she asks. "Or are you a psychopath? I mean, do you actually want to kill all these kids?"

She can feel, rather than see, open-mouthed, the students in line gawking at her.

"Get in line," Bricker tells her.

But Dany isn't getting in any line. As sure as any game of ring around the rosy, that line ends in a tidy little row. "If you do this, we're all gonna die," Dany says. Her voice, loud and clear, rings out across the parking lot. She knows, she knows, it is the same strain that got Jasper. For a second, she pictures Mary Mallon – that image of her, looking up at the camera from a hospital bed. A dozen more beds recede into the background of the picture, like a vanishing point. An endless hospital ward for a vista. But Dany pushes the picture down.

No good thinking about it. No good.

All that matters now is that people know. *This* is the new strain. Whether it has gotten out of the lab or slipped the bounds of the hospice, she doesn't know. All she knows is that, somehow, the new virus has found its way into Liz. Nothing else is this quick. She looks from the sponge to the other students. And as her mind fills with math, a differential equation chalks itself onto the pavement at her feet. When she raises her gaze, her eyes carve numbers into the VP's forehead. Blood drips into his eyes.

The VP snaps the manual against his pant leg.

His mouth is moving, but it takes a minute for him to work the words out of his moving jaws. "Calm down. Take a quiet moment," he says, enunciating each word in an all too familiar way. "Then get in line."

"Screw the line," Dany tells him.

"Mister Bricker?" Eva has pushed her way over, because she is at Dany's side now, talking to the VP. "She's just shaken. We're all a little shaken."

"You should be," Dany snaps. "He's killing us. We're all going to die. You will die. I will die." Dany looks around for George. "If you stay here, you'll die, too."

George touches the silver-framed glasses he's wearing, and Dany expects a tiny light to blink into being on the frame.

"Last warning," the VP growls.

Dany can see it. She knows she needs to stop, to shut her mouth. She bites down on a ragged thumbnail. But then, her hands are at her side again, forming fists, and her mouth is working. Now that she is talking, she can't make it stop. "You didn't see Liz. You didn't see her bashing her brains out on a school desk," she tells the VP.

Eva takes a step back from Dany and looks at her strangely.

But Dany can't make the words stop. She can't make *anything* stop. Not once, in her life, has she found the off button. Never. "I don't want you to die," she tells Eva, "but you will. And so will I and so will Mac and –"

Dany can't find any more words, so she turns and kicks over the bucket. The smell of bleach rises from the concrete and a dark stain blooms on the pavement, washing away her mental equations.

The vice principal, wordless for once, slaps Dany across the face.

For a second, a quarter of a second, the whole world spins.

Dany feels the heat of the slap – it is the kind that hurts more on the inside of your head than on the outside. The kind of slap that makes you feel ashamed, even if you aren't the one who hit somebody. She draws in a sharp breath. This time, when she opens her mouth, she lets out every curse word, every swear, every foul bit of gutter verbiage she's trawled up in the alleys of the Eastside – and, it turns out, she's stored up a lot.

In a part of her brain she doesn't need right now, yes, she is aware of Eva's hand on her arm. Eva, begging her to just calm down. But they are all going to die and it is the stupid sponge that will nail the job, and Eva's voice is lost in the white hot roaring inside of Dany's head.

| CHAPTER 0 = X + 12

One minute, she is eye level with Bricker's chest, swearing at the stupid bastard. And in the next, she is on the ground, and her mouth is filled with dirt.

The whole thing happens so fast, it's over before it begins.

The guard grabs one of her wrists, hard, and Dany screams. She feels a searing flare of pain. His huge hand grips her scarred arm, turning and tearing the flesh. Under his grip, her scarred skin cracks at the fault lines. The pain reshapes Dany, twisting her in response. And as soon as she turns, to relieve the pain, the guard has pinned her other wrist, too.

A moment later, she is zap-strapped in the dirt.

The guard knocks her head into the ground, slamming her mental suitcase shut. Dany's eyes ring in their sockets, and she stares at the ground, dazed. A trickle, warm and wet, runs from her mouth to puddle in the dirt. She can smell the blood, like pennies and salt. Rust-coloured spots bleed through her shirt sleeves.

She's been here before.

Face down in the dirt.

She's been here dozens of times.

This is why Dany can't wear her mom's old wristwatch. Never mind the scars. Never mind her hatred of time. Never mind that the stupid thing hasn't ticked in years. It is that she can't stand the feeling of a confining band around her wrist, like a zap strap. To wear anything on her wrist is to evoke, in small, the feeling of Darling-Holmes. The endless suck of the present tense, draining down your life. Guards and zap straps. Eating dirt.

| | |

Dany spits out dirt and gravel.

Face down, hands strapped behind her back, she side-eyes the guard. For the first time in two years, the world begins to make a terrible kind of sense. For the first time since Darling-Holmes, the perpetual knot in her chest – the one that beats in place of a heart – unties itself. Her body doesn't need a heart, not so long as there is enough adrenaline and anger.

"Back the hell off her," Faraday is saying.

Dany blinks up at her history teacher.

Her teacher has put himself between Dany and the security guard.

"Everyone needs to calm down," Eva is saying. "But we intern at a *virology* lab. And there are protocols, so, Dany has a point – though, yes, I can see that her diplomacy skills could –"

"Would you like to join your friend?" Bricker asks. "We have zip ties enough for all of the student body."

Eva makes a zipping motion over her mouth and sits down on the curb next to Dany.

| | |

Faraday tries – he is talking to Bricker – telling him what he's seen. He believes Dany, that much is apparent.

But Dany shuts out Faraday.

Closing her eyes, she presses the side of her face into the dirt. Inching her knees up to her chest, she works her way into a forced fetal position. Then, rolling on the balls of her knees, she digs the toe of her sneaker under her until, finally, she is sitting up in a squat. It is uncomfortable as hell, but better than eating dirt. And it keeps her wrists out of the VP's line of sight. Which is the point.

Dany can still hear Mister Faraday taking up her cause with the VP. Dany is glad for the distraction, but ignores him.

"Got a knife?" she whispers to Eva.

Eva shoots her a worried look.

"For the zap straps," Dany says, shaking her head.

Eva digs through her purse, and Dany glances at her classmates.

The secretaries have refilled the bucket, and two of Dany's classmates are splashing their faces with handfuls of the suspect liquid. After they wash their faces and hands, one of the admins sponges down each student's clothes and hair. Then the next student moves into place. Same sponge, same bucket. For all they know, those buckets are the best way possible to spread the new hybrid strain.

George, at least, gets away. One moment, he's standing by the corner of the building, but when Dany looks again, he's vanished.

She looks at the line of remaining students, and a rhizome forms in her head, a spiderweb, tracing each footstep she has taken since the day before, when she sat with Jasper at his desk.

"You want some tea with your sugar?" she'd asked him. Had Jasper taken a sip from that tea, before she'd taken a mouthful?

She doesn't want to think about the other possibility for transmission. Doesn't want to think about the red rope. Because if Dany became infected while visiting the hospice, at a distance of ten feet, then the virus is airborne, and they are all of them, every last one, dead already.

No, it has to be the tea. Bodily fluids. Has to be. And that means that the bucket is a problem. She pictures each footstep these kids will take, moving out from this moment in time. Every time a vector's path crosses with another's – a kiss, a shared glass, an open sore – there will be a role of the dice.

| | |

Finally, Eva finds a pair of manicure scissors at the bottom of her purse and gets to work. The moment that Eva finally snips the zap strap, the whole world changes.

Dany's muscles go slack, the math disappears and it is as if the sky itself has been holding its breath. Eva tucks the tiny scissors into Dany's back pocket, and, for the first time since Liz entered that history classroom, Dany can breathe.

"Keep them," Eva says. "You need them more than me," she adds, glancing at Dany's ragged fingernails. But just as quickly, Eva looks away. "I mean, for these kinds of situations. You seem to be, I don't know, some kind of a natural magnet for trouble."

Dany looks at her for a beat, gives her friend a smile. But the smile dies when she thinks of Mac. "I need you to get my sister," Dany tells her. "Before the ministry can. Take her to Bea."

"Yeah, I'll pick up Little Rabbit," Eva says, dropping her voice. "But, strictly speaking, is that legal? What if they ask for my babysitter's licence?"

Dany rolls her eyes. "Trust me, they won't. But, like, no hair dryers. There was a thing."

"Uh, weirdly alarming, but okay," Eva says.

Dany gives Eva the pickup code and then, hands held behind her back, she studies the guard's boots. Dany is once again in a world that makes perfect sense, a world of guards and zap straps. Only Dany isn't a stupid thirteen-year-old anymore. She knows better than to fight back. Not if the guard is bigger. Not if the guard is stronger. And not if there are more of them than her.

Dany will beat them where *she* is stronger – she'll use her mind. As she sits with Eva, Dany tracks the guard's boots. The boots are aimed at the halfway point between her and those kids. Still, his attention – if the direction those boots are pointing is any sign – is beginning to wane. He's already losing interest in her.

Faraday steps into her line of sight, eclipsing her view.

"You okay?" he asks quietly, kneeling down in front of her.

"Nobody's okay," Dany says honestly. She flicks a look at Faraday. Then she glances past him to the VP, who is on the phone.

Faraday shakes his head.

Dany stares at the rough yellow paint on the curb, the deteriorating pattern. And for a vertiginous moment, that's all there is, just the peel of yellow paint, the cool concrete on which she perches, the tidal sounds of human breath.

"You and your sister," Faraday asks, "do you have people? Someone I can call?"

Faraday's words demolish the centre of her silence.

His words send ripples outwards. Dozens of images flash through her brain. Liz. Aunt Norah. Mac.

Eva gives their teacher a warning look.

But it's fine. Faraday is fine. To a point.

"It's just me and my sister. When it comes down to it, we're what we've got."

Eva gives her a withering look.

"And Eva," Dany says, rolling her eyes. "We've got Eva."

Eva nods, emphatically. "And your aunt, dummy," she adds.

Dany frowns at the curb. She promised to tell Eva more. And she really should have told Eva about her aunt before now. She should have told her eight weeks ago when Norah's parole got revoked. But it's hard. Finding the words for things is just so hard. But the truth is, Dany and her kid sister are screwed – and talking about it doesn't help. She flicks a look from Eva to Faraday, and settles her gaze once more on the guard's boots. "Look, Aunt Norah's gone. So there's nobody I can call."

Eva gives her a strange look, but Dany ignores her, settling her gaze on the knot of Faraday's tie.

"I'm sorry," her teacher manages.

Then he pulls out his notebook and scribbles something. He tears out a page and puts it on her lap.

"Now there is," he says. "If you and your sister ever need help, call me."

For a beat, Dany just looks at him, then she glances down at the paper.

Eva rolls her eyes. "Oh, and I suppose you have a personal law firm on retainer?"

Dany ignores her. Nodding at the paper, she tells Faraday to put it away. For a second, a fraction of it, he looks hurt. "Numbers," Dany explains, before he can get entirely offended. "I'm just, I'm good with them."

"I bet you are," Faraday says.

| | |

Dany hears the car coming from blocks away. She's the only one who seems to notice, or the only one who gets the significance of the sound. She's been waiting for it. The police officer assigned to her high school is in need of a new muffler. He might as well have turned on the siren.

She turns to Eva. "You'll get Mac right away? No matter what. No distractions. You swear?"

"You don't have to ask," Eva says. "No hair dryers. Pinkie swear."

That isn't the kind of distraction she means, but Dany hears the misfire of the police car's exhaust, and she knows that this is Bricker's doing. In spite of what she's learned, about how it is always worse to run, sometimes *worse* is the only open pathway.

The low rumble of the muffler is a few blocks distant, but, as the car draws close, the Doppler effect will lower the tone briefly. If she has to guess, she'd say the officer's car is five blocks off. This, in a neighbourhood with as many addicts as baby strollers. Today, she is glad for each and every one. The officer can't go past fifty, not here. Forty is pushing it. She does the calculation in a flash, and knows, worst case scenario, she is cutting it very close. But she needs to wait until Bricker's eyes are off her.

Bricker, smiling, has heard the muffler now. After a glance her way, he turns his back and looks out over the parking lot expectantly.

"Mister Faraday," Dany says, "can I ask you to turn around? Just for a human second."

He looks a question her way, but still, with a sigh, Faraday does it. Shaking his head, expelling a long breath and with a look approaching regret, he turns his back on her.

Dany grins at Eva.

"Don't wait. Stay away from that bucket. Go get the kid," Dany whispers. And then her eyes find her path and Dany is up and running.

| CHAPTER ⊙ = X + 13

Brit, with its barred windows, looks more like a juvie prison than a high school. The main building is enormous. But Dany runs full out – not holding anything back. She is almost at the steps – the ones leading down to the track – when Bricker finally calls out. A beat later, behind her, she hears the guard's heavy steps in pursuit. Still, Faraday hasn't outed her – and that buys her an all-important fifty-yard lead.

The guard, she knows, will never leave the school grounds. She'll lose him once she hops the fence – but that's a good two-hundred-yard sprint.

Still, Dany can make that in her sleep.

Hitting the schoolyard fence at a run, she clambers up, and though her arms are hot with pain, she's over it in a second. In truth, using her muscles feels good, even if her scars hate her for it. She smiles, picturing the guard who follows.

Once she's crossed the street, Dany turns and walks backwards, facing the guard, holding up both middle fingers. All the while, she has a smile on her face. But the guard, far from stopping, takes that fence in a loping run. The bastard *parkours* over the fence. He pauses to pull off his N95 mask – Eva has to have given it to him – and that's when she sees it. The guard has a grin on his stupid face. She's seen it before, in the dogs, the ones who see the chase as just another kind of play. Even as their teeth punch holes into the flesh on your arms, their tails never stop wagging, not for a second.

Dany swears.

A moment later, she turns tail and runs, wishing, all the while, for the stupid guard to fall and break his neck. Her bad luck, to piss off a guard who has the heart of a dog. *You run, it chases*. Still, that doesn't make him terribly bright, just a creature of instinct.

Dany knows the back alleys better than any rent-a-cop.

She knows these streets as well as she knows her sister's face. She knows which walkways connect up to the next alley, and which ones bottom out in a dank stairwell. She knows which dumpsters will let you onto low roofs. She'll lose him quickly in the labyrinth of back streets and alleys. Once she loses him, she'll head home, pack up a bag and, one way or another, she'll get her sister out of the city.

Dany is already making plans. She'll call in every last favour she can. Eva was only the first ask. She needs to borrow money – she can ask Bea – and she'll need a little bit of help, too, from the old Russian shut-in, Kuzmenko. Hell, he doesn't even need to know he's helping her. He owes her, anyway. For the better part of a year now, she's done the old Russian's garbage disposal.

Dany races down the alley, legs pumping, lungs burning. She needs to get Mac out of the city before her baby sister goes the way of Liz and Jasper. She runs hard, as hard as she can, but the guard – running at a calm lope – is easily keeping pace.

That's when the first cramp hits.

Dany tries to pinch it away.

She tells herself it is nothing, but a bony finger is digging its way into her side with each step she takes. She can't afford to feel it. Not now. But the pain – like the thought of Liz Greene and, a half a breath after, Jasper – gets to her. The pictures bring to mind other pictures. Mac, for one. Aunt Norah, for another. The images hit her like successive blows.

Her aunt is in the worst place of all. Where the outbreak started.

If she doesn't get to her aunt, the virus will. Inevitably, more and more people who are infected with the new strain of the virus – perhaps even Liz herself – will be sent to the hospice.

Her aunt will die.

Dany can hear the guard's approaching footsteps and knows that he is getting close. She feels a hit of fear and adrenaline, and forces herself to pick up the pace in spite of the pain, holding her side as she runs.

The guard, unfortunately, is in decent physical shape. Better than Dany. Her bad luck, he is probably a runner. He gallops easily along, not seeming to tire. His legs are longer, and he is better fed. When she glances back, she sees an eerie smile on his face.

Because the guard is enjoying this.

| | |

Dany is already pushing her limits. She's been malnourished for months. As for reserves, they're what she's been living on. Running faster isn't the answer.

She has to run *smarter*.

Dany takes in the possibilities. There are a lot of RVs and converted vans in her neighbourhood, the people who live in them, one step from homeless. Dany puts an RV between her and the guard, cutting across a lawn. The RV blocks her from sight as she dodges into the space between two apartment buildings. A slim passage lets out the next street over. Before he catches sight of her, she slips over a residential fence, crosses a yard and, clambering through a hole in the cedar hedge, lets herself into another alley. In the distance, she hears the silent warning.

In one instant, there is the distant low drone of a muffler, and in the next, it is gone.

The cop is close. A block or two. Stopped by the school? She isn't sure, but it's bad luck. Now, at any moment, that cop might come creeping. He might even call for backup.

And Dany is running on empty.

Her lungs burn and her side feels like she's being stabbed with a screwdriver. She doesn't have the stores for this kind of physical work. Doesn't eat enough to run, not for long. Her legs are seizing up, and her knees are all wobbly. Still, with all the twists and turns she's taken, she's passed out of the guard's sight for the moment.

Dany glances around.

One hundred metres to the west, the long alley empties out on a busy six-lane road, the western limit of her 'hood. That strip is a desert, as far as she is concerned. Running along the six-lane, they'll spot her from a mile off.

To her immediate left, there is a small recessed parking lot and though the front is open, the back is set under a building. It is dark, cavelike and somehow looks inhabited – though no one looks to be there just now.

A dead end.

A bad idea. No, a terrible idea.

Then the guard comes into view, his back to her. There, at the top of the street, and Dany is out of steam. There is no more run in her. There is a butcher's knife planted in her side and her lungs are on fire. Before he sees her, she dodges into the underground.

And there, Dany is trapped.

| CHAPTER 0 = X + 14

Dany steps between the dumpster and the compost bins, eyes darting between nooks.

Tucked between the dumpster and the wall, there is an old foam mattress soaked in urine. And worse, much worse, down its middle is a brown slick that one sniff tells her can only be human feces. The mould-mottled and shit-streaked thing is horrific. Disgusting. There is no way she is going near that foul thing. Nobody in their right mind would.

Dany shakes her head, following her own logic through to its conclusion.

She burrows into the mattress fold, forcing her small frame into the compressed space. The whole of it is wet and foul. On the inside, the thing stinks worse than a public toilet. She chokes on the smell of rotting meat and stale sweat and the musk of dog urine and worse, the smell of human shit. She tries to hold her breath – but it's too hard. Her lungs are desperate for oxygen after the run. The smell is intense in such a small space, stifling, stomach turning. Every breath fills her mouth with water and bile. If she doesn't get out soon, the retching will give her away.

A deep long-ago memory resurfaces. The memory is very old, because they shut down public swimming pools eons ago. But yes, she finds that nameless muscle that lets her plug the passage to her nose. And that helps, a little.

The footsteps approach.

Her heart is pounding so loud she is sure the sound will give her away. She hears the rent-a-cop's heavy boots. His steps slow and then stop. The guard backs up, and Dany imagines him looking first this way, then that.

Those heavy boots clomp her way, the sound growing steadily louder. She closes her eyes and holds her breath.

The guard pauses.

"You're not a bad runner, girl," he says. "I'll give you that. But why don't you come on out now? Make it easier on both of us."

Dany pats her front pocket. There, she feels the reassuring shape of a small canister of pepper spray. Her aunt attached the tiny cylinder to her key ring months ago. But she can't risk the jangle of keys, can't pull it out, not now. Not yet.

"You know you're done. I'll pull you out of there, so why not save yourself the pain. If you make me get my hands dirty, I'll be pissed."

But in such a small space, the pepper spray will be a mistake. She'll blind herself as well as him.

"All right, then," he says. "We'll do this the hard way."

Dany hears the first of the compost bins go down, flipped onto its side, no doubt spilling out a new host of horrors.

"Eeny, meeny, miny, moe," sings the guard.

The second bin goes over, spilling out rotten veg and eggshells and, worse, a big rat that scurries past her nook.

"Catch a girly by the toe."

Dany's hand shifts. She reaches into her back pocket, drawing out Eva's manicure scissors. If that guard doesn't shut up – Dany pauses, glancing at the miniscule scissors – she'll what? Give him a pedicure? She shoves the tiny scissors back in her pocket, disgusted. A heavy creak comes next – the metal lid of the dumpster. In the silence of a held breath, she hears the guard poking around.

"I can smell you, girl," he says. "I know you're close."

Dany's heart is pounding against her rib cage. She holds her breath, but her lungs burn and a tiny gasp escapes her mouth.

The guard falls silent.

Dany hears it, too. A distant rattling. The heavy metal lid of the dumpster slams to a close, and the guard gives up the rhyme scheme.

"Little bitch," he mutters. And he takes off, footsteps jogging the other way. Chasing a sound in the distance. The rattle of a shopping cart.

Finally, as if a vanishing point has swallowed the man whole, there comes a beautiful, unbroken silence.

She counts, waiting.

| | |

Dany squeezes out of her foul hiding spot.

In the fresh air, standing in rotten vegetable leavings, she brushes at her clothes desperately, trying to wipe off the disgusting stench. Her mouth is full of water and she spits it clean. Then, taking a deep breath, she takes off her boots, quietly steals up the alley in socked feet, eyes sweeping the ground for syringes.

The alley, like the cul-de-sac, is clear. Still, she isn't scot free, not yet. If she is unlucky, the guard will double back. Or a ghost car will come silently creeping – the hybrids are impossible to hear. Or worse yet, the school cop will call in canines.

Dogs are bad. You can't outrun dogs.

She's known five or six kids at Darling-Holmes, ones who've run in the night – as she had, in her turn – and who were returned to the bunk come morning with wounds in the shape of a dog's teeth up and down an arm. Of course, not one of those kids can hold a candle to Dany.

Sure, the dogs have left their marks on her. But it isn't like anyone can tell. Because her arms are a ruin. The skin looks like it has been liquefied in places. Her arms don't hurt her much, not anymore – they were once twin beds of fire – but still, each night and each morning, she rubs lotion into her arms, or the skin cracks and lesions open up along the worst of the seam lines.

Not even a dog can make Dany's arms look much worse than they do now.

Dany pushes up her long sleeves – she is too hot to care who sees her scars. Still in her socks, she starts down the alley at a slow jog. She carries her boots in her hands, moving silently. A block up, she passes a homeless man. Is he infected? She can't say. No one can. What she does know is this – if he has the virus, it is only the regular strain, version 1.0. He doesn't look anything like Jasper or Liz.

But something about him tells her he is probably infected.

Maybe it's the water.

The man has a huge plastic sack made from some kind of tarpaulin. The bag is stuffed with cans and bottles – taken from dumpsters probably. But beside it, she can see a half-dozen dirty plastic bottles, ones he's refilled with water. By the time they're taken to the hospice, the virus has made them drink water compulsively. The shrunken hypothalamus again. At the hospice, she's seen evidence of what all that water does to the dying. The ascites, the swollen belly-bags, that develop with time.

One of the man's feet, the bare one, is encrusted with blood. The other foot is clad in a rotting tennis shoe. He is wearing a worn pair of track pants, but no shirt. Even in April his skin looks like tanned leather. His patchy beard shows a couple of months' growth. He looks a question at the boots she cradles, or maybe he looks at her arms, but he doesn't so much as glance at her face.

Dany breathes through her mouth.

She can smell him, even from ten feet away. Even through her own reek.

If he is infected, the virus will colonize his brain. And day by day, one flickering light bulb at a time, everything that makes him who he is will burn out. Until the day comes that someone glances at him in passing and decides to call him in. They'll put a yellow jacket on him. Lock that jacket up tight. Dany reaches for her hex key.

Still there, inside of her shirt.

She breathes her relief. And there, at the edge of consciousness, she just makes it out, the rattling of rickety old wheels disappearing into the distance. Then Dany sees it. A small figure.

A little girl, leaning against the wall, a single arm outstretched. Only, no, it's the same strange doll she saw the day before – the one that was propped up beside the dumpster. Yesterday, it looked to be greeting her. Today, the tangle-haired doll is standing by a wall, one arm outstretched, pointing Dany's way home.

Dany looks from the doll to the homeless man, the one with the virus, but she knows the doll doesn't belong to him. No, the doll is the creature of that woman, the one with the familiar face. The one who is always rattling her cart through the back alley by Dany's place. Always watching. Always with eyes on Dany and her sister. The sound of her rattling cart dogging them, as the two make their way to and from school.

Dany looks around for the woman – but she is nowhere in sight. Still, in the distance, she once more hears the rattle of her shopping cart.

Dany turns her back on the doll and heads for home.

She isn't far now, and as she jogs, her eyes scan the street, moving from side to side, left to right, checking the peripheries. But she doesn't cross the guard's path, doesn't see any cops, doesn't hear the low growl and near-silent padding of a canine's paws.

| | |

Dany takes in the place she lives with a stranger's eyes. First, she does a check of the shadowy spots, the corners, the bushes, and finally, she scans the approach down the alley.

Clear.

Over the years, she's lived in a couple different units. She lived in a basement flat with her mother – the one whose sole tiny window looked out on a small hole in the lawn, ringed by aluminum siding, about half as deep as a grave.

The window well.

Later, she and her aunt moved into number six, where she lives now. So, she's put in a lot of years at this building. Minus those eleven months gone – the ones she spent locked up at the work farm.

Honestly, the place doesn't look like home.

The building is a big ugly box. One look, and you know the place was never nice, not even when it was new. In the yard, there is an old cedar-railing sandbox. Each spring, the rails sink a little further into the ground. No one bothers to plant flowers in the garden, not anymore.

Dany glances at the old heritage house next door. That's where Mac will go.

Bea's place is more than a hundred years old, and, like the cedar railing of the sandbox, slowly sliding into the earth. There is no sign of the old woman. Still, her screen door is open a few inches, and the curtains are catching the breeze, fluttering through the open crack.

Dany nods. If that door is open, then Bea is home.

Dany squats down and takes the time to get back into her boots. Otherwise, all that broken glass in the stairwell, what her aunt calls Eastside rain, will cut her up. While she ties her boots, she keeps an eye on the alley.

| | |

In the upstairs hall, Dany stops outside of her door and, using a dime, unscrews the number on her door. A moment later, she is standing outside of Kuzmenko's unit. He lives in number five, right across from Dany. She undoes the screw on his door, and replaces his number with her own.

She lays her hand on Kuzmenko's door and a shadow crosses the peephole. "It's just for a bit," she tells him in English, adding, "Bal'shoye spaseeba, Kuzmenko."

Dany nods at the peephole.

Outside of her own door, a moment later, she puts his number up. Smiles. She's just given herself a brand new, untraceable address.

The rent-a-cop can show up here if he wants, the ministry, too, for that matter – but all they'll find is an old Russian émigré who is too old and sick to remember more than a few words of spoken English – and no trace of Dany.

Dany grins.

Let them piss off Kuzmenko. See what that gets them.

Then she pulls out her keys and lets herself in. Dany is safe at last. Home free. *Olly olly oxen free.*

| CHAPTER ⊙ = X + 15

Inside the small apartment, Dany sniffs at her shirt – all but vomits in her mouth – and strips the thing off, burying it in the garbage.

After taking a shower, Dany stares at the foggy mirror. After a long moment, and a steeling breath, she swipes at the mirror with a hand towel. First, she wipes away a narrow stripe at the top, revealing the face of a dark-haired girl.

"I'd say you're at a crossroads," she tells the girl in the mirror, her voice reasonable. "You can kill yourself now. But, I don't know, maybe we just play this one through, see if we get lucky?"

The girl in the mirror is without an opinion.

Dany steels herself again. This time, the swipe of her towel reveals the rest of her. But Dany loses the dark-haired girl, because her gaze is pulled inexorably to those arms.

The sight, she's never gotten used to it.

The girl's flesh is a cruel patchwork. But it's the texture that pulls Dany's gaze. The way the skin is raised in places, and there are strange little declivities, like moon craters, as if bits of the muscle have been torn away. The padding that should be around her muscles has been removed, revealing all too clearly what should hide beneath the flesh. Her eyes take in the strangely mottled colour of her skin, the lines that mark the rough grafts. The new lesions, the bloody crust. Her arms look like they've been submerged in acid, then jerry-rigged with a few spare strips of mismatched flesh. As if the doctors didn't have time to do more than a quick quilt-work job of her. To her, the arms are, in a way, fascinating. But she knows what it must be like for other people.

After it first happened, she figured the scars had rendered her moot. Unlovable. That she'd have friends, she'd have family, but she wouldn't have the kind of relationship that would mean she'd have to take off her long-sleeved shirt. She believed that the fire had set her . . . apart.

She feels differently now.

Looking at her arms now, she tells herself a new story. *I lived through the fire. I lived through it. And if a person can't look at my arms and see how that's life? How that's me? Well then, they aren't worth the breath it takes to say, Screw you.*

Dany pulls on a fresh long-sleeved shirt – and looks at herself again in the mirror. The effect is entirely different. But the girl in the shirt, the one without visible scars, is just an illusion. Not the real girl. Not the *survivor*. The real Dany, scars and all, that's who she is. *Screw anyone who doesn't get it.*

Dany sniffs at her shirt, as fresh as lemons. Like the dishwashing detergent she washed it with. She looks at the mirror – and the girl blinks back at her.

Dany shrugs.

"See ya," she tells the girl in the glass.

"Not if I see you first," the girl says.

And then the lights flicker, twice, and darkness steals the girl's image from the glass.

| | |

Dany went on a date with a boy. Once.

Ruben Ripley.

They went to the beach together, last summer. The hot sand was good between her toes, and she took off her shorts – her bathing suit was underneath – and headed to the water.

"Your shirt," he said.

Dany stared at him a beat, then got it over with. She took the shirt off and tossed it on the sand.

Ruben didn't say anything, not right away. But the look on his face, right before he turned away from her, was enough.

They were waist-deep in it when he finally looked at her again.

"Your arms," he said, "they look like they hurt."

Dany, squatting down, submerged under the waves.

Half an hour later, when she came out, she pulled on her long-sleeved shirt.

"You're leaving," he said.

Dany nodded and put the buds in her ears and the music washed him away, the way, half an hour before, an entire ocean had flooded up around her and disappeared him.

When the bus pulled up, Ruben got on first. He picked out a pair of seats near the front. Ruben sat down in one, and his duffle bag sat on the other.

And Dany walked past him like the stranger that he was.

At the back, she sat and stared out the window. The rocking motion of the bus and the warm salt air put her to sleep. When she woke up, she was at the end of the line and Ruben, like a bad dream, was gone. It'd taken her a long time to get past the shame and to figure it out. No, it hadn't been Dany who failed the test. Ruben Ripley failed the test. Her arms are a litmus test of a person's humanity.

Eva helped her see that.

But some days, it's hard to be a person.

But Eva makes that easier, too.

Eva sees her scars as part of her. The first time Eva saw Dany – really saw her – Eva looked into Dany's eyes and simply said, "Your scars are part of you. You're beautiful." A shiver runs through Dany. But she can't think about any of that, because she can't be selfish. Because Dany has to think of Mac.

| | |

When the phone rings, Dany is scribbling some math on the wall beside the window. Here, with the window open, the stench of the dumpster below is overpowering. But she has a perfect view of Bea's backyard. Only there is no sign of Eva. No sign of her sister.

And now the dead telephone is ringing.

Dany turns her back on the equation and slowly follows the sound into the living room. For a minute, she just stands there, staring at the little black box, the one they cut off days ago. Somehow, the phone is back from the dead. And it is ringing. Loudly.

For a moment, her hand hovers over the black horn, but no, no good could come of that phone, she knows. No good at all. She pulls the cord from the wall and retreats to her bedroom. But in those few minutes, the feeling has gotten worse.

Eva and her sister should be at Bea's by now.

She glances again at her math equation, the one that she is writing on the white wall with a Sharpie, the one that just won't come out right.

But this time, when her eyes fall on the math, understanding fills her mind.

It's not like every person has an equal chance of meeting with every other person, like we're atoms in Brownian motion, or a bowl of alphabet soup. Jasper taught her this, told her all about stochastic modelling. She should have remembered. *Stupid.*

Dany starts again.

No, people aren't soup, are they?

Not all people mix the same way. Plus, there has to be a delay, for the window of infection. So add a new class, here.

Dany scribbles another notation on the wall.

Now, when she retraces the resulting graph, finally, the picture looks right. The rates of infection oscillate and rise. Graph overlays graph, curve overlays curve, until a butterfly fills her wall, its wings not gossamer but a series of curving black lines.

Lorenz's butterfly.

The strange attractor. An accident of successive drafts, maybe? Something more? A pattern in the noise.

Dany stares at those lines for so long, so hard, they imprint on her eyes, and when she turns away an outline of the butterfly lifts from her wall and flutters out over the world. When the noise erupts – fists banging at Kuzmenko's door, gruff voices demanding Dany come out – she's got no other choice left. She slips on a mask and follows the butterfly.

She opens her bedroom window wide, sits on its edge and, lowering herself from the frame, hangs there a moment, suspended in air. And when she opens her hands to let go, falling the last six feet to the dumpster's lid, the butterfly is already there.

| CHAPTER ⊙ = X + 16

Lorenz's butterfly vanishes somewhere in the alley out back from Bea's place. Dany stands in the shade of a pear tree. Two long depressions, left by tire tracks, mark the alley. On either side of those tire tracks, clutches of crabgrass feed on shadow.

Dany looks everywhere, but the butterfly is gone.

She closes her eyes – feels for the strange attractor, the one that lifted from her wall and fluttered to life. But when she opens her eyes, it is Mac she sees, smiling, from the mouth of the alley. The kid's mouth is ringed with purple, like she's been eating a cartoon eggplant. Eva must've given the kid sweets.

The kid catches sight of Dany and runs, full throttle, throwing her little body at Dany's chest. Even knowing what's coming, the weight of the kid surprises her, and Dany clutches at Mac, falling on her ass.

Eva, smiling, jogs up behind.

"Oh my God," Eva says. "She's just like randomly happy to see you. I swear, I'm not that bad of a babysitter."

The strange feeling Dany had, only a minute ago, is gone. It's as if the weird feeling can be erased by the life energy that emanates from Eva and Mac. Dany grins at her friend, so entirely grateful that she can't even speak.

Thank you, she wants to tell Eva. But what she means is so bright and shiny and big, the words can't fit inside of her mouth. She looks at Eva, and maybe something of that is on her face.

"Yeah, you're welcome," Eva says, laughing.

Dany looks over the kid. All in one piece, and the nose plug there, in its customary place. Eva has taken care of everything. Mac is safe.

"We need to tell Bea," Dany says, nodding at the big house. "We need to make her come with us."

The smile disappears from Eva's face. She nods, and together they head towards the house.

| | |

The three of them stand in front of Bea's sliding glass door. Eva looks at Dany and shakes her head.

"Something's wrong," Eva says quietly.

The garden hose has been left running. This, in spite of water tariffs and badly depleted reservoirs. On the picnic table, three buckets have been set out. One is full to overflowing and the others, bone dry. The hose has fallen from the first bucket, and come to rest in a stand of Jerusalem artichoke. Half the roots have been laid bare by the unchecked flow of water, and the garden is a slimy bed of mud.

Eva shuts off the faucet, and Dany peers into the dark house.

The screen door is open and Bea's curtains flutter in the breeze. The hem is covered in muck. The whole of the house looks lonely, unpeopled. Inside, all is dark and quiet – which is odd. Always, before, there's been light. Light and music.

"You better stay here," Dany says. Without waiting, she slips through the curtain.

| | |

In the pale light that passes through the curtains, Dany can make out muddy footprints leading through the living room. "Bea?" she calls.

No sound comes back to her, not even a whisper. Just a waiting silence.

Then, from somewhere deep in the house, comes a muffled bang. It's as if someone has left a running shoe in the dryer. But Dany knows this isn't it. Can't be it. Because this is a fleshier sound. And, judging from the dead spiderweb of wiring over the living room, the power is still out. The hydro has been on and off since morning and Dany tries not to understand, tries not to put the muffled bang together with what she saw earlier today, tries not to think of poor Liz.

Dany reaches for a light switch, flicks it on and off, but there is no effect. Or, there is an effect, but it's only this – when she flicks the light switch, and it doesn't offer control over light and darkness, Dany feels like she's been plunged into a lucid dream.

"I'm dreaming," Dany tells herself, but her voice drops to a whisper.

"Interesting thesis," Eva says, coming up behind. "And if you die in a dream, then, like, do you die in real life?"

Dany takes a deep breath and looks at her friend.

Under those enormous bangs, Eva wears a silly grin on her face. She doesn't look the least bit worried.

Dany stares at Eva, but what she sees are all of the sheltering layers that, over long years, have been carefully built up around her friend. Bianca, who keeps the Wahls' house. Esteban, who keeps the grounds of the Wahl estate. The driver, who stands outside their car, modelling conservative suits. Lawyers. Private doctors. Nutritional consultants. So many people in Eva's life, all hired by Len Wahl, to keep her apart from the world.

And Eva, crazy Eva, doing her best to outflank the lot of them.

It's Eva who insisted on an Eastside micro-school.

It's Eva who parachuted herself into Dany's world.

It's Eva who followed her into this house.

She supposes, really, that's what being rich means. Being rich means you have to fight your parents to be able to spend a sliver of time in Dany's world. Being poor means it's all but impossible to scratch your way out of it.

"What'd you do with Mac?" Dany asks.

"I gave her my glasses," Eva says. "Don't worry. I opened the internet browser for her and everything. There's a lot on there that's, like . . . artistic."

"You left her alone on the internet?" Dany asks, incredulous.

"Yikes," Eva says. "User error? Sorry."

Dany looks at Eva for a beat.

"But there are some really good pictures," Eva says.

Dany shakes her head and moves into the dim interior. "You should wait outside," Dany tells her. Her eyes trace the muddy prints, but these peter out partway into the house. By the time the living room carpet becomes linoleum, the footprints are smears.

"Bianca tells this story," Eva says quietly, "about the house on Negros Island where she grew up. It was an old place, like, say, the guest house of a plantation, but falling apart. I always sort of pictured it like this."

Narrowing her eyes, Dany traces the last of the muddy streaks. Soon, though, she's lost all sign. But whoever it is, they were moving towards the kitchen.

"When she was six," Eva goes on, "Bianca saw an *amomongo* – it's like, the Negros Island version of a Sasquatch. The thing disembowelled a goat right in front of her and then draped itself in the entrails."

Dany stops and looks at her friend. "Helping?"

Eva shakes her head. "No, it's not helping me either."

Dany stares at her friend, exasperated.

But Eva has stopped moving, and she is looking at Dany with a serious expression. "Look," Eva says, "just in case we do both die, there's something I want you to know. I, well, I want to be a cryptozoologist. For a non-profit. You know, something humanitarian, er, well, sasquatcharian. But yes. I want to like work with cryptos. For, like, minimum wage." Her eyes light up at the thought. "Like, I don't know, I thought maybe you and me can like found an organization, you know, like the SPCA. But for sasquatches. Err, I mean, sasquai? Sésq'ac?"

Dany nods – but already, she can smell the danger. "Gas," she says.

The two of them head for the old stove.

Two of the gas burners are on, the pilot lights out. After switching off the burners, Dany tries to open a window, but over the years, the seams have all been painted along with the frames, sealing them shut. In the distance, above them, she hears scuffling. Now and again, another strange and muffled bang.

Dany looks at Eva and her friend shakes her head. "We turned off the gas, and now we should go," Eva says.

"I told you. Go wait in the yard," Dany tells her. "But I'm going up."

"But, like, you're my sidekick."

Dany rolls her eyes, but Eva puts a hand on her shoulder.

"I am not losing you. No way. No how."

| | |

As they move deeper into the house, up the steps and onto the second floor, Dany catches the scent of something unsettling. More unsettling, even, than the smell of gas. There is, as always, the faint smell of whisky and lilacs – Bea's scent – but under it, there is something else, something subtle, the kind of scent that comes and goes, there and then not, here and then gone. The smell reminds her of the burn ward. . . . In the air, a strange copper tang, one she associates with the inside of the body and that makes her afraid.

"Where would I be if I were Bea?" Eva asks.

Dany glances at her.

"You sure she's even home?"

Dany nods. "Somebody's definitely here."

"I know where I'd be," Eva whispers dramatically. "I'd bloody well hide under the bed from monsters."

"You should wait outside," Dany says. "Watch Mac."

"No," Eva says. "I have to protect you."

Dany can't help it. She laughs.

"Not from them," Eva says, seriously. "From you."

Dany narrows her eyes and looks at her friend, but Eva is staring straight ahead, and the expression on her face makes

Dany's heart skip a beat. She turns, follows Eva's gaze, and that's when she sees Bea.

Bea, who has always been like a grandma to the girls. A slightly terrifying grandma, but a grandma nonetheless. Bea, who brings over dishes of pasta, plates of cookies, casseroles and soups. Bea, whose tongue is sharp but whose eyes are soft.

She is wearing a flowery apron, and yes, on the surface, as always, she is Bea, their Bea. Mac's Bea. But one look, and Dany knows – the Bea they both know is gone. This old woman's face is wild with fright, and her hands are curled like claws around a pair of knitting needles.

"I'm on fire," Bea is saying, in that strange and broken way. "On fire."

Like Liz. She's muttering just like Liz.

But it is her eye that stops Dany cold. Something is wrong with her left eye. A strange liquid is leaking from the broken orb. One glance at the dark-tipped knitting needle confirms it. The eye has been perforated.

Bea's other eye bulges from her socket, looking wrong – so wrong. The swollen orb doesn't belong in a human face. Her brain is swelling. Her swollen brain is actually putting pressure on her eyes, pushing them out.

Eva is right.

There are monsters.

Little planets that consume us from within.

And they aren't creatures, just clusters of molecules. . . .

And then Bea – who Dany loves, who Dany trusts with her little sister – raises the knitting needles in her hands, but they aren't pointed outwards, they aren't pointed at Dany. And that makes it worse.

Infinitely worse.

| CHAPTER ⊙ = X + 17

Dany doesn't know this girl, the one who fights Bea for the knitting needles. The one who doesn't think about viruses or vectors – only about the soft orbs of an old woman's eyes, the sharp needles in her hands. Dany roughly tears the knitting needles from Bea and then knocks the old woman back into her bedroom.

She and Eva get the door closed, and Dany tosses the needles down the hall.

All at once, Dany is more tired than she's ever been in her life. She wipes her hands on her pants and slides down to the floor.

Eva sits heavily down next to her. With a chagrined shrug, she passes Dany a small bottle of alcohol gel.

Dany pours a glob on her hands and rubs them together. Her whole body is shaking. Dany hates the virus. Hates it. But most of all, she hates what the virus does to every last one of them – infected or not. "We need a chair," she tells Eva. "Something to hold the door."

| | |

Dany squats on the ground, her shoulder lodged against the door. The tongue is in its groove and the old woman has gone quiet on the other side.

Dany turns the handle and opens the door a crack – just a tiny bit – just enough for a whisper. "Bea? Hey, you in there, Bea?"

The old woman shoves forward.

She doesn't mean to hurt Dany. She just wants to get out of the room she's locked in. But when Bea shoves the door, the edge hits the side of Dany's face, and there is an explosion of pain.

A moment later, swearing, Eva is beside her. Together, they shoulder the door to a close. The metal tongue, once more, snicks into its groove.

Dany slides to the ground, her back against the door, holding it in place. Already, she can feel her eye swelling. Feel her mouth filling with something warm and wet. She wants to spit the blood from her mouth, but can't risk spattering blood near Eva. Instead, Dany swallows. The blood is lukewarm and salty, sickening. She tongues a tooth experimentally. It gives a little in its bed. *God*. But it was an accident. Bea would never hurt her. Not on purpose. Never.

On the other side of the door, Dany can hear the old woman muttering. Only it isn't Bea in there. It's the virus. The virus is moving Bea's puppet strings now. That's not Bea, but a life-size viral host. She hears herself think it – hates herself for thinking it – but somehow, she can't stop the word from coming. *Viral*. Bea is a viral.

Finally, Eva drags the wooden captain's chair over and together they angle it under the door handle.

"Can we call someone?" Dany asks.

"Outside," Eva says. "We should get out of here first."

Dany sits there a moment, more sad than afraid. Here she is, turning on Bea like the old woman is nothing to her. Dany doesn't want to be a bad person. But everywhere she goes, and everyone she loves, turns bad.

"Everybody, everybody around me, they all die," Dany says, her voice small.

"No, no, no," Eva says, pulling at her arm. "I need you to listen to me. This is not your fault. This is not on you."

Dany looks up at Eva.

But then Eva is looking at her strangely, as if some new thought is only now occurring to her.

Dany fingers her mask, checking the seal. Only after she is sure that her mask is in place does Dany get to her feet, get herself moving. Step follows step – exactly as they always do – and Dany, once again, finds herself walking out of the ruins of another life.

| CHAPTER ⊙ = X + 18

Outside of Bea's house, Dany looks up at the sun. The fiery ball is set inside of a big blue sky and shines down on her bruised and battered face. Shines down on the three of them. Her arms are shaking and the kid, now, is in front of Dany – tugging on her hand – an urgent question in her eyes. But Dany can't tell her, can't find the words to explain to Mac about Bea. Shame burns inside of her. She's let Bea down.

Bea has been like a grandmother to Mac – and now, Dany's let her down.

Mac stares at her solemnly. But her eyes keep flicking from Eva to Dany to the house. She wants to know about Bea.

Eva is the one to tell her.

"Aw, Little Rabbit, Bea's not up for a visit just now," Eva says. "But she's got a couple of new friends. Mister Sharps and Mister Pointy."

Mac, running tiny fingers over her nose plug, looks from Eva to Dany. Dany sees it – the worried expression in her eyes. Dany kneels down in front of her kid sister. Because she doesn't want to lie to the kid about anything. Not anymore. Not ever.

Not even about Santa Claus.

Dany lifts a single finger towards Mac's nose. Stops herself just in time. Slides that finger instead along the ridge of the kid's ear, tucking away a strand of loose hair. She feels a kind of grief for the gesture, that moment her finger would gently arc into air before tapping down on the button of her little sister's nose. A familiar gesture between them. Full of meaning, thick with repetition, a gesture they've come to and made and remade over her years on this planet. Gone.

One day, she doesn't know when, but one day, the kid would have been done with the gesture. But now, the virus has done away with it for them.

"Bea's sick," Dany tells her. "I'm sorry, but we can't help her. We don't want you to get sick, too. Bea wouldn't want that. 'Kay?"

Mac looks up at Dany and, standing on her tippy toes, reaches up, touches a tiny finger to the outer ridge of Dany's ear. A gift, that one tiny fingertip. And Dany, feeling that little tap, knows it will all be okay. Even if Jasper and Liz and Bea are gone. Because as long as Mac is okay, the world has a centre. As long as Mac is okay, gravity holds.

Because Mac, she is all of it, she is the beating heart of Dany's world.

| | |

For a few minutes, they stand there, in silence – the sun beating down on them, the world reassembling itself into something like sense.

"What do we do?" Eva finally asks.

"Warn people," Dany says, her shrug an open question.

They stand in the sun in the alley, Eva instructing the little voice in her glasses to text every last person she knows.

Finally, Eva calls Bianca. The right arm of her glasses separates into two limbs, and she slides one of these down towards her mouth, positioning the tiny microphone to pick up her voice. A moment later, Bianca is on speaker and Dany's listening to the call.

In the background, she hears a Tagalog soap opera on the shortwave. Dany can't help it. The sounds of the kitchen, they put her in mind of Antoine. And then *he* has to figure in the equation too. As little as she likes it, as little as she wants to do with him, as little as he deserves to be part of her math, because he hasn't earned it, there it is. She has to rescue her stupid father, too. On their way out of the city, she has to somehow break Norah out of jail, and then stop to pick up Antoine, too.

In the background, the soap opera falls silent.

She hears the receiver hit the hard stone tile of the kitchen floor – handcrafted, Italian – and realizes that Bianca has taken Eva literally. She's simply dropped the phone to get Eva's mother and go.

Eva clicks some invisible button on her glasses and nods.

"I'll get my driver," she says.

But it's too late. When Eva calls her driver, instructing him to pick her up, Dany hears his voice for the first time. "To hell with that," the driver tells Eva. "I'll mail the keys when I hit Alaska." The call clicks off, and Eva makes a face. "Maybe I should have called my driver before I sent that mass text."

Dany looks up at the sky. Ten digits write themselves into the blue of forever. Like wisps of cloud, there and then slowly blurring at the edges. *The answer. A way out.* The number is there, after all, in her head. And she's seen Faraday around, seen him putting groceries into his car at the local store. His old VW Bug might be a shit box, but it's a shit box with four wheels. A shit box that rolls on the ground, presumably.

"We'll go to Faraday's," Dany says.

"Uh, and stalking our history teacher, it helps how?" Eva asks.

"He has a car," Dany says. "Besides, I owe him. If he hadn't kept his mouth shut – back there – I'd be . . . I'd be . . . Me and Mac, we'd have been . . ." Dany shrugs. "Just, like, give me your glasses."

"What," Eva says in mock seriousness. "Dany is utilizing the new technology. This *is* an emergency!" Still, she hands the glasses over. Dany addresses herself to the object in her hand – one lens irises into an opaque screen – and a moment later, she can see a reverse-lookup website in small, right before her eyes. A beat more and she is blinking at their history teacher's home address.

"Someone really should teach Mister Faraday about how personal privacy works in a digital age," Eva says. She shakes her head sadly.

| | |

Dany's last call is about Bea. Isobel Lau takes down Bea's address – but it isn't Bea that Isobel wants to talk about.

"The MDC sent people to your house," Isobel says. "But somehow, we had the wrong address on file." Her voice is dry with irony.

"Why would they go there?" Dany asks.

But she knows.

The blood and tissue samples, the ones they took at the lab, they must have told Isobel what Dany is only now beginning to suspect. Dany takes the eGlasses off speaker and turns her back on Mac and Eva.

Quietly, clinically, in the cold language of a scientist, Isobel draws a line from the new, mutated virus – the one that got Jasper – to Liz and Bea. The line runs right through her. Dany has infected them. It's obvious. Dany all but knew it already.

All but for one problematic fact.

"I'm not sick," she tells Isobel.

"You're asymptomatic," Isobel says. "Your samples tested positive for antigens to *both* variants of the virus. So even if you aren't feeling sick, we need to assume you're infectious. We need you to come in."

The world spins, and all the while, Isobel offers up theories. What prior exposure to the mild strain of the virus might mean. Critical differences in T cells and immune response in the young. A recent study out of Oxford. "They're only now documenting the existence of cases like this. Children, Dany, children and early adolescents who present with such mild symptoms they're almost subclinical. Of course, that's with the earlier strain," she adds, and Dany's head spins. "We'll need to watch you, carefully, and we should run a cerebrospinal fluid analysis stat," Isobel begins, but Dany is done.

On Dany's first day at the BioGENEius lab, Isobel Lau took them to see the facilities. On the tour, she showed Dany the microtome. "This machine," Isobel said, "was a big part of our first real breakthrough with the virus. The sections that this microtome produces, when fed a viral brain – thinner even than onion skin paper."

Dany stared at the machine, thinking of a word. Three letters. Five points.

She stared at that machine, thinking of all of the people she'd ever known and lost track of. The ones who just one day weren't there anymore. Just there and then gone.

Thinking of a woman named Phil.

Thinking of a man the kids called Veg. Because of his cauliflower ear. But it was only funny if you didn't know how he got the damage. Bill was his real name. He used to run the convenience store, and he sold her mom real cigarettes for a quarter each, until those too were impossible to get.

Had Bill been infected? Had it been Bill's brain that they'd fed to that machine?

While Isobel explained the finer points of the microtome, Jasper looked at Dany, his brown eyes soft with concern. "It's a rough kind of science," Jasper added, quietly. His words had the ring of an apology.

Isobel Lau raised an eyebrow and gave the biologist a corrective glance. "In the early days," she reminded him, "with a virus of this magnitude? Well, a little rough science is called for."

Dany turns away from the memory, and looks at her kid sister, at those enormous brown eyes. "What about treatment?" she asks Isobel.

"Once we get you into the lab," Lau tells her, "we can begin to think about that. But the clock is ticking."

"My little sister," Dany begins.

"Your sister," Isobel asks, her voice brisk. "She's with you?"

"Yeah," Dany says.

"Then I'm sorry, Dany. I'm truly sorry, but she'll need to come in too. Let us pick her up. Let us see if we can keep her safe," Isobel says, her voice gentle.

But there is no "safe."

The MDC would just contain her sister. Stick her in some kind of a glorified glovebox, just like Dany and her rats. And if Mac was fine? They'd send her off to the Ministry of Child Services. They might even send both of them there. That's if they didn't feed Dany to the machine, if they didn't slice and dice her brain. She pictures deli-sized slices emerging from a microtome.

"It's not safe," Dany says.

"No," Isobel tells her, misunderstanding. "No, you aren't safe. No one's safe when they're with you." And it is like her lungs collapse, the air pushes out of Dany's chest all at once and, for a moment, she can't breathe, she just can't catch a breath.

There are prime numbers and then there are the patterns in the primes. Today, Dany skip-counts primes, leaping through the sums by the power of ten. *Two, twenty-nine, five hundred and forty-one.*

Breathe, she tells herself, *breathe.*

"You're a danger," Lau tells her flatly. "You're a danger to every living person you come in contact with."

Dany taps the temple of Eva's glasses, and with that tiny click, the tinny voice in her ear dies away, and Isobel vanishes with it.

"What'd she say?" Eva asks brightly.

And for a long beat, Dany stands there, staring at what looks like an ordinary pair of glasses in her hand. "Nothing," Dany says, finally. "She didn't say nothing."

She slides her fingers over her mask, testing the seal.

Dany is pretty sure she knows how the new virus is transmitted – the one thing that ties Jasper, Dany, Liz and Bea together. Saliva. Three tiny snapshots rise up from the swamp of her mind: Jasper's tea, a wrinkled pea in her copy of Shrewsbury and Liz's voice, asking, in a decent imitation of Bea, "Want some sparkle?"

A tiny virus has turned Dany into a ticking time bomb. And that bomb is attached to a clock that has no visible hands. She wants to tell Eva, but there are no words.

She can't find words.

"It's the new strain," Dany finally manages. "That's what got Liz and Jasper."

"People need to know," Eva says.

Dany shakes her head. "Yeah, who'll listen to a couple of teenagers?"

"I could post a video, like, of what happened to Liz and Jasper. I could put it up on the interweb," Eva says.

Her glasses, Dany thinks. Of course, she's taped all of it on her glasses.

Dany nods, and five clicks later, it is done.

| | |

As they close in on Faraday's house, the girls come to a decision.

"My father's yacht," Eva tells her, "it'll be perfect. Sort of like a plague vacay."

"Your dad has a yacht," Dany repeats.

"Fully stocked. But one small problem. It's moored out by Steveston. Len Wahl, the malignant narcissist who spawned me, is schlepping a foot model. She's got a condo out there."

"Like Chaucer meets Boccaccio," Dany says.

Eva bumps a look her way.

Dany doesn't bother explaining. "I like to read," she says and shrugs.

"And I like to survive extinction-level events," quips Eva. "In spite of my research interests, I am fond of humankind."

"I have to stop at the prison-hospice on our way out," she tells Eva. "For my aunt."

"Oh, DJ, I'm sorry," Eva says and looked at her sadly. "But if she's at the hospice, do you really think we can help her?"

"She's not sick," Dany says.

"Wait, your aunt's in jail again?" Eva stares at Dany, surprise plainly written on her face.

But Dany grips Mac's hand, picks up the pace, and the last fifty yards of their walk are spent, by Dany at least, in brooding silence.

Eva, meanwhile, calls out updates – every time she gets a new follower, every time the outbreak video is viewed and shared. "I'm going viral!"

Eva laughs an evil laugh, *mwa-ha-ha,* and then catches sight of Dany's expression.

"Too soon? Okay, yah, too soon. I'll be serious." Grinning wildly, Eva draws a giant X over her heart – and Dany, she has to turn away.

CHAPTER ⊙ = X + 19

The three girls stand in the back alley, surveying Mister Faraday's house.

"Well, let's see what our school tuition pays for," Eva says.

"Uh, we go to public school," Dany reminds her. She is holding Mac's hand in a firm grip.

"Whatever," Eva says. "I think he's in there."

Banging noises float out of the garage. Dany leads the way through the door, and there, in the middle of chaos, they find him. Their history teacher, Faraday, is sitting cross-legged on an oil-spattered floor. He looks less like a history teacher than a mechanic, one who has been set down in the midst of an exploded three-dimensional diagram. All of the small parts that belong inside of his VW Bug are strewn around him. Dany takes the whole of the scene in at a glance. To one side of Faraday, there is a vintage scooter. A Sunbeam. The bike is all in one piece, but will only hold two of them.

Dany glances from Mac to Eva and back to Mac, her heart sinking.

She frowns at Faraday. Bad luck, that's what it is.

"Can someone tell me what the hell you're doing in my garage?" Faraday asks.

"Oh, oh, oh," Eva says, one hand jigging in the air.

Mister Faraday closes his eyes, bites back a word and puts his teacher face on.

Finally, his eyes come to rest on Dany. Whatever he was about to say is gone. Faraday stands up in a clatter of car parts, and holds out the palms of his hands. "Jesus, Dany, who did that to your face?"

Her gut twists.

She feels a little sick, thinking of Bea, locked in that room. How Dany, always, is the one to survive. She hasn't seen her own face, not yet – but she can feel it. Her right eye is swelling up, and it throbs with every beat of her stupid heart.

Dany shrugs him off. "Just an accident," she says, and looks down at the floor.

"Let me guess," Eva says to Faraday. With a sweep of her hand, she takes in the mess. "This would be your car's motor and your motor would be a precursor to movement – specifically, to velocity, which, I know, implies speed *and* direction, but we know where to go, Mister Faraday. We've worked it all out."

Eva looks at Dany.

Dany shrugs unhappily. "You'd probably better sit for this," she tells him. The girls sit down on the oil-stained floor and, after a bewildered moment, Faraday sits down too. "The virus," Dany tells him, "it's made a leap. Mutated." Faraday's hands work as he listens, putting the puzzle pieces of his car back into working order.

PART TWO

| CHAPTER 0 = X + 20

Dany's right eye is swelling shut. With every heartbeat, blood ebbs and flows, and her eye pulses with pain. The sky above Faraday's dark yard slowly fills with red, and she has to remind herself of how little time has passed. Only this morning, she had history class with Liz. Only yesterday, she stood in the rat house with Jasper.

A part of her is still in that classroom. And a part of her is still in the blue suit.

And at Darling-Holmes, and at Bea's, and at the prison-hospice.

Seeing a red rope. Hearing the sound of bone dislodged from a fleshy socket.

The ringing of alarms. And always, always, at the back of her throat, the acrid taste of smoke.

But, as always, too, she is sitting quietly at home on her bed, on a park bench, in the back of a classroom, reading a book, reading so many goddamned books.

She tries to remember all of the books she's read in her life. Only the books are not just there, like pictures on microfilm. She doesn't have forever photographs of each page. It feels strange, for a reason she can't name, but maybe books aren't the same as the places a person has been, which somehow *are* forever. But yes, she knows for sure there have been times when she's tripped over a thing, a feeling, and called up a page in front of her eyes – but, today, the page she trips over is angled away from her, and she has to crane to catch a glimpse. So it's hard for her to collect up more than a few words. Tonight, she trips on a book by Frantz Fanon and catches a single line before the page fades from view. In her mind, the words light up with new meaning.

We revolt simply because, for many reasons, we can no longer breathe.

| | |

After the fire, there were police. Police and psychiatrists, doctors and fire investigators, specialists in arson. They thought that Dany set the fire.

Because, when they asked her, she shrugged and said, "It's all my fault."

The fire was all her fault. She hadn't protected Zeke, and the accelerant on her arms seemed to confirm her story. At least, until the coroner's report came in. And somehow, they went back to work, building a new story out of the old nouns, drawing completely different lines, and when all the little dots were connected up, they thought it was Zeke, that a little boy with spiky hair and enormous black eyes had doused a pillow in the stuff. Because his shoes, like his hands, had been soaked in petrol. Because his little shoes had been found a few feet from the fire's point of origin. Because marking the place that the fire had caught were tiny rubber soles, melted to the spot.

Dany knew there was only one reason for an eight-year-old boy to try to burn the world down around him. Because he couldn't stand another night of it. Another hour. Another minute. Another brutal second.

It was because, when he turned eight, they separated him from Dany – making him sleep in the boy's ward, where Dany couldn't look out for him. Night after night. Day after day. Without end.

It happened because it got to that point.

It happened because Dany wasn't able to protect him.

It happened because he couldn't breathe.

Dany tries to tell herself that she couldn't have protected him. Not really. How could she, when she couldn't even protect herself? But deep down, she knows. It's all her fault.

| | |

Ten minutes later, Dany sits at the kitchen table with Mac and Eva. The earpiece of Eva's glasses has opened up to reveal a pair of tiny wires, now clipped onto Faraday's portable battery.

"It's perfect," Dany says.

Faraday steps into the doorway, shifting on his feet. He looks a question her way, but Dany turns her gaze back to the lens-screen. A moment later, she's reeling off the sequence of digits, quick, so their imprint doesn't have a chance to fade from her eyes. Eva thumbs in the numbers. Laughing madly, Eva flips the lens so that it projects its image on the table. It's an image that, Dany doesn't doubt, means nothing to Faraday. An oceanic blue splosh. A few pixels of colour.

"What am I seeing?" Faraday asks.

"Your destiny," Eva tells him.

"We need a place that no one else will think to go," Dany tells him, eyes on the image. "A place that's isolated, but survivable."

He stares at the girls blankly.

"We've found a secret island," Eva adds. Again, the mad scientist laugh rings out.

"It's a historical site, but it's pretty much abandoned at this time of year," Dany says. "It's where they used to put the lepers."

"Hansen's disease," Eva corrects, "is the proper term now."

Dany looks at an oil stain on Faraday's shirt. How can they be any clearer?

"D'Arcy Island will be safe," Dany says slowly. "Because no one's there. Other people aren't safe."

"And now we've got the address," Eva says. "The latitude, the longitude, it's all right here." Eva taps the side of Dany's head.

"Your memory," Faraday asks, "it's eidetic?"

Eva answers before Dany can. "Her brain's picture perfect."

But while Eva is excited about it, thinking about her memory just makes Dany sad. "Nah, not perfect. Sometimes, I don't know . . . it's like I time travel. Sometimes the things I see or smell, they get . . . stuck. Or maybe I get stuck." Dany rubs her temple. It hurts to make sense of her brain. Later, she'll think about her brain later. "But, yeah, I remember stuff," she says and shrugs. "Whether I want to or not."

And for a long moment, she feels Mister Faraday's eyes taking her in, as if Dany is a problem he can't begin to frame.

Dany turns from Faraday to her kid sister. "Grab your pencil crayons," she tells the kid. Flicking a look at Faraday's mask, she explains. "We need a copy, in case."

The kid settles herself at the table, and pulls out a Ziploc baggie filled with sharp pencil crayon stubs. Five minutes later, they are looking at a pencil-crayoned map. Most of the page is a map of the Haro Strait. There, inside of its blue waters, a red dot emerges from a tiny unnamed island, a flyspeck of a place, a pixel in a sea of blue. Mac has drawn a sea monster, too, but that's probably artistic license. The kid's squared off one corner of the map, where she's done a blown-up version of the island – a detailed shoreline of D'Arcy Island – an all-but-perfect copy of the internet image, though she's only just looked at the projected image once.

Dany gets the kid to draw a map to Antoine's farm next. Dany knows there's a chance that things will go wrong before then, and she may not be around to tell them the way.

"The kid's memory, too," Faraday says, a trace of awe in his voice.

"She likes drawing," Dany says. Again, the shrug.

"Erm, our vehicle?" Eva asks.

"Just about ready," Faraday tells them. "I just need to pop the carburetor back in and then pack up some supplies for this island of yours, and we're gone. Looks like we'd better bring potable water, in case."

"We can get started," Dany says. "You know, finding stuff that looks useful." Her eyes trawl the closed cupboards.

She feels Faraday's eyes on her. And, from the corner of one eye, can see him shake his head. "Fine," he says, his voice tight. "Just, look, stay out of anything personal."

Dany glances at Eva.

Beneath those enormous bangs, her eyebrows waggle. "Personal," she whispers, and her eyes fly wide.

"I can hear you," Faraday says slowly, his expression incredulous. Eva can't help herself, she giggles. Shaking his head, their history teacher stares at her for a beat. "Look, I have some old military relics. They're not safe. Stay out of those."

The girls nod, and he retreats to his garage.

"Military relics!" Eva whispers, a Cheshire cat grin on her face.

| | |

They pack up what they can.

While Faraday packs up dry goods and ferries them out of the kitchen, Dany slips upstairs. She's supposed to grab what she can from the medicine cabinet, but what Dany needs is the key to Faraday's vintage BSA Sunbeam scooter. So far, she's come across an old Mylar blanket, torn; a couple rolls of duct tape; and a socket wrench. But no key. She's also found a really old gun. There, in his office, an ancient service revolver is hung on the wall in a case – the gun, its manual and a box of bullets are socketed in a velvet inlay.

Of course, you can't shoot a virus. But maybe you can outrun it.

So what Dany needs is a ride. And for that, she needs the key to Faraday's scooter.

Eventually, she finds what she needs. On top of his bookshelf, stashed in a folder box stuffed with old papers, she finds the manual to Faraday's old scooter. A glance through the book tells her that the early model didn't even *have* an ignition key. Now that she's read the manual, all she needs is half a minute alone in that garage.

With one flick of the toggle switch, Dany will be gone.

| | |

A few minutes later, Dany stands looking at her swollen eye in the bathroom mirror. If she wants to drive that scooter, she will have to open her eye up. Faraday's medicine cabinet has what she needs – talcum powder and an old razor blade. He also has some allergy pills and a few Tylenol 3s. Dany shoves the pills in the front pocket of her backpack and, for half a minute, loses herself, staring at an expired bottle of Namenda.

She'd almost forgotten she had the bottle in her bag.

But yeah, she always carries it in her backpack. Always.

And inside of the bottle, a broken watch and a mood ring.

These objects are literally all she has left of her mother.

After Dany was released from the burn ward, she and Mac moved in with Norah. Dany found the mood ring and the watch inside of an old pill bottle in her aunt's black medicine bag. Until she sold them off at the black market, her aunt had kept a miniature pharmacy in there – half a bottle of Percocet, a few stray tabs of Vicodin, a couple doses of Narcan, a load of *Bugs Bunny* Band-Aids and, deeper down, inside of a zip-locked hospital baggie, the half-dozen pill bottles that had once belonged to her mom, an ever-shifting series of prescriptions they'd given Phil before she'd been separated from her family. Though it was empty of pills, Dany had taken the bottle that held the mood ring and watch. Because the label was still legible. Because there, in black and white, she could see her mom's name. *Munday, Philomena.*

Of course, nobody calls her Philomena.

Everybody who knows Mom calls her Phil.

Phil always drove with the car windows open, even in winter. Because of the holes in the floorboards. Because of the creeping stink of exhaust. Phil had a throaty laugh. So low, people mistook her for a smoker. But that wasn't it. Her mom's laugh just came from a deeper place than other people's. And Phil always wore the ring. Wore it religiously.

When you needed it most, the mood ring glowed a special colour. That's what Phil had told her. When it glows, Phil said, it isn't a ring at all, but a portal to another world. A world in which you are so, so brave. That's what Phil always told Dany. That's what Dany was saving for Mac.

Dany buries the bottle in her bag and picks through Faraday's razors. One of the blades looks decent. She drops it in a Dixie cup and pours in some alcohol, stowing the bottle of alcohol in her bag. Then she looks at the girl in the mirror, the one whose right eye has swollen shut. She'll need the use of that eye, but before she touches the razor, she wants it good and sterile.

But then, what does she have to be afraid of now?

Plucking out the blade, she wipes it on her sleeve and nicks the swollen eye fold, one slim cut above her eye. But the pain is worse than she remembers. Dany bites her lip so hard that it bleeds. Finally, she dabs a bit of talcum on her cut, to stem the tide of blood.

While the blood clots – just to let herself breathe, just to feel a bit of fresh air on her face – Dany lowers her mask. Before she goes back down, she'll slip her mask back on and reform the seal. Dany isn't a fool. She knows the best way to use these N95 masks is to keep any potential virus on the *inside*. And Dany is careful. Especially since she talked to Isobel Lau.

The virus might not be airborne, but Dany isn't about to dice micrometres. Not when it comes to Eva and her sister. She isn't going to take chances. Well, she isn't going to take *many* chances. Dany is standing there, mask lowered, razor poised to make the second cut – when Eva appears in the bathroom doorway.

"What the hell," Eva says.

Dropping the blade, Dany pulls up her mask. With two fingers, she reforms the seal, then turns on the tap to wash her hands. Only when she's soaped up does she take in the reflection of her friend.

"I need to ask you something," Dany tells her. "I need to know if we trust each other. I mean with our lives? For real? *Literally* for real."

Eva looks at her friend and shrugs. "Sadly, yes, we would. Well, I would anyway. Not the smartest decision I've made, to be honest, but yes, overall, I'd say we –"

"I need you to take care of Mac," Dany tells her. "You know, like she's your own." Her voice is strange, and almost breaks on the last word.

Then, as Eva's face drains of blood, Dany tells her the plan. And what's more, she lets her in on how, exactly, Dany is going to break into prison and rescue her aunt. As she talks Eva through it, Eva doesn't look mad. Eva looks scared. She looks scared and sad and small and, worse, she won't look at Dany, not at all.

"No," Eva says, shaking her head. "You can't do this, no way. Not by yourself."

"But you'll take care of Mac?" she asks Eva, her eyes narrowing.

"Always," Eva says. She almost looks hurt to have to say it.

"And you'll keep Faraday out of the garage," Dany says, pressing the point.

Eva looks down. Her mouth starts to move – and then stops. Once, twice, it happens. Finally, she looks at Dany. Eva is breathing a little too deeply, a little too fast. Dany looks at her friend, standing there, on the precipice of a crying jag.

"Norah is Mac's only family, after me," Dany says gently. There is Antoine, sure, but Dany doesn't mention him, because Antoine doesn't count.

Eva shakes her head.

"Look," Dany says, "I have this feeling everything will work out. If I do this, somehow, everybody will be okay."

The assurance does its work – Eva takes a deep breath, a little more in control of herself. "You," Eva says slowly, "have a good feeling?" Her friend raises one eyebrow so high it disappears under her enormous bangs.

Dany gives a noncommittal shrug. She hates lying to Eva.

"We're screwed," Eva says. "We are wholly and completely screwed."

"So you'll do it?" Dany asks.

Eva doesn't answer. Shaking her head, her friend turns and leaves the bathroom, shutting the door behind her. But Eva doesn't say no, and with Eva, that's practically as good as crossing her heart.

| | |

But when Dany comes downstairs, Eva isn't doing what she promised. She's just sitting there, and no, she hasn't gotten Faraday out of the garage.

She is sitting at the kitchen table as happy as daylight. What's more, Mac is sitting next to her, surrounded by a glowing sea of tea lights. The kid's nose plug has been taken off and Mac is wearing it on her finger like a wedding ring. An old yellow manual lays open in front of the kid and there, in her tiny hands, is the gun. The one Dany saw earlier. The one that lives in the velvet display case upstairs.

Mac has that abstracted look she sometimes gets, like the time Dany found an old rotary phone in the dumpster and let the kid strip the thing down to its parts. Eva is sitting beside Mac. Her mask is dangling around her neck and she wears a grin on her face. "I've got a plan," Eva says brightly. "We're going to help with the prison break!"

Dany looks from the gun to Eva. "Your plan involves arming children with guns?"

"You said no hair dryers," Eva reminds her. "But you said nothing, and I remember this specifically, you said nothing about guns."

"I need to specify?"

Eva doesn't answer. She frowns at the table, and a little sigh of annoyance passes through her lips. "If you want to pull off your rescue," Eva says, her tone clipped, "you'll need help." Eva looks up at Dany, and a blush butterflies over her collarbones. "Look, I happen to have an interest in your continued existence, okay? We're going to help whether you like it or not." Eva crosses her arms.

But Eva doesn't understand. Because nobody can help Dany. Not now.

Nobody.

Dany glances at Mac, but the kid's hands, deft and sure, are a blur of motion. When those hands stop, the kid has stripped the gun down to its parts and one little hand is reaching out for a bottle of WD-40, just beyond her grasp. Before her, in the place where, a moment before, a gun had been, there is now a jumble of little metal bits.

Dany looks at Mac, but she doesn't see the kid.

What she sees are dead salmon fry, the grim line of Miss P's mouth, the beige suits at the Ministry of Child Services, the work farms where not just Dany but, now that she is five years old, Mac, too, can be sent. What she sees is Faraday's face, after he gets a look at his prized display piece broken down into a jumble of spare parts. *Faraday*. That's all they need. Faraday might walk in here any second and see this. Dany shakes her head. "Stop it," Dany tells the kid, her voice shaking. "Just stop."

The kid looks up at her and cocks her head.

"Don't you get it?" Dany asks. "You broke it, you broke it. God, sometimes you just don't think. The gun's not ours. It was on display. In a case. It's special."

The kid stares up at her, bottom lip trembling.

"Yeah, don't give me that," Dany tells her.

Dany takes a paper bag from the counter and, turning back, carefully puts each of the parts inside. "You're going to fix this," she tells Eva, shoving the bag her way. "And you," Dany says, turning to her kid sister. "You just, just keep your stupid paws out of it, 'kay?"

The kid looks up at her, her eyes rimmed with water.

Squatting down, Dany kneels in front of the kid and sighs. "Look, tonight," she tells her, "you have a job. A very important job. You need to stick to Eva. Like crazy glue, 'kay. You stick to her. And I'll go get Aunt Norah."

The kid looks at her out of her wet brown eyes.

"You need to help Eva and Faraday find Antoine's farm, 'kay?" Dany asks. "You're the only one who's been there. If we're not there by morning, then you need to help them find the island you drew." She looks at the kid, but Mac is staring past her now, her gaze a thousand miles distant. "You know I love you. No matter what. For always."

She lays her hand, for a long beat, on her little sister's. She takes in those big brown eyes, but they are staring past her, bottomless and near black in the darkness.

"Well, are you going to do this?" Dany asks, rounding on Eva.

But Eva just stares at her, her eyes rimmed with tears. Lower lip trembling.

"I need to get Norah," Dany says. "Please."

Eva hiccups. And nods.

"One minute, that's all I need alone in the garage. Just keep him out for a minute."

"I'm sorry," Eva tells Dany. "I really am. I'll do it. I promise."

"I'll wait in the yard," Dany says. Then, by sheer force of will, Dany makes herself turn away from the kid and go out the door. Her feet are moving now, and it'll be easier if she just keeps them moving. *Don't look back. Just don't look back at the kid.* Dany slams the door open and pushes her way out into the dark night.

| | |

Dany stands in the dark yard, alone.

Wordlessly, without so much as a glance, Eva passes by and heads to the garage.

Beneath her mask, Dany sucks her lip, tasting blood. She stood here only an hour ago, but now the world is changing, slowly filling with horror. Because now, when Dany looks out over the yard, everything is different.

The full moon illuminates each leaf on the tree in Faraday's yard, casting millions of individual shadows, each razor-edged in definition. Dany looks at the tree, but what she sees is Liz Greene. She will never forget the look on Liz's face, not if she lives for a hundred years – which, of course, none of them will.

Finally, Eva emerges from the garage, and with her is Faraday.

Dany breathes her relief.

Faraday, meanwhile, stands there awkwardly, looking from one girl to the other. Dany doesn't know what Eva has said to him, but his face is filled with confusion.

"Ah, you used ice," her teacher says finally. "Did it help your eye?"

"Nah, I cut it," Dany tells him.

As she watches, his expression changes from confusion to shock. Dany cocks her head and takes her teacher in. Out of everything he's seen today, this, nicking her eye with a razor so that she can see better, shocks him? She's just released the pressure. Sometimes, the kids back on the work farm used to do it.

She pushes out a breath and lets it go.

"I just, I just need to stow my bag," she says. On her back, she wears her backpack. She starts past Mister Faraday and Eva, but pauses. "Mac doesn't talk much," she tells Faraday's shirt, "but she's not stupid."

"Of course not," he says.

"She's gifted," Dany tells him. "Lots of gifted kids talk late."

"Einstein was a late talker," Eva adds.

Dany glances at her friend and nods. "There's something else you have to know." Dany is dancing perilously close to the truth, here, and knows it. Still, she turns to Faraday and eyes his oil-stained T-shirt. "Just, so you know, I'll *always* come back for her. I did today. I *always* will. But if something happens to me, if I'm gone, you'll do your part, you'll take care of her. You'll get her out of the city – take her to Antoine's then the island, right?"

"I love the little rabbit," Eva says simply. "I'll get her there."

"I know *you* do," Dany says gently. "I was talking to *him*."

Again, she feels his eyes on her. And from the corner of her eye, she can make out his expression. It's as if, just now, for the very first time, it has occurred to him to ask what the hell he is doing. Or maybe, who the hell Dany is.

But he'll help.

Faraday is a *decent* person, that's what he is. That is his character, through and through. *Decent*. And for a moment, Dany glimpses another line from one of the many books buried in a series of shallow graves in her head.

Character is destiny.

She takes one last look at her history teacher and walks into the garage.

| | |

The garage is dark, cavelike. Dany balances on the scooter's seat, and her fingers find the toggle. She flicks the switch and for a beat, a long drawn-out beat, there is nothing – and she's sure the thing is old, done, dead. But a moment later, the engine is vibrating under her and the garage fills with bluish exhaust.

The scooter is fast, faster than she imagined it could be. It roars to life under her and, shooting out of the garage, she passes through the alley in the space of a breath.

At the mouth of the alley, Dany pauses to glance back.

Fifty feet behind her, Faraday bursts into the alley. Seeing her, he stops all at once, and on his face, there's a comic look of utter shock. Half a beat later, Eva is beside him, her face marked with a wordless plea. "Take me," Eva mouths.

But Dany can only shake her head, see Eva's face, crestfallen.

Dany has no choice. She turns away from her friend and torques the gas, so the asphalt beneath her becomes a blur of grey.

| CHAPTER 0 = X + 21

Dany leaves Faraday's scooter by the old swimming pool. Once upon a time, the pool was a pretty blue jewel set in all the green, mountains framing it in the distance. The water was as blue as the sky and littered with hundreds of kids. But when Dany parks the scooter by the rusty old fence, all that remains of her sky-blue memory is a cracked concrete depression in the brown earth. She can't see the prison-hospice from here, but it's close, close.

Over the last two months, Dany learned everything she could about the prison-hospice. Internet searches didn't turn up much – and the internet's satellite-view of the place was blacked out – but Jasper is doing a field study there. *Was* doing one. Him and Lauren Ko.

Jasper told her what she needed to know. Jasper, who is gone now too. The place, he told her, is run by a skeletal crew of guards, the dangerous work mostly handled by female prisoners – who muck out stalls, scrub down floors, empty out buckets, herd the dying by day and, in the morning, carry the night's dead to the mobile crematorium. Inside the old coliseum, he told her, there are hundreds upon hundreds of cots. The cots, Jasper said, are the same kind used in cholera camps, the kind with a hole to put a bucket under. There, like elsewhere in the prison, it is prisoners who care for the terminals.

And watching over this forced work?

The kind of ex-soldiers the government can leverage. The kind who might, Jasper said, prefer "community service" to a court martial.

Lauren, passing by Jasper's desk, overheard them talking.

Dany remembers her face. How she looked at Jasper, narrowed her eyes and shook her head. "I swear, some of the soldiers I met were sociopaths. Keep your distance," she said to Dany. "Creepy sons of bitches. Creepier than the virals."

"Jesus, Lauren," Jasper said, giving her a look. "These are patients. People with lives, with families."

For a brief second, Ko flinched and closed her eyes. When she looked at Jasper once more, she held one hand up in apology. "I'm sorry, I'm so sorry," she said. "I just, I forgot myself." She flinched again as she said it.

Dany frowned, trying to read what was passing between them. When Ko had gone, she turned to Jasper. "What was that about?"

But Jasper shook his head. "Look," he said. "I haven't interacted with the soldiers as much as Lauren, but I did meet privately with more than one. They were having . . . difficulties with the job. I referred them to a colleague, someone who specializes in PTSD. It's pretty common among soldiers and first responders, and," he said, with a chagrined shrug, "laboratory macaques."

Standing by the abandoned pool, Dany considers all of this. When it comes to guards, Dany doesn't know what to believe. Jasper is probably right, more or less, but if she had to put money down, she'd put it on Lauren Ko.

| | |

Leaving the pool behind, Dany makes her way up the embankment and crosses the railway tracks. Before her, the busy artery, and beyond it, the old racetrack – home to a hospice and prison. Home to her aunt. Beyond the prison, barely visible in the smouldering dark, she can make out the dilapidated remains of a roller coaster, a bestial skeleton rising into the sky.

As Dany's eyes adjust to the darkness, she places prison landmarks.

She can easily make out the gates. They've mounted a couple of powerful floodlights on a pickup truck – to light up the eighteen-wheeler, spilling out its human cargo. And there, around the truck, she glimpses the telltale orange of prison suits, in among the yellow plague jackets.

The rest of the camp is dark, but for a few low and flickering lights. It's late. By now, most of the prisoners will be locked up for the night. Somewhere, at the back of the prison, they'll be interred in a row of tin boxes.

Just past the track, she sees the squat building that once upon a time housed horses. Though, no, it hasn't always been horses kept in there. Dany knows the history of the place, too. Knows what use it was put to during the war.

On this night, because of the power outage, the ones confined in the stalls will be without heat or light. She pictures them standing, shivering together, seeking out what small measure of warmth their bodies can share. She pictures stick-thin legs and waxen faces. Faces that echo earlier selves. *People*, she hears Jasper say. But it's drowned out by Lizzie's voice, muttering, *I'm on fire*.

She turns away from the past, forcing herself to take in the hospice before her. First, she finds the dark outline of a hill, the one she and her sister picnicked at. Though she can't make out details, not from here, just outside the fence she'll find the old maple tree, the one whose branches overarch the razor wire fence. And a few feet below those branches, on the other side of the fence, there is a chicken coop, with its stunned and ragged birds.

Looking to the hill, she sees them. Lazy, rising into the sky, a pair of smoke trails.

Somewhere, inside the dark compound of the prison-hospice, orange suits heft corpses onto a crematorium's charger. And her aunt? She could be anywhere. Locked in one of those tin cans, unloading the truck, loading the charger. Here and there, on the prison grounds, her eyes pick out more orange suits, glimpsed as they pass by a low and flickering light.

It is only now that the utter scale of the prison hits Dany.

Her aunt could be anywhere. *Anywhere.*

What's worse, already, she can hear them.

Even over the rush of traffic, she can hear them. Over the groans of trucks, under the rush of engines, the sound seeps up through all of the little gaps. It's like the buzzing of an enormous beehive, the sound carried on the crystalline night air. Dany stands in darkness. There are the stars above her and everywhere, all around her, is the muttering of hundreds, maybe thousands of Lizzie Greenes.

And all of them whispering, *I'm on fire.*

| CHAPTER 0 = X + 22

Dany slips into a tunnel that leads under the highway.

The dank hollow smells of piss and tainted meat. So it's not unoccupied, though she sees no sign of whoever lives in here. Still, in this tunnel, she can make the first part of her journey on foot, unseen.

On the other side, she makes her way to the hill where, only two days before, she and her sister picnicked. Finally, she stands at the base of the maple tree, the one whose branches crest over the razor wire.

Slowly, gripping the rough trunk, she climbs up. The scars on her arms, still sore from earlier this day, scream with pain as she grips the trunk. The bark is as rough as sandpaper, but she monkeys her way up, making her way out onto the overhanging branch. The maple has leaves as big as dishcloths. Dozens break off under her hands, fluttering to the ground below.

She is dangling over the prison fence when the branch she clings to dips, swings low – threatening to dump her onto the razor wire below.

Dany freezes. Becomes as still as stone. Doesn't even dare to breath.

When the branch stills, she creeps forward again. One more inch. But the branch sways, amplifying her tiny movements to a degree that, she sees only now, is too great. The branch is too thin, too slight to bear her small frame.

Clinging to the see-saw branch, clasping that rough limb, all Dany knows is that Aunt Norah is her people, one of the only ones in her life who's actually stuck around. After the fire, Norah was all that stood between her and a return to the horrors of the past.

Dany doesn't know if it is love that has pushed her out onto this slim branch, the one that is swaying dangerously over the razor wire. In this moment, she finds it hard to read the dark swill of emotion within. But she knows this much. She owes her aunt. She *owes* her.

Dany slows her breathing.

Each breath, each tiny movement of her body, is exaggerated by the branch. If she can make it another few inches, just three or four, the fall to the roof of the chicken coop, at least, will be clean . . . In the distance, a new sound is added to the muttering of the infected on the track. A low rumbling hum, the sound of something electrical . . . There is a flicker of lights and the noise evaporates once more in a whining crunk.

Dany inches out a little further, the branch once more dipping down towards the razor wire. This time, the branch swings low, and one of the barbs catches her jeans, snags, pulls and torques the branch like an archer's bow. The fabric tears slowly, and instead of shooting up, the branch eases off, quibbling its way up and down.

Dany tells herself that the razor wire isn't that sharp.

Not *razor* sharp, anyway.

The fence is psychological, she tells herself. Meant to slow you down. To scare you. A wire like this is hard to cross without tools. Of course, tools will get you killed. Razor wire, she knows, has a stainless steel core that is under constant tension. Cut it and the wire recoils in a vicious strike, slashing you, buggering you up in the loosened coils. No, this is the only way to go, slowly. Inch by inch. Over it. Just a little further and she'll have cleared her legs, too, and then she can let herself down onto the chicken coop's roof.

Another inch, and Dany knows she can make it.

But the branch begins to dip – this time, in response to no motion of her own.

The branch fails under her, cracking and bending. Dany thinks of everyone in her life, her sister, her aunt, Eva, her mom. She clutches at the branch, her hands slipping, her fingers desperately clawing, but it's too late.

CHAPTER 0 = X + 23

For a moment, Dany hangs there, half-suspended. There is the sound of her pants tearing, as one leg snarls in the coil of wire. Then, hands grappling with the branch, she pushes off, and she is free.

The sound of her impact, when her body lands on the aluminum roof, is as loud as a gunshot. Dany lays utterly still, stunned. Her entire right side is a throb of pain and her lungs feel like they've collapsed. Pulling down her mask, she gulps at the stinking night air. But for long panicked seconds, she can't draw a breath.

Finally, finally, she takes in her first breath of night air.

Dany curls up and breathes. Tentatively, she slides a hand over her throbbing side, but the roof is a tin drum and it creaks and groans with each movement. Below her, stirring to life, she hears the chickens. Long low calls, deep in each throat.

Dany looks over her long-sleeve shirt. There are new spots of blood on her arm. Then her hand gently explores her torso, and with each tiny movement, the roof groans under her. She fingers her ribs. They are bruised, that's all. Not too bad.

Dany listens for some sign that she's been heard, that even now there are guards padding towards her. But she hears nothing out of the ordinary. Just the low calls of terrified birds. That distant, omnipresent mutter of the dying. Traffic on the highway. Slowly, on hands and knees, Dany inches towards the edge of the roof. The chicken coop is roofed with old and rusty corrugated sheets, and they grate and groan under her. Beneath her, the chickens are alive with terror. Most of the birds release a low-pitched distress call, but one, at least, has begun sounding off like a goddamned air raid siren.

Finally, Dany reaches the edge.

There, below her, she sees some kind of a small hill or bump. A cesspit. A filthy pile of straw and shit. At the top of the mound, she sees the corpses of a couple chickens. The ones she saw days before, probably, dead in their cages. But it is the softest landing place she can see.

Dany rolls off the roof and lands in the mess. The pile is swampy and warm, and smells of death and shit. Inside the coop, the chickens are quieting. She hears the last few distress calls, from deep in the throat. Dany carefully stands. One side of her body is throbbing, and her right arm is on fire. Her body and boots are covered in chicken shit and straw, but she's okay. She's good.

Ahead of her, in the dim light of the night sky, Dany can see dark figures milling about. Her nose catches the viral smell of piss and shit and tainted meat. They're close. So, yeah, Dany smells the viral coming before she sees him.

The viral in his yellow plague jacket. She touches the key that hangs from the cord on her neck and knows exactly what she has to do.

Talking in low and reassuring tones, like the viral before her is a stray dog, she makes her approach. Dany slips the key from her neck. And then she gets close enough to see him. To take in his face. His eyes. His expression. And as she unlocks his jacket, she knows that she is doing something wrong. Something awful. Shameful. She wants to wrap this man in a blanket, but she has none.

"I'm sorry," she tells him, and she means it. "I'm sorry." But she takes his jacket anyway, because she has to.

| | |

The plague jacket is old, weathered, the plastic cracked and worn at the seams. The seams are spackled with dirt, a deep unyielding brown. As she shrugs it on, the plague jacket stinks of sweat, as foul in its own way as turned meat. The jacket stinks of something else, too, something worse, a smell that sets her on edge. The smell that precedes death. Still, with this jacket on, she is as good as invisible. The guards will never see her now.

The grounds are dark and keeping to the edges, she can make her way around the prison. She's taken a step away from the fence when she hears it, that distant engine. At first she thinks it's an old film projector – that it's movie night at the prison – but a moment later, the power kicks in, and she knows the sound for what it is, the rough cycling of a portable generator, a sound she will, in time, come to hate. A sound that will infiltrate her dreams and dog her waking moments. A sound that, in the days ahead, locked inside a concrete box, will become her sole companion until the darkness finally comes for her.

She hears the sound of a whirring motor – and a moment later the perimeter lights flicker to life. Dany stands pinned.

Heart fluttering, all of her is illuminated by a beam of light.

Twenty feet overhead, one of the panels is aimed her way. Every last inch of her is lit up inside that spotlight. Around her, she senses the many-eyed prison stir into wakefulness. And then Dany remembers. None of this matters, because she is invisible.

All except for her N95 face mask.

And though it goes against every instinct, Dany tears off the mask and tucks it into the back pocket of her jeans.

| | |

Dany hasn't just seen the walk. For years, she lived with it.

When the disease has progressed to its final stages, the infected walk like this.

Her own mother walked like this, with a strange clockwork gait. When Dany was eight or nine, her mother was hospitalized for a staph infection. It was there, at the hospital, that they told her mother that something in one of her skin lesions had likely leached into her blood, causing the pain in her lower spine.

Phil never walked the same again.

Dany didn't know why. If it was the drugs or a side effect of her meds or if it was the osteomyelitis or if, as far back as that, undiagnosed, her mother was already infected with the virus. It didn't matter. Her mother walked like a late-stage case long before she was taken from Dany, her joints stiff, her back almost fused.

So, yeah, Dany knows the walk.

Her mother moved on unoiled joints.

She moved like her spine was slowly fossilizing.

She moved like she was thirty-five, but her hips were eighty-five.

For a moment, there is a flicker. An image of the woman in the back alley, the one with the shopping cart. But Dany pushes the picture down. Then, slowly, like one of the broken clockwork dolls that dot this hospice, Dany walks on unoiled legs through the prison grounds, aiming for the shipping containers at the back. That's where, the math tells her, her aunt is most likely to be. Most of the prisoners are locked up in metal boxes for the night, and Dany plans to open every last can of prison worms.

| CHAPTER 0 = X + 24

The day her aunt's parole was revoked, Norah said a strange thing. She'd been arrested at a protest – the police called it a "riot" – and Dany went to the police station to see her. The lawyer brought her into a little room, where her aunt was cuffed to a desk.

"Sometimes you have to set your pain aside," her aunt said. "Set love aside, set anger aside, set all of it aside and just deal with some basic facts."

Her aunt was trying to tell Dany and her sister to go and live with Antoine.

Dany looks at the facts.

Fact. Along the back fence of the prison, there are a half-dozen shipping containers, the kind that once floated into ports on enormous freighters. The day of the picnic, she wondered what those metal boxes were for.

The next day, Jasper told her.

It was an afterthought, the question. Not important, a curiosity. More urgent, at the time, were her questions about the plague jackets. Jasper was rifling through his desk, looking for the hex key he would give to her, the one she wears around her neck.

"It's weird," she said, looking at all the junk in his drawer, the little wire kittens, shaped out of paper clips. "Those metal containers at the prison. What do you think they're storing back there?"

Jasper paused, the drawer forgotten, his hand still.

He turned and gave Dany a searching look. Touched her hand. It was gentle, this touch. She could have broken the contact with a blown breath.

"Did you lose someone?" he asked. There weren't any other people in the room, Lauren Ko was long gone. Dany glanced around self-consciously. But they were alone.

She nodded once.

"Oh, Dany," he said, searching her eyes. He shook his head, looked away from her and told her the truth. "Those shipping containers, those metal boxes, that's where they keep the prisoners. They lock them in at night. I'm told the cells are quite comfortable really," he said, a question in his eyes. "But no, they don't keep patients in there."

He was asking – she could see it in his eyes – if she'd lost someone to the hospice. But her aunt was a prisoner, not infected. At least, not so far as Dany knew.

"Memory is a strange, strange thing," Jasper told her. "Mutable, subjective, strange."

He looked at her then, for a long beat. His chest rose once, twice, and then, some invisible decision made, he went on.

"Memory has a kind of half-life," Jasper told her. "Memories are incredible. They are these transient, mutable, changeable things. When we remember something, when we call it up, well, we set that memory down again. Reinscribe it. And the next time we remember? It's a copy. And then a copy of a copy . . . and so on. Over time, imperceptibly, the memory fades and blurs."

Jasper's hands had fallen still, the drawer forgotten.

"No one mourns what they've forgotten," he said. "Our perception of the past fades just like our memories of it. So, in a way, the people who've contracted the virus are the only ones who aren't holding on to what's gone." Jasper looked at her out of eyes filled with helpless empathy. "I don't know if that comforts you," he said. "But it helps me, it helps a little. When I think of those I've lost."

But yeah, no, it didn't help. It didn't help at all.

| | |

Dany stands outside the first shipping container. But Jasper's in her head. And the night around her is alive with small sounds. With danger. And then it's not just Jasper in her head, but fear, too.

She stands, looking at the door, her heart pounding.

She's read books. She's made herself ready for the kinds of cryptography systems they might throw at her. But reading is different from doing. Standing here, with her palm flat against the door, all alone in the dark, is different from picturing it, from sitting there with her nose in a book. And worse, the noises she hears, they're not just from out there, in the night, around her. Some of the noises are coming from inside the box. A banging sound. Dim at first, but growing louder. As if the metal box has felt her touch and is waking now. As if the metal box has grown a beating heart.

The banging is rhythmic. And suddenly, she's just a kid again, living with her mother in the basement flat, staring at the popcorn ceiling and trying to understand the noises that come from the apartment above. The yells, the screams, the bursts of violence.

Dany takes a deep breath. Makes herself focus.

She can remember reading the book on locks, the book on cryptography systems.

She can picture each cover.

But all of the pictures that book had held? A jumble of lines in her head. Somewhere, in a book, there are codes and cyphers scribbled in ink. There are pictures of the kinds of locks some jail cells have. All those weeks spent studying schemata, and now she can barely remember the basics of an electric strike.

In her head, somewhere, there are dozens of exploded diagrams. She neatly filed them away, but it's like she traced the images on onion skin paper, with lemon juice, and what she sees are a series of overlapping lines, drying into nothingness on the page.

Still, she has to try.

There is a little lock compartment on the door, hidden behind a metal flange. Dany lifts the flange and slips her hand inside the compartment and knows. In an instant. No, none of her stupid diagrams will be any use. Not against this.

Solid, simple. A bit of steel.

A padlock. They've used a goddamned padlock. She's pretty sure it's illegal, but what's she going to do, walk over to the warden's office and lodge a complaint?

Dany slams the thing.

The lock bangs against the hollow wall, echoing through the container. Like lab rats when the cage door is rattled, all at once, the women inside are scrabbling to get out. The tin can lights up with screams – terror, banging, begging – and Dany, heart pounding, steps back from the human alarm, melting away into the darkness.

All she's done is touch the lock, but the sound of metal on metal is enough. The tin can is alive with terror. Dany doesn't know what's happening in there, but this much she does know. The screams will draw the guards.

Sure enough, she sees one coming.

Dany backs deeper into the darkness as the young soldier in uniform approaches the shipping container. He's not much older than her. Eighteen years old maybe. The boy – she can't bring herself to call him a man – tries, hands shaking, to open the door. But his fingers fumble and he cusses, swears. Shakes his head and tries again. He thinks he's alone, and maybe that's why he doesn't hide it. His fear. Hands shaking, eyes scanning the grounds, he looks like he hopes some other person will come and take over.

His eyes alight on her, take her in, and Dany goes still. But it's like he doesn't see her. His eyes don't register anything. It's like she is invisible. An object. Part of the landscape.

By the time the kid gets the door open, Dany's backed up halfway to the gate, her eyes never leaving the young guard.

| | |

The woman who emerges first might be wearing the orange track suit of a prisoner, but this woman has the look of Liz Greene, the same bloodied face, the same swollen eyes.

Dany freezes.

Every last instinct tells her to run, to race for the gates, to dash headlong across the six-lane and jump on Faraday's scooter. To drive far, fast. The way is mostly clear, after all. The tarmac all but abandoned.

But for the truck.

There is a truck directly in her path – halfway between her and the gate.

And then her eyes narrow in on the truck's cargo hold.

There, on the ramp leading to the hold, outlined in the perimeter lights, stands a single guard. A hulking shadow more than a man. In his hand, he holds a chain, and at either end, like a pair of dogs, are two prisoners. But Dany's eyes are on the slight, dark-haired woman.

Even in the half-light, Dany would know the woman anywhere.

Seeing her aunt stumble to her knees, seeing her aunt roughly pulled up by a chain, yanked by a man who is a full foot taller, a hundred pounds heavier, a man against whom Dany has not the slightest chance – she does the only thing in the entire world that makes any kind of sense.

Seeing that huge prison guard, bludgeon in hand, taking hold of her aunt by the neck – Dany runs.

Right at the son of a bitch.

| CHAPTER 0 = X + 25

Dany takes the ramp in two strides – her dash ending in a wild leap. She slams into the soldier's chest, full on, and then her nails find his cheeks.

For one instant, Dany is clinging to the guard, raking his face with her nails – and in the next, her body hits the far wall of the truck.

She slides into a crumpled heap on the floor.

The blow comes a beat later, out of nowhere – hard and solid, to her head. And when she looks up, dazed, she is somehow balanced on her knees, and staring in wonder at the fireflies.

One blow with that mag cell light, *bam*, and there they are. Dozens of fireflies. Little living lights.

Dany, on her hands and knees, looks up at them. Tiny luminous beings, cavorting in the air of the cargo hold. Somehow, everything in the truck's interior has a strange hue, and yes, there are fireflies in her eyes.

When Dany looks up, her aunt finally sees her. But Aunt Norah is staring at Dany in abject horror. Her aunt's eyes flicker from the yellow plague jacket to Dany's face, and something in her seems to break.

"No," her aunt says, her voice low and distressed. "No, no, no."

"Goddamn virals," the guard mutters. "I swear to God, we should smoke every last one of the bastards."

When Dany looks from her aunt to the guard, her lip curls. "Sociopath," she says.

And in that instant, Dany has *everyone's* full attention.

Her aunt's face fills with a different kind of horror; the red-haired prisoner, chained to her, raises one eyebrow and cackles; and the guard, with a click of his mag light, aims a beam of light at Dany's face. She squints up at the guard and swears.

"Jesus Christ," he says, stumped. "It's a goddamn kid."

It's only when the guard has lowered that beam of light to her jacket that Dany sees what the redhead is doing. A wary look on her face, the redhead is angling up behind the guard.

For a moment, all Dany sees is a little bit of darkness, a tiny gap of night, there, between the red-haired woman's two front teeth. And then she sees the broomstick in the woman's hand, sees that broomstick raised for a blow.

| | |

The blow is hard.

The broomstick cracks against the guard's skull – literally – and the pieces fall to the floor of the truck bed, two splintered ends of wood. The impact of that blow on the guard's skull should have taken him down. But the man's head is made of rock.

The guard, rising – smacks the red-haired prisoner.

She flies against the wall of the truck, and slides down, dazed. He's hit her so hard, so brutally, that Dany is sure the weight of the prisoner – flying against the wall – will take her aunt's hand off at the wrist. Still, the guard isn't done.

He turns that stupid smile on Dany.

Dany struggles to her feet, draws in a shaky breath.

His first punch lands deep in her gut, and her body is re-shaped by the blow. His fist steals the wind from her lungs, ruptures a thousand tiny capillaries, tears up her guts and sends her skidding across the wet floor of the truck. Sliding across a slick of filth, to land, choking and helpless.

When she opens her eyes, he's grabbed hold of her aunt by the hair.

Her aunt, roughly held aloft, is screaming and grasping at her hair – and he rounds on the other prisoner, there, at the end of the chain. The air is filled with a strange popping sound, a sound that crackles over the grunts, the heavy breaths. It's only when her aunt begins to moan that realization hits Dany. The popping noises – they are the sound a fistful of hair makes as, strand by strand, it is pulled out at the roots.

Her aunt yelps with pain, and the guard turns on the redhead. He lifts the red-haired prisoner into the air with one hand – a fist around her throat – and as Dany watches in horror, the prisoner's legs thrash out.

He's going to kill her. There's no doubt in Dany's mind that the guard is going to kill her.

Dany hears the prisoner squawk in protest, but it's strangled in her throat. He's going to kill the redhead – right here – right in front of her. He is going to squeeze and squeeze until there is no air left in her lungs.

Dany's hand scrambles over the floor – and what she finds is the broken broomstick. Rising – on unsteady feet – she jabs the splintered point against the side of the guard's neck, there, where she can see a vein, throbbing beneath the surface of his skin like a rain-fat worm.

"Let her go," she tells the guard. "Let. Her. Go."

The guard opens his hands, and her aunt and the redhead fall to the floor.

"Son of a bitch," the other prisoner says, her voice a hoarse whisper.

But Dany can't look at her – because she can't take her eyes off the guard, not for a second. Her legs are weak, and her head throbs. The fireflies have left the cargo hold, but her legs are made of Jell-O. And she is pretty sure that her mind has somehow detached from her brain. To move too fast is to risk letting go of some essential part of herself.

And then the red-headed prisoner grabs the guard's mag light. She grabs the mag light, smashes the long cylinder against the back of his head. Blood spouts from a cut – the guard slumps to his knees. And Dany drops the splintered broom and steps back.

The guard is on his knees but the redhead isn't done.

A dozen savage blows follow – all aimed at his head. Dany sees it all. The precise moment that consciousness leaves the guard. His eyes wink out, his shoulders slump and he falls. Forward. Onto his face.

A beat later, her aunt – dragging at the chain – pulls the redhead off his unconscious body. Still, for a few seconds, the red-haired prisoner keeps swinging – blows whistling through empty air. Finally, she turns on Dany's aunt, the mag light gripped in her fist.

"Keys," Aunt Norah says. "Ceci, we need the keys."

Norah snakes a hand out, but the redhead, Ceci, bats her aunt's hand away.

"I've got an idea," the red-haired prisoner says. "Why don't you try the word *please*. What does it cost you?"

As Ceci searches the guard, she swears. A long crazy agglutination of a swear.

Aunt Norah flicks a look at Dany and shakes her head.

"Your mother, here," Ceci says, searching the guard, "she's thinks she's some kind of princess. Thinks I'm her servant."

"She's not my mom," Dany says.

"You know what, screw the keys," her aunt Norah says. "I'd rather spend eight more weeks chained to you. You know what you are. You're a goddamned genius."

And then, for a good ten seconds, the two of them swear their stupid heads off.

Finally, Norah shakes her head and turns away.

The redhead stares at her aunt's back for a few seconds. Finally, she turns back to the guard. Squatting down, she searches another pocket. "I didn't know you and Harold here were so close," Ceci says, her tone light. At least, Ceci sounds like she's joking, but Dany senses something darker, a minefield in the words.

"I think we'd better go," Dany whispers.

Aunt Norah, meanwhile, bends down to pick up the broken broomstick.

She eyes the splintered end and tosses it from her. Finally, she turns a cold eye on Dany. "What the hell are you doing?"

Dany looks from her aunt to Ceci.

Dany has the plague jacket key. The two of them, wearing plague jackets, are going to move invisibly through the camp and quietly leave. No one was supposed to even notice. No one was going to get hurt. That was her plan. Because, yes, Dany had a plan. But now, here they are, the guard knocked out – and Dany knows that life is not like television. Knows that if the guard is out, if he's been out this long, it's bad. It's really bad.

But no, Dany isn't stupid. She had a plan.

"I had a plan," she says, stupidly.

"A plan," Aunt Norah repeats, "a plan."

"Not her fault," Ceci says, glancing at Dany. "I guess she takes after you in the brains department." Ceci has the keys now, and is trying one after another in the lock at her wrist.

Her aunt narrows her eyes at Dany.

"There will be words," her aunt says, her voice a hiss. "You and me will have words."

"Oh, there will be words," Ceci says, and again, her voice hits that unsettling note, half amused, half dangerous. "And not one of those words will be *please*. Because your mother, here, is a goddamned princess."

Ceci is half in a squat, fiddling with yet another key. Finally, finally, this one slides home. Ceci unlocks the cuff at her wrist – the one that chains her to Dany's aunt.

"God that's nice," Ceci says, rubbing the raw skin at her wrist.

"About time," Norah tells her. "Now me."

"I've had enough of you," Ceci says. Her voice is so calm, so emotionless, that Dany doesn't sense the danger. Ceci leans down over the guard, and Dany hears the click.

Rising, Ceci aims a smile Dany's way. "Enjoy your visit," she says.

Ceci strides down the ramp and is gone.

It takes a second for Dany to understand. First, she sees her aunt Norah lunge after Ceci – only to be pulled short by her metal leash. Then, Dany's gaze takes in the comatose guard, the one whose arm is lofting into air, the one who seems to wave, as her aunt yanks on the other end of the chain.

| CHAPTER ⊙ = X + 26

The keys, thanks to Ceci, are gone.

Dany blinks at the unconscious guard then looks up at her aunt Norah.

"Go," her aunt says. "Get out of here. Go home."

"No," Dany says. She grabs hold of the chain.

Her aunt sighs. "Go," she says.

"We go together," Dany tells her, and takes up the slack. The guard's arm lifts into the air, and it's almost like he wants to make a point.

Finally, her aunt Norah takes up the chain, and together, inch by inch, they drag the two-hundred-pound soldier down the truck ramp. Dany leans away, using her weight and gravity to leverage the body.

At the bottom of the ramp, Dany scans the prison grounds.

Fifty yards back are the tin cans. The ones that, each night, the prisoners call home. That's where most of the noise and the commotion is. And that, of course, is a good thing. Dany can see the cluster of prisoners, can see how they've drawn the guards there.

For the moment at least, she and her aunt are alone.

But it won't last. It can't. Already, in pools of darkness, places the perimeter lights can't reach, she glimpses a flash of orange. Shadows flitting in the dark of night. Here and there, a distant shout.

Aunt Norah lets go of the chain. "Don't you get it?" she asks. "I'm done. Finished. Just go. However you got in here, just go."

Dany ignores her. She'll heave the soldier the rest of the way by herself if she has to. She flicks a glance at her aunt, who is trying to catch her breath. So far, they've dragged the guard down the ramp, but now, Dany has to drag him across the flat prison ground. Her hands are shaking, her knees are filled with water and she's pretty sure that, before this is done, she's going to throw up.

No, they probably won't make it.

And what are they supposed to do when the guard comes to?

Dany looks at the prison's gate. It's only thirty feet away – but all of it is illuminated by bright white lights. Even if they do it – even if they cross the distance – her aunt is chained to a soldier, who, the moment he wakes up, will kill her. Will kill them both. Or, worse, send her aunt to the judge and Dany back to the work farm. Still, they are in the shadow of the truck right now. For the time being, at least, they have a chance.

With a sinking feeling, Dany leans in once more against the chain – and for a long beat there is nothing. Her aunt takes up the chain once more and, heaving together, the guard's dead weight slides forward another painful inch.

"This can't work," her aunt mutters.

"Try," Dany says. "Please, just try."

| | |

Dany and Aunt Norah are fifteen feet from the gate when it happens.

"No," her aunt says in horror. "Why did you bring her? Why?"

Dany looks up, and sees something that makes her heart stop in her chest.

But what she sees makes zero sense.

Dany left all of them behind – Eva, Faraday, the kid. She left them all back at the house. They should be on the highway by now. They should be in that old VW Bug, heading out of the city. But here – making a beeline for the spotlights just outside of the prison fence – is her little sister, Mac.

Have they come after her? But then, where are Eva and Faraday?

The kid trots towards the pool of light, there, just on the other side of the gate. She looks to be headed to the spot, just outside the guardhouse, where the light is the brightest of all.

Mac's holding a paper bag in one hand. On her face, she has that look she sometimes gets when working on a mechanical problem – a look of utter focus. It is the look that Dany imagined when the teacher told her that the kid took apart the fish tank motor. It's the look Dany saw when her sister rewired the hair dryer, setting off a small supernova on their bathroom counter.

Eva and Mister Faraday are close; Dany knows they have to be close. But Mac must have slipped away. And now, holding a bag filled, no doubt, with the little metal bits that sum up into a gun, she is heading to the bright light like a suicidal moth.

Dany's heart skips like a stone over water.

Dany, completely focused on the kid, doesn't notice at first that Mac is on a collision course. But yes, there, exactly where the kid is headed – just outside of the gate – is the red-headed prisoner.

Then Ceci, down on her knees, starts cussing – and Dany's gaze takes in the scene one stroke at a time. First, she sees the woman, on her knees. Then she sees the arm, drawn up behind her back. And finally, she sees the prison guard. The one who is torquing Ceci's arm in a backwards wrench.

And her kid sister?

Completely oblivious. Stumping ever closer to the redhead, there, at the place where the perimeter lights are brightest. From its nest in the kid's backpack, Mac's doll peeks indifferently out at Dany, head lolling to one side. Little wooden eyelids descend lazily over glass eyes, only to rise again with each step the kid takes.

As Dany watches, Mac sits down cross-legged in the dirt, just a few feet from Ceci. Oblivious to the guard and the kneeling prisoner, Mac carefully pulls half a dozen pieces of metal from the paper bag and lays them out in the dirt.

Dany drops the chain. Takes one step, another.

The guard, at least, has no idea what those little metal pieces might amount to. It's obvious to Dany that he has no idea why a five-year-old has wandered off in search of light. No, he's staring wide-eyed at the kid, his eyes a pair of blinking question marks. The soldier loosens his grip on Ceci's arm, his eyes on the kid, who is just sitting there, completely focused on all of those metal bits.

"Go," Aunt Norah says. "Jesus, go."

And then Dany's eyes catch the glint of metal – there, on the ground at the gate.

"The keys," Dany whispers.

She sets off at a jog and then, by force of will, slows her pace. She won't run. Because she will have to pass directly into the guard's line of sight. Now, more than ever, she needs to be invisible. For a little longer, she needs the illusion that the plague jacket will give.

Dany makes her way to the gate, slowly, as if her legs and hips are fossilized.

Ahead, there is Ceci, kneeling, one arm drawn up behind her back. And there is the guard, his grip on her looser now as he leans forward, looking at Mac.

"Hey, kid," the guard is saying. "Hey you, kid."

Dany scoops up the keys, and with a backwards glance, tosses them to her aunt in a long loose arc. Without waiting to see how they land, she makes her way to the small gap in the fence. Dany squeezes her head through the gate, but the metal fence pinches and holds her at the shoulders.

As she struggles through, Dany's gaze takes in the kid once more.

Mac sweeps up each of the tiny pieces and, like a tiny magician, fits them into place. The girl's hands move fast. Dany hears it clearly, hears it travelling on the crisp night air – the sound of metal clicking home. And, those tiny hands moving so quickly that they are no more than a blur, the child makes a gun out of all of those disparate parts.

The gun is in the child's hand – only she isn't pointing it. For a moment, she dangles the thing by the grip, holding it out from her, like a dead frog, and then she takes it into both hands and opens the chamber. Mac has no idea of the danger she is in, because there is a grin on her little face, and she's laughing – well, huffing, but yes, her whole face is lit up with pure delight as the first bullet clicks into place.

Before her magic trick is finished, the guard's smile has wavered and died. He lets go of Ceci's arm – palms raised before the kid.

Dany's shoulders are through the gate now, and she's working on her hips.

"Easy, kid," the guard is saying. "Just take it easy." He lifts his mag cell light from his belt and looks at Mac warily, blunt instrument in hand.

But in that instant, the redhead is moving. Pinned in the gate, Dany has no choice but to watch as Ceci launches herself forward, grabbing up the kid's gun. Ceci roughly grabs hold of Mac by one arm. In her other hand, she holds Faraday's revolver.

The barrel zeroes in on the guard's forehead.

"Kneel," Ceci tells him. "Look, I'm sorry. I know how awkward this little role reversal must be for you. Now, kneel on the ground, like a good dog, or I'll put a hole in the place your brains should be."

Dany is through the fence. She stands there, in the light, knees bent – a cat, intent on her prey.

Ceci flicks a casual glance Dany's way. "Nice of you to join us, princess," Ceci says, and the gun swings round to point at Dany.

| CHAPTER 0 = X + 27

Dany's eyes are on her kid sister, taking in how small Mac's arm is, held in Ceci's grasp. So she doesn't see him at first.

Faraday, her history teacher, steps out of the shadows, and slowly makes his way towards the redhead. He's coming up behind Ceci, holding up the flat of his palms.

For a moment, Dany feels a flare of hope. The redhead hasn't seen Faraday. So, he has a chance. Coming up on her, from behind, he can take down the redhead before she's even seen him, before she can hurt her sister. And if the gun goes off, well, it'll only take out Dany.

Faraday catches Dany's gaze and nods, as if to say, *Don't worry, I've got this,* then he turns his attention back to Ceci. "Let the children go," Faraday says, "and everything will be okay."

Dany's heart sinks in her chest.

Her teacher's words may be calm, measured, but they do not have a calming effect. Ceci leaps back – yanking Dany's sister with her. Her gun swings wildly from Faraday, to the guard, to Dany. Then a smirk crosses her face and she lowers her pistol – to Mac's temple.

"We can work this out," Faraday says. But Dany can hear it, uncertainty. He darts a nervous glance from the prisoner to Dany, and Dany sees that his eyes are filled with alarm. "Let the kids go. Let both the kids go. We can sort all of this out."

"I'll kill her if I have to," the redhead says dryly. "I mean, I won't like it. I'd rather not kill a kid. That won't end at all well for me. Or her. Or my jumpsuit."

Dany can't think of anyone or anything but Mac. The kid is held by one arm, her body taut, and that gun, that gun is aimed at her temple. Ceci's grip on her sister's arm is firm, but measured. When Dany sees that grip, she knows that the redhead is being careful not to hurt Mac, and all at once, she wonders if Ceci is bluffing. Even so, it's a dangerous, wrong-headed bluff, a bluff that could go wrong. Still, maybe she doesn't mean to hurt the kid.

"You best take a step back," Ceci tells Faraday. "Move."

Behind her, Dany hears the rattling of the fence. And there, pushing her shoulders through the gap, is Aunt Norah – the chain gone from her wrist.

Turning back to the kid, Dany sees one thing and one thing alone: her sister's eyes. The kid has a faraway look. Then, Dany knows. Mac no longer sees the prisoner, doesn't feel the grip on her arm, doesn't see the perimeter lights above her or even her sister, Dany, rooted to the spot. The kid has an absent look, the kind of look that sometimes comes over her when she is about to bolt. She's always been a bolter, only her arm is held in the prisoner's grip. For now, the kid is held in place. But Dany sees it. The girl's taut posture. Her legs, trembling. The kid will bolt the second the prisoner lets go.

If the prisoner lets go.

If the prisoner doesn't accidentally kill her first.

"That isn't a gun," Faraday is saying. "It's a historical relic. A museum piece. A one-hundred-year-old service revolver from the Boer War."

The redhead raises an eyebrow and, sighing heavily, looks at Dany's history teacher.

"Shoot that thing, and it'll take your hand off at the root," he tells her.

And what will it do to her sister's face, so close to the redhead's hand?

Aunt Norah lays a hand on Dany's shoulder. She's made it through the fence. But Dany doesn't look at her, because she can't take her eyes off her sister. Finally, the redhead swivels on the ball of one foot, and makes her choice. She aims at the guard's head and pulls the trigger.

Dany thinks her heart will stop beating – she reaches a hand out for her little sister, but nothing. Nothing happens. Panicked, Ceci turns the gun on Faraday, clicking again and again. But nothing.

Dany hasn't realized it, but she's been holding her breath. All at once, the air expels from her lungs. The redhead, cursing, throws the gun at the guard. The gun rebounds from the guard's face, hits the dirt at his feet and, a beat later, Dany hears it. A single gunshot.

Dany's gaze is riveted. A small and inelegant hole has opened in the redhead's neck, and spits out a jet of red. There, just above Mac's head. The rough little hole in her neck is a ragged valve, ugly lipped and raw. Like a faucet, it pours out a stream of red paint.

Dany's gaze drops to the gun.

No puff of smoke. No telltale whisper of dust, raised from the earth. And then she knows her mistake. It wasn't the revolver that went off. That was the sound of a rifle.

Dany hasn't done the math.

She hasn't thought about the guards, plural – the *other* guards – who run this place. The guns, she knows, are kept in a single locked trailer, Jasper told her that much. But by now, the guards must have retrieved their guns and, confined to shadows, come creeping up on the gate.

That wasn't Faraday's gun. But a soldier's rifle. They *know*. They know and they are armed. Dany hasn't thought. She just hasn't thought.

In that instant, Mac's sneakers kick up a puff of dirt from the ground.

For a long moment, it is too slight, too little, the kid can't break the redhead's grip – but those little legs are pedalling and the kid is tugging. And it's then, while Mac is still held in the prisoner's reflexive grip, that the second shot rings out.

Ceci's head is a water balloon, bursting. One filled with red ink.

The blood showers the orange track suit, drizzles the dirt at Mac's feet, freckles her hair and face. Dany's mind is opened up so wide that it's impossible not to see, not to witness all of it, not to take pictures with her eyes, no matter how much she wishes she wouldn't.

And the kid, released from the redhead, is running – straight for the six-lane.

Dany acts on pure instinct.

She doesn't think of guards. Doesn't think of guns. Doesn't think of her aunt. Doesn't ask who is shooting and who is being shot. Because her eyes are on Mac, running from the bloody thing that is, even as she watches, falling to a crumpled heap in the dirt.

The kid is running. She is the sole point of movement in a still and dead world. And then Dany is running too.

Only someone has painted the child's hair red.

But it is only when she's caught her sister up in her arms, when she's kissed the sticky crown of her head, that her brain can formulate the question.

How is it that blood can be so red?

Because the blood is *unnaturally* red. Red like a child's crayoned picture of a tulip. Red like a cartoon flower. Redder, even, then the redhead's bottle-red hair. Later, she'll wonder if it was a trick of the perimeter lights, because all of everything about that night is set into such stark relief, Mac's face most of all, freckled with all that red. But now, she presses the kid into her arms, kisses her bloody hair, and Dany feels it, she feels it, the fluttery-beat of the kid's tiny rabbit heart.

| CHAPTER 0 = X + 28

A beat after Dany pulls her sister into her arms, the world erupts around her.

A volley of gunshots sets off a world of chaos.

She doesn't hear the screams. But she sees the open-mouthed prisoners.

One pair of prisoners is working their way through the fence, bound at the wrist. Another pair, angry and gesticulating, is stalled behind these two. And in the murky distance, she can just make out two others as they tackle an armed guard from behind. And all the while, a voice is crackling on the loudspeaker, telling everyone to lie down on the ground, though the words sound like gibberish, as if she is translating from pig Latin.

And that's when the old VW Bug materializes in front of her.

The Bug doesn't roll onto the scene so much as leap from the shadows, landing on all four wheels in the light, right there, between Dany and Faraday. The car leaps into place, and the engine stalls out.

Eva leans out the driver's window, wild-eyed.

Small dust clouds detach from the ground, exploding outwards from each wheel – all of it playing out in the filmic white light of the perimeter panels – all of it unfurling so slowly that Dany can trace the path of each individual dust mote as it eddies and floats up from the ground to dance with fireflies.

Suddenly, the volume comes on, and now Dany hears the screams.

She hears screaming and gunshots and time is moving forward, moving fast. In all of the world, in every last place around her, people are screaming. As she is pulled into the car, Dany turns back. Sees the guards with their rifles, straining forward. A dozen gunshots ring out in close succession, the sounds coming closer and closer together.

But the world is a sea of red, and time, time has finally found her, time has caught her up again. Dany finds herself shoved into the rough shelter of Faraday's old VW Bug, and she presses her little sister down low, into the footwell in front of her feet.

She turns to Faraday, beside her, but the back window is exploding, and Faraday, looking out the back window, is suddenly awash in a spray of broken glass.

Dany looks around her wildly.

And when it's done, when those bright splinters have fallen like stars, her history teacher slumps forward, and though the car is speeding into the dark night, somehow, the screams follow them, because something dark is leaking out of Faraday, the night is leaking out of him, and it's spreading across the back seat, a puddle of it, not as red as a child's tulip but as black as the night sky.

| CHAPTER 0 = X + 29

Dany looks at her aunt.

There is a goose egg rising on Aunt Norah's forehead. A cartoon circle and stars revolve around her head. Mac is curled up in the footwell, and Eva, hands gripping the steering wheel, is pale with panic.

Only then does she dare to look at Faraday, beside her.

Dany sees the dark blossom of blood on the teacher's pale blue shirt. Too high for the heart. Too low for the throat. His chest is rising and falling. *Breath. Life.* But there is blood dripping from his open mouth too.

The wave of panic dims – and she feels it, the descent of dead calm. With calm comes reason. First, she pulls her mask out of her pocket, and slips it on her face. Her fingers, practiced at the motion, reform the seal. "Knife, scissors. Something sharp, now," Dany calls out, holding her hand out towards the front seat.

"Manicure scissors," Eva says. "You have them."

Cursing, Dany grabs the nail scissors from her pocket and forces Faraday upright.

And then the nail scissors are the letter opener and Faraday is the envelope. She slices his shirt away. Dany can see it now, the wound, a deep fissure in his shoulder. She breathes. For the first time, she breathes. He must've bitten his tongue, that's all. A little investigation and yes, that's all it is. And yes, there is a little hole in the skin of his shoulder, and it will not close. Out of that deep black wound pours blood.

"You have to stop the bleeding," her aunt says.

"Give me something," Dany tells her.

Faraday reaches up towards the wound, his dark face is now an ashy grey-green, and he falls back against the seat.

"Whoa there, Faraday," Dany tells him.

Already, she's cutting up the kid's blanket with her tiny scissors. She makes a little cut, tears off a strip and, balling it up, jams the thing into place.

"Can you see me?" she asks, leaning into his face.

A pair of brown eyes blink back at her.

"Can you see me, Faraday?" she asks him. "Are you there?"

Her aunt, meanwhile, has clambered over the console, making her way into the back seat. Dany is on one side of Faraday, and now Aunt Norah is on the other. "Help me," her aunt says, and together, the two of them ease Faraday forward, so that her aunt can get a look at his back.

"No exit wound," she says.

"How about a hospital?" Eva asks – her eyes are huge in the rear-view mirror. "You know, like, doctors and machines meant for the prolonging of human life?"

"They'll arrest us," Dany points out. "Any other day, I'd be okay with that."

Mac is shaking on the floor of the car – and Dany knows she has to get her sister out of here. "Go up front, little monkey," she tells the kid. "Be the co-pilot for Eva."

The kid wipes her eyes and, after blinking at Dany, nods and climbs into the front seat.

In the front seat, the kid is still crying, Dany can see that, but her sobs are near-silent things, just the racking of her chest and some tiny hiccups. She'll be okay. But Dany keeps glancing up front. How much? How much is too much? Where is the line? But if they've crossed a line, it was a long time ago. Maybe even years.

Her aunt, meanwhile, is painting her hands red with Faraday's blood. She's wadded up another ball of fabric and, pressing it to his shoulder, she's trying to staunch the unchecked flow.

Dany looks into Faraday's face and sees it.

He's discovered it for himself now. He's found that category of pain that Dany once believed had been invented for her alone. But someone has planted a white-hot piece of metal in her teacher's shoulder and, when Dany looks into his eyes, she can see that it burns, it burns.

| CHAPTER ⊙ = X + 30

Dany and her aunt spend what feels like an hour getting the bleeding under control, but when Dany glances at Faraday's watch, it's only been a few minutes. Already, up in the front seat, Mac is calming down.

The kid's eyes, though, aren't focused, not on anything Dany can see. There are flecks of shattered glass sparkling in the kid's hair, twinkling in the light of oncoming cars. The kid, she only notices now, no longer has the nose plug on her face. She thinks back. Had the kid even had it on at the prison? But she can't remember.

The kid is sucking on her thumb. "Fingers out of your mouth, now," Dany tells her.

Eva asks something then – but her words come out so fast, it takes a minute for Dany to disentangle them.

"She wants to know where to go," Dany translates.

"Just follow the highway," Aunt Norah says. "We'll go to their dad's place. It's twenty minutes past the bridge."

Dany looks at Eva – she is holding the steering wheel in a death grip. The whole of her is shaking. And she's talking so fast that her words run together. It's as if Eva has lost her mental space bar.

"Slow down," Dany tells her.

And then she feels it, hears it. The car grinds down into a lower gear.

"No, no," Dany calls out. "Don't *drive* slower – *talk* slower."

"I've got this driving thing down," Eva is saying, "but, like, it's better if we choose one speed. Fast, slow, I don't care, but change is bad, okay. Change is very bad. So let's just pick a speed and stay there, 'kay?"

Dany looks in the rear-view.

Eva's eyes are darting from mirror to road, mirror to road, as the car zigzags down the highway, as if the wheels are tied to her friend's gaze. There are cars on either side of her, and Eva is pinballing from near collision to near collision.

"They painted lines on the road for a reason," Aunt Norah says. "Ignore everything else. Ignore the other cars. Just follow the lines."

"Hey, Little Rabbit, check the glovebox for me," Eva tells the kid. "See if there's a manual or something. It'll have, like, a picture of a car on it."

"She can read," Dany says, exasperated, and shakes her head.

The kid opens up the glove compartment and sorts through papers.

"Hey," Dany asks. "When did you get your license?"

"Next year," Eva says. Her voice drops to a whisper, and she asks, "Is Mister Faraday . . . dead?"

"Nah, he's all right," Dany says. "When we get to Antoine's, we'll just sew him up . . . or something."

"Is he going to die?"

"No way," Dany promises. "He's just got a leaky pipe. Drive a bit more. Then, if we pull over a minute, I can get the duct tape out of the trunk."

Then Faraday is mumbling, muttering, but Dany can't make him out.

Aunt Norah, she sees, is still holding the balled-up fabric to Mister Faraday's wound.

It'd been blue, the blanket, but as Dany watches, the fabric turns black. "Hold this a minute," Norah says to her. And it is then, only then, that Dany gets her first good look at Aunt Norah. She's aged, these last couple months. And her eyes look strange and saggy. Worse, there is that loose flap of skin on her forehead – that'll have to be stitched up too. And below the flap, it looks like a goose has laid a prize egg.

"I'm okay," Faraday is saying, over and over.

Dany nods at him. "You are, you're okay."

"I think someone hit me," he tells her.

"I think maybe you're right," Dany says slowly, her eyes narrowing.

Faraday isn't okay. His eyes look strange, like they've been pinned to his face. Like someone has sewn dark buttons onto a doll. Norah, meanwhile, is still trying to get out of her orange track suit. And then Dany sees her aunt's face, sees her eyes, dull and unfocused. Her aunt, too, is shaking it rough.

Dany looks from her aunt's track suit to her own sad outfit, the plague jacket she is still wearing. Holding the balled up fabric with one hand, she takes the key from her neck with the other. It's awkward, but Jasper's one-handed test tube lessons help. Finally, she unlocks the thing, and shrugs it off. The jumpsuit and the plague jacket go out the window.

In the low beams of oncoming cars, Dany sees the bright flashes of colour – the orange of the bloody prison uniform, the yellow of the plague jacket – as they scuttle over the highway, tossed lifelessly up by the wheels of oncoming cars.

| CHAPTER ⊙ = X + 31

Dany takes the bottle of sanitizer from her aunt and cleans her hands. Then she turns to her teacher. He isn't going to like this.

"I'm sorry, Faraday," Dany says. "But this might sting."

He shakes his head, but Dany lifts the blood-soaked blanket and, as fresh blood oozes out, Dany squirts alcohol gel directly into the wound. A dollop on her hands too, for good measure.

A beat later, the car is swerving in time with his ratcheting screams.

"Eyes on the road," Dany calls out. "Faraday's fine. He can handle it."

And then Aunt Norah presses a new ball of blanket against her teacher's shoulder. Her aunt talks quietly to him, gently touching his hair, but Faraday is done. Dany can see that he is done. As Dany watches, whimpering, her history teacher squeezes his eyes shut.

| | |

Finally, when they've put enough distance between them and the hospice, Eva stutters to a stop on the shoulder of the road. First things first, Dany finds duct tape and pain pills, and heads back to Faraday.

"Here, take these," she orders.

When he doesn't respond, she thumbs open his mouth – and drops a couple pills in. A second later, she shoves the bottle of water in his mouth.

"It'll help with the pain," she tells him. "Swallow."

Eva, up front, is reading the manual out loud.

"It is advisable," Eva reads, "to read the first part of this instruction manual, which deals with the operation of your Volkswagen, *very* carefully. You will then . . . start off your first trip with complete confidence."

Dany tears a long strip of duct tape from the cylinder.

"I could really use a sticky for the gear shift," Eva mutters.

Dany looks at her work-in-progress. She's set a fabric bandage in place, and now she duct tapes it to his chest. It won't feel good coming off, but it'll do the trick. She nods. He'll hold for a little while. "There now, Faraday," she says. "I fixed your leak."

Next, Dany digs through the trunk, finding clothes for Aunt Norah. Her aunt can't just sit around in prison-issue underwear and a tank top. She finds a pair of Faraday's rugger pants and an old Cornell shirt that look like they'll do. When she gives them to her aunt, Norah tries to stand up, but as soon as she does, she vomits on the gravel.

"Sit," Dany tells her. "Don't stand up."

Up front, Eva is studying the VW Bug's manual like she's about to be quizzed on it. "One minute," Dany tells her, "and we go," but Eva doesn't take her nose out of the all-important book. She doesn't even look up.

Dany taps Eva on the shoulder, nods at her aunt. At first, Dany thought the problem was the goose egg. But now, she sees it's more than this. She can see it, in her aunt's eyes and skin. Aunt Norah is sick. Dany thinks back to what Jasper told her, about the hospice-prison, and ticks off the likely possibilities. Dysentery. Cholera. She hopes it's neither.

"She looks like shit," Dany says quietly.

"She needs to hydrate," Eva says. "Electrolytes," she adds and turns back to her book.

Dany finds what they need in the console between seats. A few ancient packets of sugar and salt, the kind that once came with fast food. A faded cursive *M* on each packet. They're probably as old as the car itself. Taking a bottle of water, she empties one sugar and one salt pack inside. Then, with a second look at her aunt, she doubles it. "Drink this," she tells Norah. "It'll help. Electrolytes. But no gulping. Take it slow, 'kay."

Norah nods.

In the front seat, Eva flips another page and then she is staring agog, her mouth wide open. "Holy mother of moly," Eva says. "The gears work according to vehicle speed. That *is* logical. Of course, if they want my advice, they should automate the whole process."

"I could try driving . . ." Norah offers.

"I think we're better off with Eva," Dany answers. Not only does her aunt not have her license, but one look, and Dany can see she's in terrible shape. She glances from Norah to Eva. Eva frowns back and shakes her head.

"I figured out the scooter pretty quick," Dany says and shrugs. "I could take over if you need me."

"Look," says Eva. "Duct tape makes me extremely uncomfortable." Even just the one glance, back at Faraday's bloody shoulder, has left Eva looking pale.

"Go on, then," Dany tells her friend. "Before Mister Faraday decides he wants to take the wheel."

| | |

As they drive, Dany talks to her history teacher.

"You got lucky," she tells him. "I think the bullet might be in one piece."

One finger hovers over his duct-taped shoulder.

"It's right here," she tells him, her finger lightly hovering over the fleshy part of his shoulder, where shoulder meets arm. "Honestly, it doesn't look too bad. But you've lost a tiny bit of blood. And we can't leave the duct tape on forever. We need to sew you up at some point. As soon as we get you to Antoine's."

"I'm bleeding less," Faraday says.

Dany smiles and nods, but then she sees her aunt's expression. Aunt Norah doesn't say anything, but the look on her face tells Dany that this isn't the good news that she hopes it is. Still, she doesn't need to relay that to Faraday. Her aunt, after all, would know. Dany's heard the stories about her aunt and her mom and Antoine. Still, she doesn't share her aunt's resume with Faraday. Most people only know about people like Antoine from the news, so they don't get it, not really.

Besides, her history teacher, she can see, is struggling to stay conscious.

Looking at him, now, for the first time, she wonders how all of this will affect him. She's been so caught up in everything, it hasn't even occurred to her to ask. Here, beside her, is a man who tried to save her little sister, who tried to help her, and now he is bleeding out in the back seat of his own car.

And it's all Dany's fault.

His teaching career is probably over too, plague or no. Of course, he was given a simple choice – they all were – survive or die.

He'll never set foot in a classroom again, at least, not outside of a prison. The old Faraday died back there on the prison grounds. And this new one, he'll bear the scar of that gunshot for the rest of his life.

In his flesh, now, is buried evidence, awaiting discovery. A prison guard's bullet.

And then she sees it – how all of them, in this car, are fatally connected. Somehow, their lives have intersected in blood, and now they are bound together. For better or for worse. Worse, probably. Dany takes a steadying breath. She focuses on the dark windshield. The lines of the road ahead of them. No, Faraday will never forgive her. Not ever. If he survives this – who is to say she hasn't infected him in the last five minutes? A part of his life, along with a good amount of his blood, is gone. Irretrievably. One way or another, Faraday's old life has as good as leaked out on the back seat.

And then she knows something else. She knows Isobel was right.

Dany is a ticking clock – a danger to everyone she comes near.

She stares at the dark road, wishing, wishing, but then, she did a lifetime's worth of wishing back at Darling-Holmes – and where had that gotten her?

At once, the answer comes to her: *Here. It's gotten her here.*

| CHAPTER ⊙ = X + 32

Eva is having trouble keeping her eyes – and the car – on the road. Every time she looks at a road sign, the car veers towards the shoulder.

Dany presses forward between the front seats. "How's the driving going?" she asks. But when Eva glances at her, the car swerves. "Whoa. Eyes on the road."

Eva nods and stares straight ahead, gripping the wheel in two fists.

"I'm doing the best I can," Eva says, "but every time I slow down, to put two *full* chevrons between us and the car ahead, some budinsky moves into our lane and obliterates my safe zone. One point five chevrons," she says, sighing. "It's the best I can do, okay. God."

"Uh, okay," Dany says. "What's . . . a *chevron*?"

Eva looks at her and swerves.

"Road," Dany calls out.

Slowly, Dany retreats into the back seat again. Safer for all of them.

In the opposite lane, a flood of bright white lights zip past.

Dany has been aware of them zinging past for a while, those cars headed back into the city. But only now does it occur to her to ask where, exactly, they think they are going. Heading into the middle of a deadly outbreak is the obvious answer.

"See the traffic?" Dany asks.

"Oh dear," Eva says. "Everybody's going back. Should we turn around?"

Dany sure as hell hopes not. Back there are police officers and prison guards and by now, who knows. Maybe even the national guard. Back there, worse than all of that, is the virus, version 2.0, the one that has made the leap.

Eva reaches over to turn on the radio, but nothing comes out.

"Hey, Little Rabbit," Eva says, "do you think you could fix the –"

"No," Dany and Aunt Norah call out in unison. Things out there are bad enough, without giving the kid access to a novel source of electrical power.

Eva risks a glance in the rear-view, the car careens towards the shoulder, Dany screams for her to watch the goddamned road and then Eva, finally, is face-forward again, her hands stiff on the wheel, her mouth clamped shut.

Dany wriggles up between the front seats and does all she can. She jiggles the radio in its casing, pushes at the thing and, finally, gives it a good bashing, but it's no use. Whatever loose connection once bound the radio to its power source has fallen away.

"My Sunbeam," Mister Faraday mutters.

Aunt Norah narrows her eyebrows, looking a question at her niece.

Dany shrugs and adds one vintage scooter to her mental list of debts, along with the things she already owes Faraday, like a working shoulder, what looks to be a couple litres of blood, a car with an actual back window and a first edition of Shrewsbury, signed on the occasion of his receiving a Ph.D.

| CHAPTER ⊙ = X + 33

Next to Dany, Mister Faraday is time travelling. Sometimes, he's giving a history lecture. More than once, he calls her either Graham or Gran, she isn't sure which. She gently pats his cheek and looks up, ahead of them, searching out the source of the bright white lights.

The lights shine even more brightly in the general darkness. The power isn't back anywhere else, and Dany guesses they are running these lights with a generator. Soon, they see a line of stopped cars ahead and, as they close the distance, she makes out soldiers carrying what can only be automatic rifles.

The soldiers are, every last one of them, wearing biohazard masks. And then she notices something else. Their uniforms are all wrong. The fade of the fabric, the cut. They don't look the same as the soldiers back at the hospice. Dany takes in the front pockets, the shoulders, too, but if these soldiers once wore insignia, they've been removed. "Are these even real soldiers?" Dany asks.

"Oh, they're real. I just don't think they're Canadian," her aunt says.

Dany closes her eyes and her heart compresses, the blood suddenly too thick to pump. Still, there is a picture in her head. In it, a cable-stayed bridge is blocked off by a coil of barbed wire, itself spiked with huge asterisks of twisted rebar. Between the traffic directions, a series of concrete piles. In the picture, there is only one place to turn back and it is where those soldiers are.

This, this was what she was talking about in history class. Because the Port Mann Bridge has been remade into a cordon sanitaire, and a line of soldiers, at the point of guns, are trying to keep a fatal plague from crossing a line drawn by some bunkered politician on a piece of paper.

"Cordon sanitaire," she says.

She leans forward, taking in the rest of the place.

Just past the checkpoint, there look to be car spikes. The soldiers have set up a temporary gatehouse – a mobile unit, half obscured by the sandbags they've piled in front of it. But it's too elaborate to be in response to the prison break. She counts soldiers and deployment patterns, takes in all of it. This isn't for them. Whatever this checkpoint is, it has to have been set in motion hours ago. As Dany watches, a soldier meets car after car. After a brisk inspection – at point of flashlight – each makes a slow U-turn and heads back into the city.

"Sugar, sugar, sugar," Eva is saying, "what do I do? I have to slow down."

But Eva soon figures it out. Dany hears the gears grind slowly down into first. At the end of the line, their car chokes to a stall.

"Everybody stay calm," Aunt Norah is saying.

"This isn't about us," Dany tells her aunt. "This is about the virus."

Her aunt looks a question at her, but Dany nods at an old rusted van. There, the one that is trying to jump the line – bypassing the checkpoint and turning back to the city. The side panel on the van proclaims its owner to be a *Drywall Genius*. Drywall genius he might be, but checkpoint genius he is not. The van pulls out of the line and turns back – only to be lit up by floodlights.

Soldiers range into place, rifles at the ready.

A single warning shot brings the rusty van to a slow stop on the other side of the road, facing the city, right across from them.

The van is forced to the shoulder of the road under the gaze of four riflemen. Dany keeps her eyes on the man driving the van.

"It's okay," Aunt Norah says. "It's not about us. This isn't about us."

But it doesn't have to be *about* them to kill them, Dany knows.

"*Can* we turn back?" Eva asks.

"I think that might draw the wrong kind of attention," her aunt says.

"That's not what I mean," Eva says. "I mean it more *literally*. Like, how do you turn a car around? In cartoons, you just poke your legs out the bottom and swing it around."

"I don't know," Dany says. "Did you try the steering wheel yet?"

Eva doesn't turn around. She lifts one hand from the wheel and, cranking with the other, slowly raises her middle finger.

Dany grins, but she knows what Eva means. "I can do the turning part if you need me to," Dany offers.

Norah leans between the seats.

"Get the blood off Mac's face," her aunt says. She hands Eva a box of Kleenex and a bottle of water.

The attention of the soldiers may be on the *Drywall Genius's* van for now, but they'll get to the VW Bug soon enough. "The window," Dany says. "We need a story."

Dany looks around. Faraday is slumped, half conscious, in the back seat. Aunt Norah looks like warmed-over goose shit. And the kid? She's covered in blood, hair spattered with broken glass. Christ, she looks like she's been in a car accident. And there it is.

"Car accident," Dany tells them.

Eva picks the story up from there.

"We were driving along," Eva says, "quite competently, I might add, when a cryptid emerged from the treeline, a sasquatch – well, cryp*tids*, let's say a breeding pair – which is pretty unusual for this time of year, and, when we slowed to look – naturally, I mean, who wouldn't? – we were rear-ended by a truck. That would explain *every*thing."

Dany pulls the ragged remains of the fleece blanket up to Faraday's chin, trying to hide some of the damage.

"We got rear-ended," Dany says. "That's all they need to know."

| CHAPTER ⊙ = X + 34

Across the way, Dany sees soldiers interrogating the driver of the van.

The fireflies may be gone from her eyes, but her world is evaporating at the edges. She's been running on force of will. When the adrenaline in her bloodstream runs out, she'll drop like a rock. She's been there before. For now, fear is her friend.

Eva grinds the car forward again and stutters to a stop. They are two car lengths from the checkpoint, now, and her gaze keeps tripping over the soldiers. "We need a map," she says. Mister Faraday, next to her, is nodding. He says something that might mean glovebox. "Check up front," Dany says, and her hand finds Mac's shoulder.

Mac's face is no longer freckled red. Her face a stain of pink, Mac rifles through the glovebox. She passes an old map back. Then she curls up again, her thumb, once more, in her mouth. "Hands out of your mouth," Dany tells the kid, her voice tight. "Sterilize her hands and get a mask on her," she tells Eva.

Dany flicks on the overhead light and takes in Faraday. Her history teacher is not looking good. One glance at Norah's eyes, and she can see her misgivings. No, her aunt doesn't like what she's seeing, not any more than Dany does.

She and Aunt Norah have wedged Faraday between them and

now she spreads the map over his lap. The map, she sees, is years out of date. It probably came with the car. The thing is ancient. No sooner has she straightened it out, then the map comes to pieces. Dany lays out first one section and then another, flipping through them until she finds what she is looking for. She leans forward over bloodied paper, her fingers tracing roads.

"Nobody's getting through the checkpoint. Nobody," Eva whispers.

Dany glances up front – an oversize mask now covers most of her kid sister's face. She nods. Turning back to the map, Dany traces her finger over a pair of promising lines on the map. "What about this," she says aloud. But there is no one to ask, really, nothing to do but choose.

Dany taps the twin lines, thinking. Even Faraday is looking down at the map now. Her aunt, too, is peering over, eyes on the twinned set of lines. "The smaller one, here, you think it's a railway bridge?" Dany asks.

"Looks like it," Aunt Norah says. She meets Dany's eyes. "It's a chance," her aunt tells her. "That's what it is, a chance."

"Old swing bridge," her teacher whispers. "Train tracks."

Coldly pragmatic, that's what they need to be. "Looks like the power's out all over the city. We'd have the dark on our side, right?" Dany asks. *Just like at the prison camp*, a voice in her head adds.

"I can do it," Eva says. "My housekeeper, Bianca, she has a story about this time she saw a car driving on the railway tracks, back on Negros. I know I can do it. We have to try."

For a moment, as she glances out the window, Dany's mind holds an image of the map, but already, it's fading from her eyes. Out there, the *Drywall Genius*, who has to be in his fifties, is standing outside of his van. His hands are raised, and he's talking, fast. At least, his mouth is moving in a blur, though none of his words are audible. But another space has opened up in front of them and Eva, once more, starts up the car.

Again, the car leaps forward. Again, Faraday cries out in pain.

"Oops," Eva says. "Neutral. You have to put it in neutral. You know," she adds, not for the first time, "I honestly think that I could design something much more user-friendly."

Dany reaches up and clicks off the overhead light. Soon, they'll reach the soldier at the front of the line. She doesn't want him seeing any more than he has to.

The big guy, the one by the drywall van, is begging the soldiers. She can see him holding up his hands and pleading. Then the car ahead of them is given a pass. It makes a U-turn, heading back to the city, passing by the van. And Eva, she skids them up to the checkpoint. Her eyes dart over the soldier, leaning in the window, and her hands tap dance across the steering wheel.

"Sorry, sugar junky," Eva says. "I need a fix."

But the soldier just holds up his palm, staying them with a single gesture.

His eyes are on the drywall van, and Dany's gaze follows. She sees a flurry of motion by the roadside. Soldiers swinging into position, and the *Drywall Genius*, he lowers his hands, putting himself between the soldiers and the side panel of the van.

Dany looks at him. Really takes him in. Balding, a few thin threads of hair combed across his pate. He's large, a big guy, but the flesh on his upper arms hangs loose, as if he's used to eating a lot more than he's getting. It's a look she sees a lot these days. Hungry. The man is huge, but scared. She can see sweat dripping down from his wispy hairline. The soldier who has been standing by their car, the palm of his hand holding them in place, drops that palm. He raises his hand to his rifle, swinging it round towards the *Drywall Genius.*

Across the way, another soldier is edging towards the cargo hold. He swings the side panel wide open and, from twenty feet, Dany can make out the girl's bulging, skittering eyes. It's the virus. But here? So far from the lab and from Liz?

Her aunt shakes her head, but she doesn't look surprised, just sad.

Dany looks at Aunt Norah. "You've seen that before?"

Aunt Norah looks at Dany, and narrows. "They've been showing up at the hospice, more and more."

Norah shakes her head, eyes once more on the sick girl, and Dany chases the math.

She's always been quick to see patterns. And the pattern, thus far, is all too clear. And the thin thread of hope this new dot offers, in her constellation of math, isn't going to change her story. So, maybe someone else was the first to carry the virus out and into the world – but Dany has already been told. Isobel has told her what she is, what's in her. Adding more vectors is not going to change Dany's story.

Dany looks at the girl in the white van. Is she fifteen years old? Sixteen? Framed by the van's open door, she sees a picture of her own future. Dany and her are probably about the same age. It is so unfair, for a girl's life to be put out like a cigarette. She's just a kid. And what's worse, the thin thread of hope Dany has been hanging onto – Isobel's words about her immature immune system – is wearing thin.

Because if there is no hope for the girl in the van, then there is no hope for her.

The girl has been bound.

Her arms are tied behind her and she's been gagged, to keep her quiet. The man out there, sweat pouring from his forehead, must be her dad. He's trying to protect his kid. The guard outside of their car takes a step forward, his rifle now level with the man's chest. The four soldiers outside of the van level their rifles at the man's head.

But the girl's father is brave. Or stupid.

At any rate, he doesn't just hide from all his problems at some stupid farmhouse in the country. He does whatever he has to do in order to protect his kid. In spite of the guns, he walks over to the van, pulls the side door to a close.

It isn't just sweat, Dany sees. Tears are pouring down the man's face. Because he loves his daughter. Dany hears the soldiers warn him, but the man turns his back and retreats to the driver's seat of his van. They call out the warning once, twice, a third time. But the man gets up into the driver's seat, and the van rolls slowly forward, making its way towards the city.

A warning shot rings out.

"No," Dany whispers. "No, no."

In the front seat, Eva's hand shoots out and she covers the kid's eyes. Just in time. Because, as the van creeps slowly forward, picking up the pace, the soldiers shoot the driver dead.

"And that's what love gets you," Aunt Norah says. "Every goddamned time."

Dany looks at her aunt, but Norah has turned away from them. Looking out the car window, her aunt just shakes her head. Not for the first time, Dany finds herself wondering about her aunt and Antoine. Wonders just how close it is that they've become.

Dany fixes her eyes on Eva. "Car accident," she reminds her.

"Yeah," Eva says, "I got it, I got it."

"No sasquatches," Dany says.

"I mean, I get why people like sasquai for the plural. It sounds Latin-y," Eva says. "But sésq'ets is probably better. Better for the singular too, since the word's Halkomelem and –"

"Eva."

"As an anarchx-feminist," she says, "I am adept at decentralized consensus, but in this instance, I have to say –"

"Eva," Dany says.

"Okay, okay," she says. "No sésq'ets. Pinkie swear."

And then Dany is blind. The soldier's flashlight hits her square in the eyes – and Dany's caught in the glare. When the light turns on Faraday, she blinks, taking the soldier in. Only his eyes are visible through the lens of the biomask. He looks over each of them in turn, staring into their eyes, examining their pupils for signs of the virus.

The soldier, luckily, is more interested in Eva's eyes than in her story.

"Turn around up here," he says, waving them on.

Eva looks back at Dany – her eyes panicky. But it's too late to switch drivers now.

"You can do it," Dany tells her.

"And then it is all on her," Eva says. "*Eva versus the steering wheel.* Hands shaking, a determined look on her face, she grinds the gear forward and –"

Slowly, Eva makes a U-turn.

It isn't a perfect semicircle, but she does turn the car around. And then she drives. She drives past the blood-soaked driver, the one whose corpse is hanging half out of the front seat of the drywall van. Dany focuses ahead of them, where, painted onto the highway, a pair of lines gird their car like an infinitely long isosceles triangle, one that will gather them up and shoot them into the future.

"Okay," Eva says. "Now for the small matter of gearing up."

But Dany can hear it. This time, when Eva depresses the clutch, she finds the sweet spot and they smoothly pick up speed. Eva grins, and her eyes flick to the rear-view mirror.

"Road," Dany and Norah call out in synchrony. And Eva straightens out the car and drives on. A half a click after they've passed the van, they hear the second shot.

| CHAPTER ⊙ = X + 35

Dany leans forward between the front seats. They're on Columbia Drive now, easing onto the small dead-end lane that fronts the swing bridge. As Dany watches, the car rolls to a stop next to a squat brick building that looks like an enormous Lego cube.

Dany is the first one out of the car.

The night air smells of creosote, dust and a hint of something green. But everything about the place is coated in a film of ashen dust. In the distance, Dany can just make out the river. There's the sound of rushing water – and in its empty noise, she can almost hear the voices of children, playing just out of sight. The quantum amplitude. In some other world, Mac is down by the river's edge. In this other universe, unsplattered by blood, hair free of broken glass, night is day, and the world is filled with sunshine and dragonflies. And in that world, her little sister, Mac, is playing by the river.

Only they're not in that world.

Slowly, Dany's eyes adjust to the present tense, to the blanket of dark. Blinking away the ghostly image of her sister, only happy, Dany takes in the bridge.

Bridges, really.

First, there's the railway bridge, rising into the dark sky ahead – then, a few hundred yards on, its distant twin – a proper bridge, the kind that cars are *supposed* to drive over, but just now the car-bridge is filled with people. A lot of people. A huge crowd has gathered at the checkpoint there.

Turning back to the swing bridge, she searches for the metal railway tracks, the ones that are supposed to be here. Eva, moving towards the railway bridge, is a little ways ahead of her, muttering and walking an invisible line. Following her friend's gaze, Dany finally picks out the tracks. The twin rails are sunk into the concrete here. Closer to the bridge, the metal tracks rise up from their gutters. So, no, they aren't going to know if their plan will work, not until they are committed, not until their car is partway up the bridge.

"I don't know," Dany says.

"I'll straddle the rails," Eva tells her, "so they act like guides. If I do that, I won't even have to steer. Theoretically."

Eva walks the sunken rails, muttering, and the kid follows after her, sliding one little hand into Eva's. Norah takes her place beside Dany, laying a hand on her shoulder, eyes on Eva and Mac.

Together, Dany and her aunt look out over the railway bridge they plan to cross. But the bridge looks unfinished. All those metal girders holding it in place, they remind Dany of one of the dinosaur skeletons you see hanging from the ceiling at a natural museum. It isn't a bridge so much as the outline for one, a dangerously incomplete sketch.

"We've done all we can for your teacher," Aunt Norah says quietly. "We've got to get him to Antoine's."

Dany shrugs, her eyes on Eva and Mac. "Faraday will be all right."

All Dany can think about is all of the things she should have done for her sister but hasn't. She should have brought Mac to a place like this, maybe, sometime during the day.

In the daytime, the place is probably full of birds and dragonflies.

Only Dany never seems to have time to do the kind of things for her little sister that she should. When Dany was little, before her mom got sick, Phil would take her to the park all the time.

Once, when she was six, she ran down to a river like this, and she stumbled on a dozen ducks, scaring the birds into flight. Dany stood stock-still, frozen like a statue, the only still point in a world filled with crashing wings.

She should have found a way to do that for Mac.

Dany takes in her aunt and she knows, she just knows. "You're good with Mac," Dany says, her voice breaking on the words. "You're a good mom. Better than me."

Her aunt's face falls.

Aunt Norah pulls Dany close so that her mask nuzzles Dany's forehead. "You've been a tremendous big sister," her aunt tells her. "Amazing. God," she says. "If I'd known – if I knew that day, if I knew that going to that protest would cause all this, I wouldn't have gone."

Dany looks up at her aunt, but it isn't her fault. They were just looking for an excuse. "Nah," Dany says. "They would have revoked –"

But the night shatters into pieces – and, as she turns to the bridge, she knows the sound for what it is. The crack of another rifle shot.

CHAPTER 0 = X + 36

Most of the people are on foot. A couple have signs, writing roughly scrawled on cardboard and skewered with a stick. A few are banging on pots and pans. A checkpoint has been set up at the entrance to the Pattullo Bridge, where it rises up over Front Street. She can see more of the unmarked soldiers there – not an insignia in sight – and now one of them has fired a shot over the heads of the crowd, the people who want to get across. No, who *need* to get across.

Dany doesn't need binoculars to see the effect that gunshot has on the crowd. People duck down, covering their heads with their hands – as if that'll help.

A riot, they'll call it. A mob. But when Dany looks out, she sees families. Desperate. The ones at the front of the crowd are backing away. But the ones at the back, heedless with distance, are pressing closer to the checkpoint, pushing the people ahead of them closer to the soldiers' guns.

Dany shakes her head. This is going to get bad. It's going to get bad fast. She wants to be out of here long before that happens.

Eva, Mac's hand firmly in hers, comes trotting back to Dany and her aunt.

"The Liz video, it did all this?" Dany asks her.

"Er, perhaps it was the shooting at the last checkpoint," Eva says. And when Dany looks at her friend, she sees that, even now, the little light on her glasses is blinking. Her best friend, Eva, is live streaming the apocalypse.

| | |

Dany's still looking at the crowd on the main bridge, so she doesn't see them coming. Two SUVs. As the first driver slows to a stop, Dany hears the wheels on gravel and turns. The driver is already rolling down her window.

She's an older woman, working class. Something about the lines in her face speak to a lifetime of days spent under the sun. "Great minds," the woman says.

Eva nods. "I drive stick," she tells the stranger.

The older woman narrows her eyes a second and then smiles. "Good for you, honey. You mind if we head over now?"

Eva nods, a big grin on her face, and Dany shrugs.

As Dany watches, the first SUV drives onto the track, round the rising arc to the swing bridge. The other follows – though it's a little slower. The vehicles have their main lights off, but she hears the SUVs rattling their way across the trestles, sees the red lights of their brakes, flashing now and again.

Her aunt comes striding over to them.

Norah is shaking her head. Not good, her face is saying, not good at all. "Let's get a move on," Norah says.

Dany looks from her aunt to Eva and nods.

She isn't sure Eva can do it – a VW Bug is not an SUV, not by a long shot – but then, Eva doesn't have a choice. Eva *has* to get them across, whether the car is capable of crossing or not.

"You *can* do this," Dany tells her. "You can."

Eva frowns. "Those SUVs won't be the only ones crossing," she says.

Dany follows her friend's eyes to the crowd by the main bridge.

A few have already broken off from the main group and are headed their way. Dany focuses on one of them, a man pulling a red wagon piled high with what must be every last thing in the world he owns. He's rolling the cart down Columbia Street, heading their way.

"We gotta book," Dany says.

Her aunt nods. "The soldiers, they're going to notice that sooner than later."

Dany takes one last look at the SUVs on the railway bridge.

Already, the first one has made it to the other side. But the second SUV is moving slower, and is only now approaching the halfway point.

| | |

Getting into the car, Dany's half-surprised to see Faraday. She's all but forgotten about him. She hopes that his pills have kicked in, because if they haven't, Faraday's about to be in a world of pain.

Up front, Norah settles Mac onto her lap, and in the back, Dany gets Faraday ready. As ready as he can be. She takes hold of his hand, the one on the good side, and wraps his fingers around the grab bar on the car's ceiling. A numb expression on his face, her teacher nods and takes hold.

Already, Eva is easing the old rattletrap onto the sunken tracks.

Dany glances out.

They're in position now, and once they start, the rails will guide them – or so Eva's theory goes. They're supposed to be in third gear. Dany knows that. But Eva is scared and she's moving slow. Too slow. And they're still in second. The car is crawling on the tracks like a drugged beetle, but the trestles are a hazard. If Eva drives too fast, yes, they'll damage the car. But if she drives as slow as this, the car will get stuck in the gaps between.

"Um, I'm not sure if anyone can actually see the rails," Eva asks. "Because, well, I don't see –"

As soon as she says it, they hit the trestles. The rails might not be visible, but they can hear them now, scraping metal from the underside of the car.

The first violent jolt pins Dany's seat belt in place, holding her fast.

Up front, Aunt Norah is sharing her seat belt with Mac. She has her arms around the kid and is using her body as a cushion, trying to lessen the impact of the jolts. She can see that her aunt has given the kid a knotted strip of blanket to bite down on.

Mac's scared, but she'll be okay.

It's bad, bad enough, but this is just the start of it. Soon, they hit the spaced wooden trestles of the bridge, and Dany, shocked, feels what amounts to a physical assault. She turns to Faraday. Already, blood is leaking through his duct tape. The patch job is barely holding, but there's nothing she can do about that now. They've hit the trestles. They're committed.

Dany is hoping that the noise of the crowd will drown out their passage, but she doesn't know how long their luck can hold. If the soldiers on the Pattullo Bridge aren't all deaf, they'll be gunning for them soon. Still, she hopes the din of the crowd overpowers the noise of their passage. But sound moves in strange ways over water.

Dany glances up front and stiffens. In the front seat, Mac's crying, but it's different. The cries aren't like anything Dany has ever heard. Mac's face is bright red, and the sobs coming from her aren't silent, but fully voiced. The kid's wailing.

This is the first time she's heard Mac's little kid voice. The first time she's heard anything from Mac – since before the ministry, since before her mom, on the coldest, longest night of winter, put the two of them in the window well, muttering in tongues. Since before a continental divide opened up in their lives, dividing it into before and after. The sound makes something crack open in her chest.

Eva, meanwhile, slows down to look at Mac. Dany slips out of her seat belt – there's no other way – and she leans forward over the console – her head slamming the roof with every thud. "Go, go, go," Dany yells at Eva. "We'll get stuck. We'll founder. Go."

Her voice, though she's yelling, is barely audible over the grinding of metal. But Eva glances at her and, when she looks forward once more, she's already picking up the pace.

Dany tastes blood. At some point, she's bitten the inside of her cheek and her mouth is filling with blood, but she has no choice. For the sake of everyone in the car, she swallows the red stuff down.

| | |

From somewhere below the car – the axle on the rails, she guesses – there comes a terrible grinding of metal. She's sure, now, that the soldiers on the main vehicle bridge can hear it. They have to hear it. In the darkness, she sees sparks flashing up from either side of the old Bug. The noise is sure to draw the soldiers' notice, and the sparks will tell them where to aim their guns.

Up front, the blood has drained from Eva's hands. Her grip on the steering wheel is so tight that Dany can see every last muscle in Eva's arms – but she's doing it – already, they are a third of the way across.

And then she sees it. There. A ways ahead of them. The flickering red lights of the SUV's brakes. The car ahead of them has slowed to a crawl. With a sinking feeling, Dany watches as the SUV rolls to a stop.

The five-ton hunk of metal sits on the tracks like a dead elephant, barring their way.

"Hold on to your hats," Eva yells.

Dany feels the car speed up. "Like hell," Dany screams. "Stop, stop." She can hear Norah yelling, too – and Dany's eyes lock onto the SUV ahead, the one blocking the tracks. The little VW Bug will never move that thing. The front end of the VW will be smashed and them with it.

But Eva must see it now, because a few feet behind the truck, they roll to a stop. Dany lays a hand on Eva's shoulder. "You did good," she says.

In the newborn silence, a child's sobs fill the air. Norah undoes her seat belt and cradles the kid close, holding her against her chest, rocking her. And slowly, the child's terrified crying eases off.

Only then does Dany remember Faraday. She looks over, half dreading what she'll see. But Faraday's still with them. He's sitting there, staring numbly ahead, blood leaking out from under the duct-tape bandage. Dany is aching and every tooth in her mouth feels like it's been loosened with a pair of pliers. She can only imagine, then, what he's feeling.

Then she sees it. From the corner of her eye. Motion, in the SUV ahead of her. Dany leans forward, one hand on her sister's shoulder, peering ahead, into the dark. Yes, someone has slipped into the driver's side door – the brake lights flick off, and the SUV is in motion again. It rocks, back and forth on the trestles – finds its traction, and is gone.

| CHAPTER ⊙ = X + 37

Dany is the first to accept the inevitable.

Unlike the SUV, their old VW doesn't have the driving power necessary to get them moving, not now that their wheels have come to a rest between two trestles. They'll have to push – and that means that whoever pushes the car will have to walk over the terrible gaps between trestles. In the near-total darkness, they'll have to walk fifty yards, stepping from plank to plank, while suspended hundreds of feet over the Fraser River. At this height, the difference between water and concrete is negligible.

Still, there's no point arguing about it.

Eva finally gives up and shuts off the car. "I think we're going to have to push," she says.

"You better tape him up again," Aunt Norah says, and Dany glances at her history teacher, taking in the damage. Faraday looks like he's been shot. Well, like he's been shot or like he's wandered into the beam of the Large Hadron Collider.

Dany slowly peels the fingers of his right hand from the grab bar, and the arm falls slack. She applies two long strips of duct tape to his wound. The patch job isn't perfect, the bloodied skin makes for a poor seal, but Faraday, like a leaky pipe, will just have to hold.

| | |

Dany opens the back door, letting it swing wide and looks down. Through the gaps between trestles, she can see the dark waters of the Fraser River below.

Aunt Norah and Eva are out of the car and looking ahead – some fifty yards, that's all that stands between them and the other side. But the distance is impossible.

Her kid sister curls up on the front seat – pushing her mask aside so she can get her thumb in her mouth. Dany doesn't even want to think about what will happen if Mac bolts on this bridge. If one foot, for one second, slips between trestles, the kid will break a leg. She is so tiny, she might even slip through the trestles and fall to the river below. Mac can't run, she just can't. Still, for now, at least, Mac seems willing to sit in the car, her eyes intent on her big sister, her thumb socketed in her little mouth.

And then, in the distance, Dany catches sight of them – back there, behind them. The first people to break away from the crowd are now mounting the arc that rises up to the bridge. Others, more and more now, are breaking away from the mob, headed for the railway bridge. "We have to go," Dany says. "We have to go *now*."

Dany's standing there, precariously balanced between two trestles, when she feels a tiny hand reach up and take her own.

| | |

Mac won't get back into the front seat.

Refuses, even, to sit on Eva's lap while she drives.

While the main mob hasn't yet hit the bridge, already, those few who were the first to see the opportunity are quickly approaching. Seeing the half-dozen men and women already picking their way across the railway bridge, Dany relents. The kid can stick with her. Faraday, she'll leave where he is. For now, it's all on Dany and her aunt. They'll have to push the car across.

Eva rocks the gas, and Dany and her aunt lean their weight against the back of the car. The motion is eerily reminiscent of what she and her aunt did together at the hospice – using their weight to inch the unconscious guard forward in the yard. Dany wonders if her aunt is remembering the same thing she is.

Dany glances back.

The people behind them are getting closer. So close, she can see faces. The first one is young, a teenage boy. His hair, long and thin, is in need of a wash. Beside him, she sees an older woman. His mother maybe, her grey hair swept up in a messy bun. They look like people, but people aren't people – not when they can get away with taking what they want. This is the truth that Darling-Holmes taught her. The primary lesson the institution existed to impart. Because it was there that she learned of the dark things that human beings are capable of.

And soon, the pair would overtake them.

Dany puts her shoulder into it, counts out with her aunt, *one, two, three*, and again, they heave. She's breathing heavy now – and pushing as hard as she can. But she and Norah might as well be a pair of ants trying to move a lead brick.

A moment later, the teenaged boy gets his hands on their car.

She flicks a scowl at the teenager, the one who's put himself between Dany and her aunt, who's put his hands on the car. But then the grey-haired woman puts her hands down too, and Dany blinks, taking a moment to understand. Counting down, together, they lean into it and, together, they push.

The tires catch and Eva in her VW Bug is off and moving.

Dany looks up from the boy to the older woman, uncomprehending.

The woman nods at Dany, a sad smile plays on her mouth, and then she moves on down the bridge. By the time Dany thinks to say thank you, it's too late. The pair are ten feet ahead of her, picking their way down the trestles.

Dany and her aunt move more slowly.

The two walk on either side of Mac, each with a death grip on one of Mac's wrists. With each step, Dany is conscious of the deadly drop, of each terrifying gap between trestles. Glancing behind, Dany makes out the crowd closing in, some fifty feet back. Only now, she isn't afraid. She doesn't see a mob. What she sees are people. Here, as at the hospice, what she sees are people still.

| | |

When they hit the bank, Dany looks around for the pair who helped them, but the woman and her son are long gone, vanished into the trees. Still, solid ground has risen up to meet her, and she feels like she's been returned to the world of solid things.

From the long grasses on either side of the tracks come the songs of crickets, dozens of tiny cellos that fall silent as they approach.

"It's noise," Aunt Norah says.

The kid is gripping Dany's hand, her aunt's, too. As they walk, Mac propels herself along the railway tracks, held aloft for an instant in time by Dany and her aunt, as if, so long as Norah is there, it will all be okay, and yes, Mac can fly.

"We can't hear the music that the crickets are really playing," her aunt goes on. "It's on a frequency we can't hear. So, what we're really hearing is the noise at the concert, the shuffling of chairs in the concert hall. The sighs, the turning of pages. Your mother told me that. She must've read it somewhere."

"It's beautiful," Dany says, though the word feels strange in her mouth. But why should it? Why shouldn't all of them, even the crickets and the ants of the world, have a little share in what is beautiful?

Another rifle shot rings out.

The world flips, background becomes foreground, and all Dany can hear is the sound of her own breathing, the blood rushing in her veins. Dany tightens her grip on the kid, looks down. Sees that her sister is calm. The kid is looking up at Dany, and waiting. And for that second, for that sliver, she sees the kid the way a stranger might.

Mac is slight for her age, but then, so is Dany. Maybe they haven't been fed enough. Maybe they've been stunted by their time in ministry care. But this isn't how a kid should *be*. The kid shouldn't be so goddamned calm about all of this. The kid shouldn't listen so well, because kids aren't supposed to listen. They're not little soldiers.

Ever since her aunt's parole got revoked, she and her sister have lived like criminals, not kids. And that's on Dany. All at once, she knows that she's been lying to herself: She's not been making sacrifices for the kid. She's been selfish. For Mac's own good, no matter what it cost her, she should have taken her somewhere safe.

She should have taken her to Antoine.

And for a moment, just a moment, as she stands there in the dark – looking down at Mac, holding her hand – something changes in her.

She can't exactly say what and she can't exactly say how – but she senses that things can't go back to the way they've been. Survival might have been her goal, but now, looking at Mac, she wants more. Because Mac deserves more. And maybe, even, so does Dany. But even here, in the quiet aftershock of the rifle's report, she hears it.

Not her heartbeat, but the ticking of a tiny clock.

| CHAPTER 0 = X + 38

At the old VW Bug, Eva has the driver's side door wide open. She is sitting sideways in her seat, long legs visible – the car manual in one hand, flashlight in the other.

"Hey," she tells Dany, "Mister Faraday is fifty-eight years overdue for a lube." She shows the owner's manual to Dany and grins. "Oh," Eva adds, "I've got more than fifty thousand followers, I mean, at last count – but the interweb, it's, like, slowly disappearing into the Borg." Eva tries to sound casual, but her excitement is plain. Yes, it's the apocalypse. Yes, the world is probably ending, but in terms of social media, Eva's hit a high point.

Dany narrows her eyes for a second. She thinks about Eva and her follower count – actually, truly thinks about her answer – before she speaks.

Eva is proud of herself.

"That's good," Dany says.

There are trees, all around them, and the slow undulations of tree limbs strikes her as strange and otherworldly, oceanic. The way the wind moves through the trees almost makes Dany feel like she's underwater. There is the song of the crickets, Mac's flying steps. And the whole of the world is filled with people, after all.

"The walk was good, too," Dany says.

Eva gives her friend the side-eye.

"We left the muffler back there," says Eva, pointing at the river. "At least, I think that was the muffler. The illustration could be clearer."

Her aunt gives the girls a look. "We need to go."

"There's a big crowd coming," Dany says. "Followers, from your page, maybe."

"I finally got a chance to check out the transmission specs," Eva says, getting into the driver's seat. "Seriously, I have some much better design ideas for these people."

Eva grins at her friend then, like her old self, and Dany, seeing that crazy smile, can't help it. In spite of the ticking clock, the one that is counting down somewhere inside of her, she grins.

| | |

Eva is ready for her learner's permit. She puts the car into neutral this time, before starting it up.

Behind them, the main body of the crowd is pouring off the bridge and a couple of them raise their arms and call out, waving. Dany waves, sadly, from the back seat. But their car is moving, and Dany, she makes herself first see and then unsee the faces of those behind them. She mentally wishes them good luck.

In the front seat, Aunt Norah has the map out again.

"The tracks hit a crossroad in half a click. We turn there," Aunt Norah says, folding up the map. "Antoine's got an artesian well," she adds. "And there are chickens and eggs and a huge vegetable garden, acres of food. Preserves in the root cellar. We don't have to leave right away. We can hole up a while until your teacher heals up."

Antoine's.

A rest at the farm will be good for her sister and good for Faraday, too.

Though whether or not it will be good for Dany, well, that remains to be seen.

When she turns, Aunt Norah is looking at her, a speculative expression on her face. Dany keeps her gaze on the T-shirt, the logo for Cornell. She flicks a glance at her aunt, but already, Norah has turned to look out the window.

She tries to find Eva in the rear-view, but the mirror is askew – and instead, Dany finds her own face looking back at her. The wind, through the shattered rear window, is teasing locks of her dark hair, lifting small strands and framing her pale, bruised face. She takes in the soiled N95 mask that covers her nose and mouth, then looks out of the window, her eyes on the dark path they are travelling.

Outside of the car, the crickets have fallen silent.

| CHAPTER 0 = X + 39

Dany is hoping that, as they drive from one power grid to the next, they'll find lights. Now and again, Dany sees brief flickerings of light – a candle in a window, the confined light of a torch, a lantern. And about five clicks from Antoine's farm, they pass the perimeter lights of the federal penitentiary, the one that Antoine once called home. But she knows that the perimeter lights here, at the prison, have to be running on generators.

Antoine's farm backs onto a national park, and to reach it, you have to pass through a small town. There, about a mile outside of the town, at its limits, they see it. Some kind of makeshift barrier. The signs that have been hoisted onto the pickup truck are handmade. Locals, obviously. Even so, Dany feels a kick of adrenaline when Eva slows the car down. In her head, she's already rehearsing for a fight. But then, Dany's always ready for a fight.

But no one comes out of the trucks. No one tries to stop their car.

Seeing the trucks blocking the road, Eva simply eases the car onto the shoulder and passes around. The silent trucks, abandoned in the dark, are as creepy as hell. Something about the trucks, how they've been simply left here, gives Dany an uneasy feeling.

Her aunt must be feeling it, too.

"Change of plans," she says. "We'll bypass town. Take the service road, up here; runs through the national park. Just an extra five minutes."

"Okilly Dokilly," Eva says.

Dany turns to look at her aunt. "Is something wrong?"

"No, honey," her aunt says. "Nothing's wrong at all. I'm just being cautious."

But Dany knows her aunt well enough to taste the lie in her words.

| | |

Her aunt is right. The way through the national park is clear, and only adds a few miles to their journey. Soon after they emerge from the parkland, the car's high beams light up an old A-frame, and on the porch, she sees a huddled figure.

Antoine has obviously heard the news from the city. Who knows, maybe he's one of Eva's new followers. Seeing him here, waiting, Dany almost feels bad for him. The old man has been sitting out on his porch, all of this time – doing what? Hoping that Dany and Mac will somehow get to him? Of course, she reminds herself, if they've made it out it is no thanks to him.

Eva pulls up and the low beams spotlight the old man. She sees her father clearly.

Antoine, standing on the porch, holds his lantern high, eyes shielded by one hand, trying to see past the headlights. All at once, leaning into his cane, he limps towards them. Mac's already unclipped her seat belt and is out of the car before it comes to a full stop. The kid flings herself at Antoine's chest. Dany follows, to keep an eye on her sister.

She gets out of the car and, when Antoine sets down the lantern and takes in her face, his gaze zeroes in on the bruises. His eyes move over Dany's bruised eyes and swollen mouth, and he opens one of his arms to her – the other wrapped tight around Mac. But Dany stays where she is, merely nodding at him with her chin. There is nothing he can say, nothing he can do. Just looking at his arms, wrapped around Mac, has made the anger well up.

Maybe she thought, for half a second, that he might be some kind of answer to their problems, but seeing him, she knows that isn't the case. Because no. It isn't that *she* hasn't forgiven Antoine for not being there. His absence was *unforgivable.*

There's a big difference.

Eva stands at Dany's side, taking her cue from her friend. She nods at Antoine. But even Dany can see it, Eva is keeping her distance.

"It's you I have to thank," Antoine says to Eva. "You got my girls out."

"It was a joint effort," Dany hears Aunt Norah say.

When she steps into the light, you can see, as clear as day, that her oversize Cornell shirt is soaked with blood.

Antoine's face changes.

Still holding Mac in one arm, Antoine raises his lantern with one hand, casting its light over Aunt Norah. Behind her, barely distinguishable in the darkness, Dany can just make out the slumped form of her history teacher. And in the lamplight, for the first time, she sees just how much blood he has lost. There is a math she might use for this, calculating volume from the area of the bloodstains on the back seat.

"Salut, Antoine," her aunt says.

"Mon Dieu," Dany hears him say. "What have you done?"

"You sure you can be out here?" Dany asks. "You don't want to set off the alarm."

Dany, of course, knows that the monitoring device he wears around his ankle isn't as unforgiving as that – he is allowed to walk to the property line – but her words do their job. They remind him of what he's done to earn that ankle bracelet.

Antoine looks at his daughter, but Dany refuses to meet his eyes.

"I need your help," her aunt says, "to stitch up a wound."

Antoine holds the lantern high and examines the torn flap of skin on Aunt Norah's forehead, the goose egg emerging beneath.

"Not me," she says. "Him."

Antoine walks to the car, and the lantern casts its soft glow into the car's interior. "What's this?" he asks quietly.

"Gunshot," Aunt Norah says.

"My history teacher, Mister Faraday," Dany says, because the man is, after all, more than a walking wound.

Dany looks at her aunt's face. It's neutral, like her own, but there's a tension in the muscles of her face, and Dany knows that her aunt is bracing herself for Antoine's reaction.

"Postscript: There's a killer virus outbreak," Eva adds. "So, just FYI, a little context for the whole prison break thing."

Dany turns to look at her father, watches, as his expression completes its journey – and the welcome in his face slowly dies.

| CHAPTER 0 = X + 40

Eva is standing in the kitchen, trying to get her mom on the phone again.

"Nothing," she says, setting the phone down. "I just wish Mom was more . . . mobile. I wish I knew she and Bianca were safe."

Dany touches her friend's shoulder. "Bianca will get her out. She'll take care of your mom. She will."

"I know," Eva says and smiles sadly. "Yeah, I know."

Between attempts, Eva tries to use her eGlasses – and though she juiced them up while they were at Faraday's, a lifetime ago, the little thing is unable to connect to the invisible ether-world that binds every last one of them together. And so, useless. Except, maybe, as glasses.

So, no more updates on her follower count.

"Let's check on Faraday," Dany says.

Eva shrugs and the two of them make their way to the doorway of the small guest bedroom where Antoine is preparing to stitch up a wound the size of a dollar coin.

Eva peeks in, nods weakly and backs out. "Yeah, no," she says. "The surgery channel was never my thing."

Dany looks at her friend. The blood has drained from Eva's face.

"I don't like needles," Eva adds. "A fish hook of a needle, driven repeatedly through human flesh? Not my jam."

| | |

Dany leans against the door frame at the edge of the room.

She is finding it hard to breath. The room is too small and smells like a wound. Still, the bloody passage of the needle doesn't bother her too much, it's the smell that does. But Dany has to be here. She has to see that Antoine does right by Faraday.

Antoine's huge form is perched on a dainty stool next to the bed.

The sharp metal hook pierces the bloody lip of the wound, pulling the pucker wide, and then the black thread is pulled taut. Over and over, stitch after stitch, as he sews the bullet up inside of her history teacher.

Dany's little sister is sitting cross-legged on the end of Mister Faraday's bed, right next to his feet. There is a look of utter fascination on her small face. She's taking all of it in. Every last bit.

"People aren't machines," Dany tells the kid, just in case.

Mac looks up at her big sister, a frown on her face.

"You can't take people apart and put them back together – not until you've gone to medical school, 'kay?"

Mac crosses her arms. Antoine grins at the kid, then goes back to his sewing. Stitch follows stitch, as if her history teacher is a sock with a hole in the toe.

Aunt Norah comes into the doorway. "Could you do that?" she asks Mac.

The girl nods, her expression grave.

For a moment, Mister Faraday looks like he is aware of his situation – because, for just that second, his face changes to a look of alarm.

"Don't worry," Dany says. "She's really smart."

"I've got a different job for Mac," her aunt says. She turns to her little niece. "Later, 'kay."

"Can he just leave the bullet in Faraday like that?" Dany asks her aunt.

"It won't hurt him," Norah says. "He can use it to tell the weather."

| | |

When Antoine sets down the needle and the thread, Mac loses interest – as if humans are not nearly so fascinating with the holes in them stitched up. The kid heads for the door and Antoine gives her a pat as she goes by.

Dany scowls. "Why do you do that?" she asks.

Antoine sighs, but doesn't look up from his patient.

"I mean, act like her dad," Dany clarifies. "Why?"

"I'm as much of a father as she'll ever know," he says with a shrug.

"Not much," Dany says and looks at his face. She wants to see her words land.

Antoine sighs again. She can see it, a flicker of hurt, but the hurt doesn't satisfy her half as much as she thought it would. Instead, she feels a momentary shame.

"Your mother," he finally says, "she took my sentencing hard. After I was gone, there was a patch, where –"

"I was there," Dany reminds him, her voice rising in anger. Then she eats it, she eats the anger and the bitterness and swallows it down. Dany shakes her head and picks at loose paint on the door frame.

"Yes. Oui, vraiment," he says. "But you must remember this too. We loved each other, and I don't know. I would like Mac to be mine. Ça va, Danielle?"

"It's Dany now," she says. "Just Dany." She shakes her head, examines the flecks of paint on her fingertip. "What, so you just decided one day. You're Mac's father now, click, you're a pacifist, click, is that it?"

"Yes, that's the sum of it," Antoine says. "Now, tell me everything there is to know about this virus."

And Dany, looking at the old man, knows that if she tells Antoine she's infected, he'll drop Dany like she is nothing. Because Antoine always saves himself. Always. Here's a man who gave up his kid so he didn't have to betray his activist friends, and then gave up his activist friends to save his own skin.

So there is no way she is telling him what's happened to her. No way. She tells him about the new variant of the virus and about the island, but she doesn't tell him that she's infected. Because if she tells him the truth she knows exactly what he'll do.

For a long time, Antoine is silent.

"So, we'll go to this island," he says. "Bien. Done."

Dany looks up at Antoine through narrowed slits. Because for the first time ever, she and the old man agree on something.

"Is he going to be okay," Dany asks, with a quick glance at her teacher.

"He's going to need strong antibiotics," Antoine says. He shakes his head. "You don't happen to have any?"

"No," Dany says quietly. "Nothing like that."

Antoine passes a glance over Dany before settling his gaze on Faraday.

Dany leans in and examines the black thread that is holding Faraday together. Her teacher's shoulder has been darned like a sock. Soon, the skin will heal, and Faraday, he'll carry with him a little bit of history. There, in his shoulder. Probably carry it the rest of his life.

"Get some sleep," Antoine tells her. "I want to keep an eye on him for the next bit. What is it he's called?"

"Faraday," Dany says quietly. "He's my history teacher."

Antoine nods and Dany, she grabs her copy of *The Wizard of Oz* and heads off to find the kid.

| | |

That night, she reads to Mac for a long time. She's read *The Wizard of Oz* to the kid twice already, but weirdly, when she picks up the book, she finds herself reading it as if for the first time, as if each line is new to her, a tiny revelation.

But she's tired, that's all. She's just wiped clean.

Finally, when she's sure the kid is good and asleep, and the house is silent, she sets down the book and heads in to check on Faraday. On the bedside table, beside him, Antoine has left a glass of water and a couple of OxyContin. Faraday will find them in the morning.

She looks at her history teacher. He isn't unconscious, but sleeping. She doesn't know how she can tell, but she can. Dany unzips her backpack and digs deep, pulling out the pill bottle that holds her mom's mood ring and broken watch. She looks at the name printed on the worn label. *Munday, Philomena.*

She opens it and puts the ring on. Waits for the warm blue glow.

There is a wrought iron chair at the end of the bed, and it's as good a place for her to wait as any. She sits down, checks the seal of her mask and, thoughts on a woman called Phil, settles in to watch her history teacher sleep.

| | |

An hour later, when her teacher calls out Dany is by his side in an instant.

She takes the glass of water in hand and holds it to his mouth. "Thirsty?" she asks. Without waiting for an answer, she tips the glass. "Drink this," she says. "You need liquids to make blood."

The water hits his mouth and Faraday chokes it down. "Thanks," he says, holding up his good hand. "But that's enough."

"Pain?" she asks, and he nods. So she gives him the OxyContin, too. She plants the pills in his open mouth, and holds the water for him.

"If you need anything," she says.

"Sleep," he says.

Dany sits back down in her chair and, seeing his gaze, lowers her own.

"It's not your fault." His voice is a hoarse whisper.

Dany leans the old wrought-iron chair back, angling it so it tips against the wall of the room and holds. Just barely. And for a long beat, she looks at the wound on Faraday's shoulder, gives it a look of deep skepticism.

| CHAPTER 0 = X + 41

Dany wakes just before dawn.

She's slept, yeah. But that sleep hasn't been empty. In her dream, Dany's head slowly filled with words – but the words were a kind of fire.

It was a dream about Zeke.

Dany barely ever dreams about Darling-Holmes anymore – at least, not dreams that she can remember. Or, maybe it is this: in her dreams, Darling-Holmes, the source of her night terrors, is made so strange, so surreal, it's hard to connect the dream up to the real place, to the real people, to the waking world.

And this dream was strange. The dream felt like it came from somewhere outside of her, like a message from another world.

In the dream, Dany was stuck on top of a pole – like one of those medieval hermits. Pillar saints, they called them. The pole was so tall that there was no getting down.

In the distance, she could hear voices – people calling out to her, but she couldn't see anyone. Still, they were voices she knew, like Jasper and Liz and Bea. But as hard as she looked, she couldn't see anything but the endless drift of the river below.

And Dany, she was stuck on her high pole – and, in the distance, there was Zeke's voice. And she turned towards the sound of his voice and he hadn't spoken to Dany then, so much as placed the burning word in her mind.

"Hello," he whispered. But in the dream, Dany knew something.

She knew about how, in some languages, the word for hello is the same as the one for goodbye.

| | |

When Dany wakes again, it's morning.

Someone has been into Faraday's room, to prop open the window with a wooden dowel. She hears a strange chirping sound, like crickets in a glass jar. It takes a minute for her to figure out what the sound is – but yes, Antoine's in April means peepers, those tiny frogs that call out when the sun warms the skin of the land.

It's a weirdly hopeful sound.

In the bed, Faraday has propped up the pillow and is sitting up.

Her history teacher, who yesterday looked to be at death's door, is sitting up, his nose buried in a book on trauma and the human brain. Her book. Jasper's book. Dany grins at him. "You're okay," she says.

He snaps the book to a close, looks at her and smiles. "Good morning," he says.

Someone, she sees, has already been in to change his bandage. The cloth is fresh and white and, but for a tiny red line on the fabric, you wouldn't even guess the extent of it.

Here, in the hush of dawn, Dany can hear all of it, the singing of the peepers, the sound of blood running through her veins, and quieter still, that weird and eerie static, the math in her own neurons – the quiet and constant stream of numbers that runs through her brain. And, for a second, she remembers the dream and remembers Zeke.

What is it the little boy said?

Something about hello. Or goodbye. But the dream is gone, and all she can hold onto is the overwhelming feeling of the dream, that Zeke is okay and it's time to step off.

But step off what?

"Take another Oxy," her aunt says, stepping into the doorway. "You're going to feel like you've been hit by a sledgehammer when Antoine's happy pills wear off."

"I'd like a clear head," Faraday says. "I missed most of yesterday and I think I have a lot of catching up to do."

"Take half a tab then," Norah says. "Think, with a bit of help, you can make it to the kitchen?"

Faraday nods, but before her aunt can get in the way, Dany is there, by his side. She runs her fingers over the seal of her mask, and steps up to help Faraday out of bed.

| CHAPTER 0 = X + 42

The rough walls of the kitchen still wear the original paint. Though it's been forever, they're just like she remembers, milky green, the paint worn and blistered with age. In the kitchen doorway, Eva's waiting for them, her hair tousled with sleep.

Seeing Faraday on his feet, Eva grins and steps aside. Dany helps their teacher into a seat at the kitchen table. And as soon as she steps in, the smell hits her, hits her hard. Dany isn't hungry. She's ravenous.

Antoine is stirring a ridiculously large pot over a pair of burners on a Coleman stove. Mac is at his side, wide-eyed and alert, a big wooden spoon in hand. Dany takes her seat at the old pinewood table.

The kitchen table is heaped with vegetable scrapings.

With a single stroke of his broad arm, Antoine sweeps the leavings into a bin for the chickens, and Mac sets down half a dozen bowls. This, this is no breakfast. This is a fully fledged dinner. Eva sits there, a grin on her face and a spoon in each hand. She looks at Dany, raises her eyebrows. Dany has caught the mood, too. She grins right back. She's going to demolish some rabbit stew.

Norah joins them a minute later. Seeing her in the full kitchen light, Dany notices the difference. The goose egg is now half its previous size, and the loose flap of skin? Neatly stitched. The prison chain, she sees, has chafed the skin around Aunt Norah's wrist, leaving it red and raw.

"Your stitches," Dany asks. "Did you do them with a mirror?"

"Oh God, no," Norah says and smiles proudly at Mac. "Mac's good with her hands. A quick study. She really just has to see a thing once to get it."

Antoine smiles down at Mac, the pride on his face clear.

"What's that thing," Eva wants to know, "about hair dryers."

But Dany shakes her head once, sharply. Luckily, Mac doesn't seem to be paying any mind.

Eva raises her shoulders. "Okay," she says. "Again, alarming."

But by then, Antoine is ladling out huge servings of the stew. The stew is thick, rich with meat. She's dipped her spoon into the bowl and gotten it halfway to her face when she remembers her mask. Glancing at Eva, she sees that her friend has just ripped her mask off. The mask dangles from Eva's neck, and she is shovelling the thick stew in.

But Dany leaves her place at the table, bowl in hand, and sits on the floor in a corner of the kitchen. Only then, sitting on a different plane, does she remove her mask. It's taken all of her will not to just tear the thing from her face and dig right in. She's lifting the spoon to her mouth when she feels it. His eyes on her. Antoine has stopped what he's doing and is watching Dany, taking in how she's sitting on the floor, a little bit apart from everyone.

Dany shrugs off his gaze and digs in.

There's a gamey taste to the stew, but that doesn't bother her one bit. She eats three full bowls. When she's finished, she stares down at her empty bowl, suddenly at a loss. She can't put it in the sink with the others. Can't take that risk. In the end, she just gives the bowl and spoon a rinse, slips them in a plastic bag and puts the bundle in her backpack.

But Antoine – with his preternatural attention – has eyes on her again.

She puts her mask back in place, reforms the seal and takes a seat at the table again. Antoine isn't eating like the rest of them.

No, her father's just sitting there, in a chair, his bad leg jutting straight out, eyes on Dany. He looks deep in thought.

But Mac is on him in an instant. She works her way between Antoine's legs, her tiny hands on his knees, eyes wide, a smile on her face.

Dany can't help it. She grins too. Not at Antoine, but at her kid sister. The kid's okay. Here, in a halfway normal environment, she's coming out of her shell again. Resilient, that's what the child workers always said about kids. It's what they said on the burn ward too, though she doubted the coroner agreed.

Kids are resilient.

Dany figured that was their excuse. That little word pretty much let you do to kids whatever you wanted.

"All right," Antoine says, beckoning to Mac with a finger. "There's time for one story before you go get dressed and brush your teeth. Allons-y. You'll like this one. There's a bear in it. A big fat grizzly like me."

Norah spears a homemade pickle and, holding it up at the end of her fork, smiles. "This, I want to hear," she says.

Eva nods, her eyes big and happy. "Me too," she chimes.

Dany doesn't say anything, but she doesn't leave either.

Antoine has plucked her little sister up into the air. Turning her in mid-air, he settles the kid on his lap. Antoine spins out his fairy tale, as Faraday and Aunt Norah sip a thin black liquid meant to approximate coffee. Antoine makes the stuff from roasted chicory roots, the pretty blue flowers that litter the edges of the property here. As Antoine unfolds the tale, Dany recognizes the shape of the story, but it's as if it was a new skin hung on much older bones.

Mac loves it. And when Antoine is done, he plucks Mac up once more and sets her down on her feet. "Be a good one and go get ready," he tells her.

But Mac doesn't move, not an inch. She holds her doll tightly in her arms, and looks up at Antoine with wide eyes.

Dany can't help it. Half of her wants to be like Mac, so at ease with Antoine, feeling all of that affection shine on her, and part of her can't let go of the past, of the places she's been because he wasn't there to prevent it.

"C'mon," Norah says. "You heard him. Brush your teeth and get dressed."

But the kid ignores her too.

"Miracle Grace Munday," Norah says to the kid.

"I'm not Miracle," Mac says clearly.

Dany stares at her sister.

These are the first words she's heard her sister speak since the ministry entered their lives, since a continental divide came down in their lives, neatly slicing them into pictures of before and after.

Her voice is strange, a little. Like she's got an accent.

Hearing her voice, so small, so sweet, it nearly breaks something open inside of her. She can't explain it. Just the feeling that there, inside of her chest, some little thing is going to burst. Still, Dany doesn't cry.

Because Dany doesn't cry.

Under the table, Eva's hand finds Dany's and she is squeezing so tight that it hurts. Eva hasn't yet pulled up her mask, and there is such a big stupid grin on Eva's face that Dany can't help it. She breaks out a stupid grin, too.

She feels it then, that little pill that has broken open inside of her? That little burst skin? It's filled with pure sunshine. Still, she doesn't want to freak the kid out. So, Dany sets the tone. She lets them know, by her example, how to handle it.

There's nothing weird, after all, about a five-year-old girl speaking. And though Dany can't help but grin, she takes a deep breath and shrugs. "Okay," Dany says, "you don't like Miracle. What should we call you?"

The girl holds up her doll, looks into its glassy eyes and considers the question.

"Mon chou," says Antoine.

"Little rabbit," offers Eva.

"My love," says Aunt Norah.

"Love," Mac says, clutching her doll. "You can call us both that."

A moment later, Mac skips from the kitchen. They hear the door to the bathroom close behind her, and a second later, the water is on.

Eva beams at her, wide eyes brimmed with tears. Grinning at Dany, Eva reaches towards her, but Dany folds her hands into her lap. "I told you, I told you," Eva says. "I told you."

Dany can't help it, she's grinning too. Norah is smiling too. Or she was smiling. But the instant that she turns to Antoine and Faraday that smile slips from its place. "How's the wound?" Norah asks.

The light goes out of Faraday's eyes. He stretches his arm and winces. "Not bad," he says.

"We're going to need antibiotics," Antoine says to the room. "Soon."

"I feel fine," Faraday says.

"Infection's a risk with any puncture wound," Norah tells her teacher. "Bullets aren't usually the worst. They're white hot – self-sterilizing – but given the old blanket we used to staunch the bleeding, well, I think Antoine's right. We should get you on something strong, soon."

Antoine shifts in his seat. "This town," he says. "It's no good. I don't know how it is elsewhere. But here, this place, it's basically a prison town," Antoine shakes his head. "The local gun club has organized. They've shut down the hospice," he says, and again, he skips a glance at Dany. "What that means can't be good."

Dany juts out her chin. "I'll go into town," she says.

Antoine's face darkens, but Eva is nodding. "You'll need a driver," she says.

"I think we all have to go," Antoine tells them.

Aunt Norah reaches across the table and grabs the man's hand. "You can't," she says. "Six months, less. And you're done. We can't take that from you."

But Antoine just shakes his head. "We all go."

Dany feels Mister Faraday's eyes flick over her way, feels him ask a silent question.

Dany shrugs and nods at Antoine's ankle.

"Show Faraday what's keeping you here," Dany tells Antoine. Her voice has a harder edge than she intends. "Show him your ankle."

Reaching down, his eyes on his daughter, Antoine pulls up the cuff of his pant leg. Now even her history teacher can see it: the monitoring device the old man has to wear.

"Wait," Eva says. "Does that work in a power outage."

Antoine gives Eva a half-smile. "I am afraid so," he tells her. "If I cut it, take it off, they will come. But maybe I have an idea or two about it, a way to get us through this." Antoine looks around at each face. "So, do we head for Dany's island?" he asks. "On la grosse barge of Eva's?"

Eva is the first to nod.

"Don't worry about me," Faraday says. "You can just give me a couple Oxy and throw me in the back like the luggage. It's pretty much how I've ridden this whole way."

Even Aunt Norah has to admit, finally, that they have nowhere else to go, and that, in any event, an isolated island can't be a bad thing. When it's done, when it's all agreed, Mac comes barrelling back in, wearing a pair of oversize rubber boots.

Eva grins at her. "When Mac puts on her big girl boots," Eva says, her eyes on Dany, "you can be pretty sure that adventure's on its way!"

Dany smiles at her friend. For a moment, she feels lucky. Really, truly lucky.

And a beat later, that hand is around Dany's heart again, squeezing it tight, and she hears it. The ticking of a clock.

| CHAPTER 0 = X + 43

Eva's in the driver's seat, and Aunt Norah and Faraday are up front, next to her, in the cab of Antoine's old truck.

Dany is sitting on one side of the cargo bed, the road vibrating into her spine. Still, it's safer – for her to ride back here in the open air. Mac, across from her, is tucked up under Antoine's arm.

Antoine prefers it back here, he says, where his bad leg has a bit of room. He's got his leg jutting out in a straight line before him. In his hands, he's holding a book of stars. Pitching his voice over the engine, he's talking to Mac, explaining how to make a sextant, using a protractor, a ruler and say, for a plumb line, that hex key hanging from a bit of string on her big sister's neck. Mac is looking at a spray of stars, pictured there. She touches a little point of light with one tiny finger.

Together like this, Mac and Antoine almost look like a real family.

All you'd have to do is X her out.

As Antoine talks about the stars in his picture, the little bear and its tail, Polaris, Dany's eyes are tracing the distant smudge of smoke blossoming into the sky, there, ahead of the truck. Dany turns to her father, then, and nods to the monitoring device on his leg. "Why haven't you taken it off?" she asks.

"Soon," he says. "I want to leave a trail to the hospice. Maybe then they'll forget me."

Dany shrugs, but she has her doubts. They've crossed a line. Already, in some distant office, an alarm is sounding and time has begun to tick down. The same way that in her, too, time is ticking down like a bomb.

She fingers the mask on her face, testing the seal.

There is a map to the stars on Antoine's lap, and her sister's finger, tracing the tiny points of light. The kid's finger stops on Polaris again, the little bear's tail, and she looks a question up at Antoine.

Antoine leans towards her ear. "When you do it, you need to hold the thing like this. You need to be comme ça," he says, demonstrating with his hands. "Let the ruler find the star, and your plumb line, hanging down – that will find the angle. It's simple."

"I don't do simple," Dany calls out.

"Ouais," Antoine says, laughing. "I see that."

Dany lets go of the side rail and inches a little closer.

"Why?" she asks, and that word, it holds everything. She glances down at Mac, still tracing stars. "Why'd you become a pacifist?"

Antoine looks at her, his expression soft, contemplative. But he doesn't answer for a long time. Finally, he shakes his head and, meeting her eyes, shrugs. "Perhaps, for a man like me, the only truly revolutionary act," he says slowly, "is to relinquish violence. Ça va, mon chou? Answer enough?"

But children aren't cabbage seeds, Dany knows that.

You can't just leave a kid in the dirt and expect her to grow herself up out of it.

Antoine reaches out, touches her arm. "Because I do. I aspire. For better. For my kids, no?"

"While you were so busy aspiring," Dany reminds him, "I got put at the work farm." She hears the sarcasm in her voice, the raw hurt beneath it, too, but there is nothing she can do about that. "You weren't there," she says, spelling it out for the old man. "Norah was."

Mac looks up at her, eyes huge, and Antoine shakes his head, eyes on the distance.

"Ouais, non, pas vraiment," he says and stares at the trees for so long she doesn't think he will answer. "How do you think Norah got released, that first time?" he finally asks.

Dany's eyebrows narrow and she studies, hard, the lines in the road behind them.

He tells her then, all of it. How he agreed to renounce his former comrades.

Dany saw the video – someone uploaded the thing to YouTube. Sometimes it feels like everyone in the world has seen what Antoine did, because the video is on the internet, but of course, nobody much cares. Except for those involved. Just the people he's betrayed. And that, she guesses, was the point of it.

"I don't get it," she says. "What does betraying your activist friends have to do with me?"

"We made a deal. I make the video, and you get a parent."

Dany chewed on that.

So, long before they granted him house arrest, the government took away his power. But what did Antoine get in return? What did Dany get? "I didn't get a parent," she reminds him. As if he needs reminding, but maybe he does.

Antoine nods at her aunt, in the cab. "You got Norah," he says.

Dany looks at her father.

In exchange for the video, Antoine explains, they released Norah – they granted her early parole. "There was no way they were going to let me go," he said. "Not then. Now? I don't know, maybe. Maybe they would, in six months."

The pieces are simple, a child's puzzle, and though there are only a few fat pieces to negotiate, still, it's hard for her to put together the picture in this new way. To reshape her understanding of the past. So, okay, Antoine made a deal. He betrayed all of his friends. He betrayed them for Dany. For Norah. All of this, around the time Darling-Holmes burned to the ground.

All of this, while Dany was unconscious in the burn ward?

"When the work farm burned down, there was chaos," she says slowly. "All those bodies. Norah said they didn't identify me right away. That I was out of it for a couple of days, but then she came and identified me."

He stares out at the trees in silence.

"But Aunt Norah came before I woke up," she says, glancing at the back of her aunt's head, up there in the cab. "So you made the deal – not knowing if I'd survived."

Antoine nods once, a nod so subtle she could have missed it.

Dany turns and, for the first time, looks her father in the eye.

She reaches out. Her hand hovers close to his face – but she doesn't touch. But yes, she could. She could reach right out and touch that pear-shaped tear in wonder.

Mac looks up from her book, a question on her little face.

"Norah made a home for you girls," Antoine says, giving Mac a reassuring pat.

"I don't understand," Dany says. "How come they put Norah back inside?"

Antoine shakes his head, a bitter expression on his face.

"Parole violation," he says. "The agreement they made her sign, it said she wouldn't attend a violent protest." Again, he shakes his head.

"It was peaceful," Dany says. "I was there. It was a memorial for murdered women on the Eastside," she says. "But they arrested her anyway and put her in the hospice."

Antoine nods.

She steals a look at her aunt, up front. She's squeezed between Eva and Faraday, but the cab of the truck might as well be another world and her aunt's face is turned away from her.

For a long time, Dany says nothing. Still, she thinks she understands.

When Dany looks at her father again, something in her has changed. Some tension, one that's always felt like an essential part of her, eases. She looks at Antoine, measures this change, and then she turns away, her eyes once more on the line of trees.

"Let me show you one more time," Antoine says to Mac.

"She gets it," Dany tells him. "Little Bear's tail is Polaris. A protractor, a ruler, a plumb line."

"And the angles?" he asks.

But Dany just points at the kid's head and looks away.

"Well, maybe you can find your way around, at that," Antoine says. A smile plays at the corner of his mouth. "Sometimes, it's just good to just look up at the stars."

And then, looking ahead, he nods to it.

In the distance, ahead, a water tower. The large structure proclaims the name of the town in red paint. Once they pass it, Dany turns back, watching the big old bulb of a thing recede into the distance.

"C'est là," Antoine tells her. "A few minutes, now, we should see your checkpoint."

Dany leans over the side rail, looking up ahead – but the truck, under Eva's hands, is swerving from side to side. She glances at Faraday in the cab up front. Like her aunt, he's green.

Eva, behind the wheel, is doing her best impression of a zig-zag.

Dany can't help it. For that one moment, she forgets all about the checkpoint and grins.

| CHAPTER 0 = X + 44

So far, Dany has seen nothing on the road. Not one sign of life.

They haven't passed another car or seen so much as a shadow behind a curtain. The only creature they've passed is a skinny dog, chained up outside an old farmhouse. The dog is too lazy or tired to raise its head and bark. Years from now, Dany worries, someone will find its bones chained in the grass.

She sits back down in the cargo hold and turns to Antoine.

"It's weird," Dany calls out. "I don't see anybody. But I feel like we're being watched."

Antoine looks at his daughter sharply and nods. "I feel it too," he says.

Ahead of them – somewhere on the far side of town – the sky is blossoming into a dark flower – all that smoke. Whole houses must be burning to produce so much smoke. On the wind, though only for a moment, there and then gone, she smells Darling-Holmes. The place is there, in the toxic fumes given off by burning clothes, in the sickening stench of burnt meat.

Dany's heart races and all of a sudden, she's tired and chilled to the bone.

But it's just like the dark, she tells herself. An illusion. A person's fear is almost always focused on the wrong thing. She doesn't need to be scared of the smoke, any more than she needs to fear the dark.

She tightens her arms around her chest. The wind is cold, that's all. It's just that the wind has picked up and it's blasting across the cargo hold. Her breathing slows, her heartbeat slows, and Dany catches sight of a billboard ahead.

From here, she can see the picture on the billboard. A little family. Behind them, a strange sun is setting. Only the sun has been painted in a vaguely ovoid shape, like it's one large burning eye. And that eye is staring at Dany with a look she knows all too well.

Your fault, the burning eye says. *Your fault.*

| | |

Trying to understand her own feelings has always been like staring at an impressionist painting, one that has been cut up into jagged bits, remade into a collage. In the back of the pickup, sitting next to her sister, is a man named Antoine. But who is he? An environmental activist? A criminal? Billy the goddamned Kid?

A liar?

A snitch?

My Dad, the eco-terrorist.

Maybe a little bit of all of them.

When Dany was really small, her aunt told her all about Antoine. How he'd lived in the squats. Sometimes, when she was really little, she and her mom lived there too. Dany's heard stories from her aunt, about the time Antoine and his friends blew up a pipeline construction site. Most of the stories are about the activism they've done. But even seeing through her aunt's eyes, Dany is always confused on a certain point. Somehow, none of the stories reveal *who* Antoine is.

She honestly can't say.

Dany looks ahead, watches as that baleful sun – the burning eye on the billboard – grows huge. Slowly, the words below that burning eye come into focus. In a heartbeat, she knows, they will be past it and the eye will wink out and disappear.

But before the billboard disappears, she sees the full picture. There, darkly outlined against the eye of the sun, there is a family: a dad, a mom and a little girl.

The billboard is a government ad for vaccines.

"Protect the ones you love," the ad proclaims, "from an invisible threat."

She sits all alone in the cargo bed, looking from Antoine to Mac, and she knows, she knows, there isn't any room for her in this picture.

| | |

The thing about Dany's brain is this.

Dany is quick to see patterns.

Dany hears patterns in the rush of water, sees mathematical figures in a sky filled with clouds. Dany senses patterns in the arrangement of skin pigmentation on a human hand and she hears words in the broken language of the virus.

She sees a pattern in the way the virus leaps, from one person to the next, always in a concentric circle, always moving outwards, and in its centre – the rock that displaces all of that water in rounding waves – a single variable, a constant, an X.

There is only one way to see her sister have a life.

Only one way to solve this equation.

With subtraction.

Dany knows that if she gets taken at the checkpoint, her family will be safe. But Dany isn't ready to be taken, and, as the checkpoint comes into sight, all at once Dany knows two things. First, Dany doesn't really want to save her sister's life. Not if it means she will lose her. Because as they pull up to the checkpoint, Dany knows that she doesn't want their truck to get stopped. She doesn't want to get taken away. That she isn't ready to let go.

Second, Dany knows she has already infected her sister. Not with the virus. Not that. But in a way, she has infected her with something worse.

Fear.

Because, over the last two months, Dany has turned her sister's world inside out. She's let her past overtake Mac's present. And this is almost worse than the virus. Darling-Holmes is the worst place Dany has ever been, and the place has gotten to Mac through her.

In her blood, there is a virus. But it isn't even the virus that has ruined everything. In a way, it isn't even Darling-Holmes.

It's Dany.

She is the vessel by which the past has overtaken the present. That's on her. Her. If fear is the disease then Dany is the vector, and through her, the horrors of the past return.

She sees her sister's smiling face, and the smile is new to Dany, and she knows, she knows, that is all on her.

| | |

As they draw up to the checkpoint trucks, Dany sees that there is no one there, no one to cull her from their little herd, and she takes a deep breath. In an instant, there's a flood of relief, and a beat later, because of the relief, there is shame.

And then Dany is sad.

Impossibly goddamned sad.

Because she knows, she'll never have the strength to do what she needs to in order to protect her sister. Their truck slows, drives onto the rough shoulder of the road – passes the two pick-up trucks – and they're on their way.

Staring out at the line of trees, Dany knows what she should do. Dany should do the math herself. Subtract the X. Save her sister. But she can't. It isn't in her; it's just not in her to do.

| CHAPTER 0 = X + 45

A few minutes later, Antoine calls out for Eva to pull over. Here, on the stretch of road that fronts the rural hospice, where the stench of burning flesh is at its worst, Eva drives onto the shoulder and, as Dany watches, Antoine lowers the back gate and eases himself down. "Here," he tells them. "I'll leave the monitor here, where the bodies are, they'll assume I'm . . ." But his sentence falls away, and he flicks a self-conscious glance at Dany's arms.

"Burned to a crisp," Dany finishes.

The old man digs into his tool box, looking for a pair of wire cutters.

The kid is looking up at her sister with big questioning eyes. "I'm okay," she tells Mac, though she's still shivering. "I'm just cold."

Dany closes her eyes and then she feels it. A sudden snuggling warmth. The kid is cozying into her, that warm little face nuzzling against her, so that the seal of Dany's mask peels away from her cheek.

Dany reacts without thinking.

She shoves the kid – hard.

The kid is so slight, so small, that Dany's shove sends her flying. The back of the kid's head hits the metal cab of the truck. Already, Dany can see it. Fat tears are welling up in those big eyes.

The kid rubs the back of her head and, through narrowed eyes, stares at her big sister, eyes full of betrayal. Dany reaches out for her, but the kid scoots away, retreating to her corner of the cargo hold.

"I'm sorry," Dany whispers. "I didn't mean to. It was an accident."

But the kid has backed up as far as she can go and, from her little corner, looks at her sister warily. Antoine is holding the wire cutters in his hand, staring at Dany. It's a long look, cold and penetrating. As if he sees right through her.

"You and I will talk," he says to Dany.

Antoine shakes his head, turns his back on the girls and limps off into the smoke.

| | |

Antoine's gone for what feels like a long time. Dany and her kid sister have time to stake out opposing corners of the cargo hold. "You want me to read?" Dany finally asks.

But it's like she's dead to the kid.

Still, Dany digs into her backpack, coming up with her copy of *The Wizard of Oz.* Dany flips through the book, finding the page with its corner folded down – the place the two had left off the night before. Dany doesn't know if it's the smell of the smoke or if somehow the virus is beginning to affect her, but her hands are shaking, badly. It's hard to hold the book. A few sentences in, the kid scooches over, reaches out for the book, but Dany shrugs away from her. "I've got it," she says gently.

Dany forces the feeling down, the impulse she's got. To push her sister away again. Instead, she trusts the seal of her mask and trains her eyes on the book. *How much risk is too much? How close can her sister get to her and still be safe?*

Dany is reading the words aloud, but she has a weird feeling – like she's fallen out of time. The passage is weirdly familiar, and she knows she's seen these sentences before. But her memory of the page is dim, a ghostly wisp. It's just a feeling. And all around them, there is swirling smoke and the smell of burnt skin and meat. All around them is Darling-Holmes.

"Did I read this part already?" she asks the kid.

Her kid sister gives her a wary look, as if she's ready to dart away. After a moment she nods. One skinny finger points at the page.

"Read some more," the finger says.

Dany's voice falls to a whisper as she reads. Yes, she's sure of it. She was reading this part out loud to her sister the night before – the part where the group gets separated, and they lose the Scarecrow. But when she tries to call up her memory of the page, the picture is distant and fuzzy. Dreamlike, strange. But yes, she remembers this much: Dorothy and the Scarecrow are rafting down a river. The night before, she read this when Mac was all but asleep. Still, though she read it – read it aloud – somehow, she just doesn't remember very well.

So she doesn't see what is coming.

"'We must certainly get to the Emerald City if we can,' the Scarecrow continued."

The night before, Mac looked a question up at her big sister, and Dany, she said, "Yeah. That's where we're going. Only it's an Emerald Island."

Dany has forgotten how hard they can be, the stories grown-ups weave for children. Dorothy and the Lion and the Tin Woodman, they simply accept the Scarecrow's loss and go on. It's seriously screwed up.

"We must certainly get to the Emerald City if we can," Dany reads, and Mac closes her eyes to better picture it. Dany pictures Scarecrow, too, pushing "so hard on his long pole that it stuck fast in the mud at the bottom of the river."

"Then," Dany reads, "before he could pull it out again – or let go – the raft was swept away, and the poor Scarecrow left clinging to the pole in the middle of the river."

That's what Dany dreamed the night before.

In her dream, she was left clinging to a pole.

And for a moment, Dany has to close the book. She looks out to the smoke-filled ruins of the village hospice. Because she wants the book to turn out different for the Scarecrow. She wants to *make* the book come out different. She wants there to be some other answer than minus X.

| | |

When Antoine gets into the back of the pickup, Mac abandons Dany and scrambles to his side. Norah pushes open the window between the cab and the cargo bed, looking a question Antoine's way.

"It's done," Antoine tells her with a shrug. "There were a lot of bodies. More than a hundred. Hopefully, when they find my monitor here, that's that. Take them weeks to work through the dead. If they do."

So, yes, she hears Antoine telling Eva she should go – and she feels the shudder of the truck as they drive on, past the burning remains of the rural hospice, and glancing up, her eyes take in the charred remains of the infected they've burned, ashen, stiff in death, like the blackened bodies of Pompeii, and she wraps her arms around herself and turns inwards, shutting her eyes against something even worse.

One single burning image.

A body, burned black, trying to drag itself away from the burning human pyre.

All around them now, closing in on all of her family, those that she loves most in this world, there is the smell of smoke and burning flesh. The past made present.

Darling-Holmes.

Dany closes her eyes and tries to remember a different past.

It's the night before and there is the sound of Dany's voice, and she's reading to her little sister, Mac. She'll have this, at least. For as long as she lives.

Along with all of the bad, there are little bits of good, as well. She'll always have the feeling of it, as long as there is a Dany to remember: the nights, reading to Mac, the spray of stars overhead, the night song of crickets, the memory of Phil's throaty laughter and this last gift, given only today – the sound of her little sister's voice.

| | |

As she looks out of the truck at a meadow, greening with spring, she sees a girl, about her own age. As the truck rolls up to where she stands, the girl, by the side of the road, drops the small bundle she's carrying in her arms and runs. The thing, whatever it is, is wrapped in a soft fleece blanket. But the little bundle is still. So terribly still.

The girl tears across the field, barefoot. Dany sees the girl's pinkish soles, flashing as she runs.

"It's just a doll," Antoine tells Mac.

But when Dany meets his gaze, she sees the dark cast of his eyes. He gives a subtle shake of his head, silencing her question. As their truck bumps over the road, she comes back to that image again and again, pictures that tiny bundle and both does and doesn't want to know.

When the Scarecrow is lost in the river, what is it Baum says? "And they were very sorry to leave him."

Dany's eyes blur and though these aren't tears, because Dany doesn't cry, she brushes roughly at her eyes with her sleeve.

| CHAPTER 0 = X + 46

The marina is a ruin.

The dock is littered with suitcases and bags. More than one case has been broken open, spilling out a trail of clothes and cans of food and kitchen utensils and books and even some fine, if now dirty, lingerie.

They collect up cans as they walk. Here and there, she sees evidence of violence. A smear of blood. A broken plank of wood. Bloody footsteps. Traces of violence. Each picture is a story. An equation. And every equation has its X.

Only four boats, the least seaworthy, remain. Eva's father's yacht is not among them. "Oh dear," says Eva. "This might be a problem."

"So which one do we steal?" Dany asks.

Eva walks along the dock, looking over their options, and Dany follows.

"There, let's take that one," Eva says finally and nods at the boat before her.

Dany's eyes come to rest on a rusted old tug. The word *Dogpatch* has been painted in homespun letters on its side. The thing floats, that much can be said. Dany stares at the rusty blue vessel Eva has pinned their hopes on. It's salty and barnacled in the soft light of day.

Dany looks from her friend to the boat. "It'll do," she says.

"The *Dogpatch*," Eva says and smiles.

Antoine, she sees, is staring at the pair of them, watching them – and there's a weird look on his face. The kind of cold and calculating look people get when they're doing math. Only Antoine doesn't do math with numbers. He does math with people's lives.

"C'mon," Eva says. "Let's find the manual!"

"I'll catch up in a bit," Dany tells her. "I got to take care of something first."

Her eyes slide over to Faraday. Aunt Norah has left her teacher roughly balanced on a milk crate. He's shaking it rough today. His eyes are half closed and his posture's got a lean to it. Every few minutes, he startles, before setting himself straight.

Dany raises her hand to him, in a wave. But he doesn't seem to see her.

| | |

Dany rifles through every last abandoned suitcase, every sodden cardboard box. Eventually, she finds what she needs – or close enough. By the time she's done, she's found not just amoxicillin, but half a bottle of erythromycin, too. The bottle was in a bag with a breast pump, and Dany doesn't want to think about who the antibiotics belonged to, or what it means, that they got left behind.

She's been aware of Antoine for a while now.

He's got his pipe out, but he's all out of tobacco. Eyes on Dany, he absently pats at his pipe bowl. It's an old and familiar gesture, one as much a part of him as his arm itself. Finally, shaking his head, he puts the empty pipe back in his pocket and approaches.

"You know what you have to do?" he asks.

Dany shrugs, but doesn't answer. There's an obvious answer to this question – and it involves giving the antibiotics to Faraday and stowing her backpack on the *Dogpatch* – but she's pretty sure that's not what he means. So she waits him out.

"How long?" he asks.

Dany's heart skips a beat, races. He knows, she thinks. He knows. "I'm careful," she says quietly. It's a generic phrase – and it could mean anything.

"Yeah? How long before something goes wrong with that?"

"I'm, I'm –"

"Careful, yes. I heard you," Antoine says.

"I'm not coming," she says, but the words don't come out as a statement, they come out as a question.

Antoine shakes his head. "No," he says, "you're not."

Dany takes in Antoine's expression and, for the first time, understands him. Gets him. She knows who and what he is. Her father has a hardness in him, a willingness to do hard things, so long as he thinks they're right. He's willing to make sacrifices, too. And yet again, Dany is the sacrifice that Antoine is willing to make.

"I don't hate you," she says, and Antoine's eyes shift to hers. There's a softness in his eyes, for a moment. A hope. But then Dany finishes her thought. "I don't *anything* you," she says. "I don't love you or hate you or anything. I look at you and . . . nothing."

Antoine doesn't flinch, he doesn't get angry. But she sees something close off in his eyes, like a door being shut. And she's on the outside again. Alone.

Dany looks out across the dock, sees her aunt talking to Eva. But when her aunt sees Dany, she looks guilty. Her aunt meets Dany's gaze for a moment, and then lowers that gaze to the dock.

All at once Dany knows. Norah and Antoine have already talked this out. Worked it all out. Without her. Antoine and Aunt Norah have already made the decision and this is not a negotiation – it's her final notice.

"I'll be fine," Dany says and looks up to meet Antoine's eyes. But what she sees is his back. Because he's already walking away from her.

On the deck of the *Dogpatch*, Eva, oblivious, grins and waves her over.

| | |

After Dany tells her friend, she watches the play of emotion on Eva's face. First, there is denial, then understanding, and finally, Eva just looks sad. Impossibly, inconsolably sad.

"They can't do this to you," Eva is saying. "They can't."

Dany shrugs. "They are."

"I'll stay with you," Eva says.

Dany rolls her eyes. "What, you want to donate your body to medical science?"

"Okay," she says, straightening her shoulders. "I will if you will."

"You only do that after you're dead," Dany reminds her.

"No," Eva says. "Let's not do that."

"I don't plan on it."

"It's funny," Eva says. "It's odd, but suddenly, I'm not feeling very much like me. Isn't that weird? I always feel *so* much like me. But right now, I don't think I'm me. I'm not me at all. Are you you?"

"Yeah, I'm me," Dany tells her, and she means it. "I'm like Dany version 2.0. I mean, Antoine's right, I guess. I still hate him though."

Dany unfolds the map in her hand, the one that Mac drew. The lines her little sister sketched out with pencil crayons. *The Emerald Island.* Once more, she finds herself staring at the small sea monster. Carefully, she tears the monster from the map. Because if Dany stays behind, then the monster stays with her.

She presses the map into Eva's jeans pocket. "Here," she tells her. "You'll need this."

Eva nods and asks, "Is it safe to hug you?"

Dany traces the seal of her mask. "No," she says and shrugs. "I don't think it is."

"Just, like, I wish," Eva says.

"Me too," Dany says and looks at her hands. Eva looks at the ring on Dany's finger, and touches the stone, gently, and there is another picture in her head, one it won't hurt too much to remember.

"I wanted to tell you something," Eva says. But her voice breaks on the last word.

"I wanted to tell you something, too," Dany says quietly.

"And then this whole end of the world thing sort of happened," Eva goes on.

"Which sucks," Dany says.

"Definitely."

"So, like, do we talk about that stuff later?"

"When the world's not ending," Eva says, "and you're not completely screwed. You call Isobel, she cures you, and then you come to the island and we talk. We finally talk."

Dany blinks at Eva. Because Eva doesn't get it. She really doesn't. But some lies are easier. "Yeah. We'll finally talk when I'm cured," Dany says. And the lie might be easier, but it feels a lot worse. She looks down at her feet.

"You want me to come," Eva says and this time, it isn't a question.

Dany looks at Eva's beautiful face – and that act of subtraction, that quiet "no" – it is so much harder than anything she's ever done before.

Dany looks at the mood ring on her finger. Pulls it off.

"This is the ring my mom used to let me wear," she tells her. "Phil told me that when you wore the ring, you could be brave. It always made me feel better. If I give it to you, can you tell Mac? About Phil, about her ring, so Mac can be brave too. She knows about the ring already, I'm sure I told her, but kids . . ."

Dany places the ring on Eva's palm.

"I won't let her forget," Eva promises.

"She can wear it on a necklace, til her hands get bigger," Dany says, folding the ring into Eva's hand. "Or not. I mean, she can forget about it too, if she needs to."

| | |

Dany says goodbye to her teacher, too. Sort of.

Before Faraday gets on the tug, she asks him to lift the edge of the bandage. Already, the wound has begun to heal. The small black hole has been stitched up into a frown. It's a bit red, and Dany's glad she found the medicine.

"I think you got lucky," she says to Faraday's shoulder. "See ya," she adds.

She tucks the two bottles of antibiotics into his jacket pocket. And he looks at her, and again, it's as if Dany is a knot that he doesn't know how to untie.

| CHAPTER 0 = X + 47

Somehow, she can't say goodbye to Mac. She just can't.

When the last chain has been unmoored from the salty old tug, Dany is standing on the dock, Antoine beside her. He's put his hand on her shoulder – but it doesn't feel like he's reassuring her. No, it's more like he doesn't trust her not to jump on board at the last second, and so he's standing here, holding her down. The engine is rumbling, and the little tug is ready to go. In a moment, she figures, Antoine will jump onto the deck and then she'll be truly and entirely alone.

Norah stands on the tug's deck, by the door to the small cabin, looking down at her and her dad. Aunt Norah's eyes are wet. Big fat tears roll down her cheeks.

"It's not too late," her aunt calls out. "Come with us."

Hope flares in Dany's chest – and she looks up at her aunt. But then she sees. Her aunt is not looking at her. She's looking at Antoine. And a moment later, the little tug chugs forward into the sea.

Dany turns, looks at the old man, not understanding. "What are you doing?" she asks him.

But Antoine doesn't answer. He just rests his arm on Dany's shoulder.

Her eyes find the deck of the tug, where Norah and Mac stand. As Dany watches, Norah leans down, whispers into the kid's ear.

And then she sees it. There, on Mac's little nose, the kid's wearing the nose plug that Dany gave her. The gift from an imaginary mermaid. It's like the kid thinks it's better than a life jacket. The kid reaches up, touches the plug, glances at the sea and then looks at Dany. Then she holds up the palm of her hand – and her eyes meet her sister's.

Dany's lip trembles.

She mirrors her little sister back. Reaching up, she touches her own nose. Then she, too, holds up her hand. If somebody drew this moment on a piece of paper, Dany thinks, and then folded the page in half, her and Mac's hands would touch.

Half an hour later, Dany is still on the dock, watching the people she loves most grow small as a speck in the sea. She keeps her eyes on the smallest of the dots until, at last, she disappears from sight.

| CHAPTER 0 = X + 48

Dany's mind is an old bookstore, crammed floor to ceiling with old almanacs and books. All of everything is in there, she's sure of it. But try finding a particular book – try finding a passage – Jesus, it might take years.

Dany sorts through the mess, combing through the memories closest to the surface. She calls up a picture of her aunt and Eva and her sister. Then she adds Faraday at the edge of the group, a human afterthought. She tries to picture them landing on the shore. But it's impossible. Already, the image she once held of the faces of those she loves has begun to fade.

| | |

When Antoine is done with the door to the marina clubhouse, it's hanging from one hinge.

"Think we can get in now?" she asks dryly.

Antoine nods. "Oui, bien sûr," he says and chuckles.

In the front lobby, Dany finds an ancient pay phone. She and Antoine both search their pockets, but neither has a quarter. She finds herself laughing – there's an edge of hysteria to the sound. The two of them have gotten this far, done all this, but neither of them thought to borrow a stupid quarter.

Antoine solves the dilemma. Taking hold of a fire extinguisher he smashes a vending machine. Three brutal blows and the glass shatters. A few hits more and an explosion of glass sparkles up from the carpet. While Antoine fills his pockets with loose change, Dany scoops up junk food, stuffing her backpack with Doritos and Cheetos and corn chips.

Every apocalypse has its silver lining, as Liz would say.

"You ready?" he asks, and holds out a single quarter.

"No," she says. "No." But her hand reaches out and she takes the coin.

| | |

Dany makes the call to the Ministry of Disease Control. As she fills them in, her eyes are on a little display case, its hundreds of glossy brochures. One of them, she's surprised to see, is for D'Arcy Island.

When Dany is done for, when the phone is hung on its cradle, she picks up the glossy little pamphlet and looks at the image of the shoreline.

"Do you think they got there okay?" Dany asks.

"I imagine, by now, they've got a fire going," Antoine says.

Dany looks down at the brochure. Among the images of D'Arcy Island is a picture of a plaque. The fourteen names on the old brass marker are like sounds from a song, one that hasn't been heard in a very long time. Maybe her kid sister will find the plaque, there, at the site of the old colony. Fourteen names are listed. There are other names, too, she knows, but they're lost to time.

The thought of that, of winding down to dust and of forgetting and being forgotten, it's not so bad. It's weirdly comforting.

Dany stares at the picture of the shoreline. She wants to imagine Eva there, taking little Mac by the hand, and leading her to the fire. And she can almost do it. First, she pictures a trace of smoke, the beginnings of a cook fire, a place for a little kid to warm her hands. But when it comes down to it, she can't put people in the picture. It's like, in her memory, the people she loves have all turned their backs on her.

But then she's tired, impossibly tired.

And maybe she should simply go back to the dock. She could lie down on the dock, the sun hot on her face, the boards warming her back. And looking up, she could empty her mind like the sky.

| | |

As they wait for the ministry, Dany and Antoine sit on the dock, watching the sun lower itself into the ocean, and the last of the day's sun gives itself over to night. And then she sees it, emerging in the waves by the shore, a strange blue-green aura. Otherworldly. A glowing curtain of fluorescence filtering up from the depths in shimmering waves. The luminescent sea is ethereal, unreal, and steals her breath away.

"And they were very sorry to leave her," Dany says to the waves.

Antoine looks up, takes in his daughter. Asks the question with a nod of his chin.

But Dany just shakes her head, because there's no explaining. And, for a long time, the two are quiet. Antoine, in his own thoughts, and Dany, like the Scarecrow.

But now, looking at the glow of the sea, her mind makes a subtle connection. From *The Wizard of Oz* to the *Epic of Gilgamesh.*

Like the Scarecrow, Gilgamesh tried to pole himself across.

Grieving, he made his pole into a mast, his rotting clothes into a sail, and he drifted alone. The death of the man he loved, so much like a kid brother, left its mark on Gilgamesh, he was a man *divided.*

Is this what the virus is doing to her mind, Dany wonders, a kind of division? Her mom was divided, and their family was divided, and in a way, she figures, all of that is of a piece, all of everything is of a piece, and she sees it now.

Life's basic truth. Life *is* the patterns we make of the noise.

"Do you think we'll ever see them again?" Dany asks. Her voice is so very small.

Antoine looks at his daughter. And she sees it. She sees that he is here, sees what he has given up to be here. Sees that maybe he even loves her a little bit.

"Without question," Antoine says. "We will all meet again."

And in his words, she sees something else. That maybe he even loves her enough to lie to her. Still, his words are almost believable, and Dany wants to believe.

"Are you ready for this?" he asks.

"No," Dany says, but she nods.

As they wait for the ministry, Dany makes a strange geometry out of Antoine's coins – stacks and stacks of shiny silver quarters and dimes. Dany is just finishing up when they hear the truck. The engine cuts out, doors open and slam shut, and voices cut the night air.

Her hand flies to Antoine's, and she shakes her head, no.

Because she's not ready, not ready at all.

She can hear voices calling out for her – but they've come too soon. All at once, she knows that she isn't done. Her grip on Antoine's hand is so tight she's sure her nails are digging into his skin.

"Tout va bien, c'est bon," Antoine says quietly, reassuring her under his breath.

She leans forward, her eyes fixed on the first sliver of the moon as it slowly rises over the horizon, and her mind reaches out across an ocean of distance.

Is Mac looking out on the ocean like this?

When Mac looks from the night sky to the ocean, does she, too, see the way that the stars themselves have taken root in the water?

From her side of the ocean, does Mac see the same sea? But of course she doesn't. Her sea will be both the same and impossibly different.

"Stay down," Antoine tells her. "Stay quiet. Let me get a closer look at these soldiers."

And silent as a cat, Antoine makes his way towards the truck.

| CHAPTER 0 = X + 49

Beams of flashlights criss-cross in the distance, a tangled spider's web of light.

Heart racing, Dany counts primes, *eighty-three, eighty-nine, one hundred and one,* but something is off, something is wrong. Her mind tries to skip along that well-worn path, but the numbers aren't lighting up for her the way they once did.

Crouching, in her little patch of darkness, Dany tells herself that it won't be so bad. There will be pain – change always means pain – but, after scraping out a few of her cells, they'll probably even let her go.

They'll have bits of her in a lab somewhere.

They'll have her blood, her cells, her tissue, her variant of the virus. They won't need *her*. But she's breathing too fast. And Dany knows it; she's on the edge of something bad.

She tries the Fibonacci sequence. Because it's easier. A matter of simple sums. *Zero, one, one,* she begins, her eyes on the beams of light. *Thirteen, twenty-one, thirty-four.*

Dany stops counting and frowns.

Because no, something isn't right. She can hear men yelling, and though it's hard to pick out, she thinks she hears Antoine call out a warning – "*Run,*" he screams – and then the first of the flashlights catch her and a beat later, she is blind – blinking up at a dozen beams of bright white light.

"*Eighty-nine,*" she whispers, shutting her eyes. "*One hundred and forty-four.*"

| CHAPTER 0 = X + 50

She hears the pounding of boots on the wooden dock, and before she can explain – before she can tell them that *she* is the one who called – someone slips an evac hood over her head, but backwards, and she is blind.

Dany screams, kicks, scratches – but it's too late.

She feels the prick of a needle, and time is a suitcase that opens in her mind. Time is a suitcase brimming with soft silk scarves and she is standing alone in a room filled with light, and holding one scarf and then another up in her hand as the wind catches the soft fabric, blowing softly, a world of light and water.

| CHAPTER 0 = X + 51

Time is a cottony and fibrous thing.

An itch at the edge of her mind, slipping.

Sometimes, she hears voices, but time pours cool water and the voices blur like watercolour paints.

And even pain, she realizes, can be soft at the edges.

A forgetting, half-forgotten thing.

| CHAPTER 0 = X + 52

She opens her eyes, opens them wide, and finds herself alone inside of a concrete cell. One side of the room is a mirror, and there's a girl inside the looking glass.

She calls out to the girl, but her voice is a whisper and in her mouth there is the taste of stale blood. She knows, somehow, that they've taken some little unnameable piece of her. Dany's fingers trace her neck, feeling stitches, in the place where a lymph node should be.

Dany takes a deep breath and stands on uncertain legs, but when she tries to cross over to the girl who lives in the glass, it's like her spine has fossilized. Like time has gotten into her, somehow, and rusted all of her joints.

| CHAPTER 0 = X + 53

Dany knows that she is deep underground, knows that her cell is a large version of the kind of BSL-4 laboratory box that her Wistar rats once lived in.

In here, Dany has nothing but time. She doesn't even have herself anymore. Because the moment that stolen quarter was dropped into the slot, Dany wasn't Dany.

She was a collection of cells.

Something to be collected, taken, harvested. To be drawn up in a needle bit by bit.

Only, it's not just a few of her cells. No, they want Dany whole, like she's some kind of hairless macaque. An oversize Wistar rat.

Because they don't want a bit of finite tissue.

They want the source.

| CHAPTER 0 = X + 54

Sometimes, she can almost see it. The gas leaking in through the vents.

And then time passes – an unknown measure – and when she opens her eyes once more, her eyelids are made of lead.

Her head is a dull and drugged ache.

When she wakes, she knows that they've done something to her, taken something from her and, in place of whatever it is they've stolen, they've left another little gap – not just a few cc's of blood – but time. They have put a needle in her vein and drawn out a little more of her time.

Gone, vanished, never to be seen again.

| CHAPTER 0 = X + 55

Sometimes, time moves forward in a predictable line, from *a* to *b* to *c.* But every now and again, a little bit of it disappears into a bloody gap, never to be seen again.

Time and again, they knock her out cold. And when she wakes up, drugged and disoriented, some small piece of her is gone.

Sometimes, the pieces they take are nothing. How can she miss an ounce of blood? A few strands of hair plucked out by the roots? A tiny patch of skin carefully sliced from the inside of her cheek? But yes, there are gaps in her timeline – and most of these gaps can be tied to a hole in her.

Sometimes, when she opens her eyes, the changes they've made are obvious. But at other times, she doesn't know what it is they've done.

Making a tent of her bedsheet, she looks over every inch of her body. She wants to know what they've taken from her. But sometimes, there aren't obvious signs. Sometimes, they have to have done something to the *inside* of her.

The kind of thing that doesn't leave marks.

But there are limits to how close they are willing to get.

They refuse to breath the same air.

Dany isn't stupid. She knows what that means. Fear. Their fear is something she holds onto. A consolation prize.

CHAPTER 0 = X + 56

When Dany next wakes, a cold white sun has dawned in her world. The bulb shines so bright that her eyes water and, at first, she doesn't even see the typewriter.

The thing is ancient. A sky-blue Underwood, legs bolted to the metal table. The sort of thing that belongs in a museum. Next to it, a tidy stack of forms, waiting to be filled out. Dany glances at the mirror-wall, but the girl who looks back at her is just as bewildered.

So, they don't trust her with a computer.

Suspect she'll open a vein if given a pen.

She knows it isn't pain her captors object to, but escape. By any means. Over the last week, they've left dozens of puncture marks, long blood-bruised lines on the back of each hand. And now, they've done something to the small of her back, to a vertebra. They've put a toothache in her spine, and when she turns her back to the mirror, there is a bloodstain the size of one thin dime on the bandage.

And in exchange, they're giving her a typewriter?

Overhead, the speakers play instrumental versions of soft rock. It's almost enough to make her wish for the good old days of straight-up torture.

Almost.

Dany is shuffling to the typewriter when she hears the screams.

| CHAPTER 0 = X + 57

There are moments in a person's life that are like a dividing line, a line that neatly separates all of everything into pictures of before and after.

There is the night that her mother puts her and her sister into the window well.

There is Darling-Holmes itself, a great black dividing line that wipes out close to a year of her life.

And then there are the kind of lines that take a while to settle in, the slow kind, that form in your life over minutes and hours and days . . .

| CHAPTER ⊙ = X + 58

When the alarm comes screaming, Dany's body tightens up like a fist. She knows, right away she knows, whatever's triggered the alarm, whatever's gone wrong – it's got to be a lot bigger than her.

Dany looks at the mirror.

When the emergency lights flash, the mirror turns to glass, and for a second she can see the other side. A theatre. Two rows of seats. She can see her captors, too. Not two men, but four. They're clustered at the back of the theatre, fear written all over them. While she watches, they pull on heavy respirator masks. A black filter covers each mouth – like the baleen plates of a foraging whale.

In the flashing lights, her world becomes a stop-motion film.

A long moment passes before Dany understands – and by the time she does the last of her captors has stepped out of the small theatre and is gone.

Dany bangs on the glass, but there is no one left to hear.

| CHAPTER 0 = X + 59

In the flashing lights, the mirror dissolves into glass and blinks back again, so that Dany is one and then zero, here and then gone. Only now does it occur to her that there might be something worse than being locked up in a tiny cell. Something a lot worse.

There is what happens when all of that stops.

Her captors, in leaving her here, might as well have sealed her up in a concrete box and dropped it at the bottom of the ocean. Because Danielle-Jean Munday is going to die in this box, alone.

| CHAPTER 0 = X + 60

Over the next few days, Dany comes to know every inch of the two adjoining rooms. In the sleeping area, a metal slab for a bed, covered by a thin foam mattress. A small stainless steel sink – the size of two cupped hands. A metal toilet. So it probably won't be thirst that kills her.

Dany ticks off the other obvious possibilities. Hunger. The virus.

But then she hears the walls.

The walls in her box should be as silent as gravestones. But leaning her head against one, she feels a quiet thrum. A generator. And if the generator's fuel runs out – *when* the fuel runs out – the vents will shut down. Then the room she's in? It will become a vault.

In science class, they learned about the sealed jars used to kill butterflies. That way, there's no damage to the delicate wings. But when the darkness cocoons her – here, in this room – Dany will be the butterfly.

Still, for now, the generators have fuel, and fuel means time.

Time during which her body will turn on itself. Time during which her appetite will turn inwards. Dany doesn't have much fat to spare, so her body will turn to muscle for fuel. *The heart is a muscle*. For a moment, a sliver of a second, Dany pictures Mac.

She sees her sister's tiny hands and her big eyes. Anguish hits her so hard that she has to pinch a finger's worth of flesh, has to twist the flesh, has to make her nails bite into the skin.

Finally it comes. Hours later, days later, she can't be sure. But it comes.

A silence so small, so slight, she's all but chalked it up to her imagination. A tiny gap in the nearly inaudible thrum, a small blip in the pulse of the engine that runs through the place. A hesitation in the machine.

A hiccup.

When that tiny hiccup comes again time flashes into existence – and she realizes that each life has a length. That days can be counted. Heartbeats, numbered.

| CHAPTER ⊙ = X + 61

Dany has never been big on writing before. But the letter is her final say. She addresses her words to her kid sister, Mac. But the letter is for all of them really. For those who tried to save her, for those she tried to save. The words are for a little girl who can't talk, and a little boy who can't breathe. The words are for Aunt Norah and Mister Faraday and Jasper and Bea and Liz. The words are for Eva, and her mom and dad.

The last earthly words of Danielle-Jean Munday.

I probably won't be around by the time you get this, she types. *If you get this. They don't exactly have postal service where they've got me. I guess if you're reading this, you'll be a lot older than five.*

Old enough, I hope, to understand.

So, yeah, I made mistakes. I screwed up. I might have even screwed up the world.

Jasper told me about the virus. That it's old. Older than most species. For hundreds of thousands of years, fragments of the virus lay dormant in DNA. Who knows? Maybe two hundred and fifty million years ago, a caddis fly sneezed on a prehistoric chicken – and from that moment on, I was completely and totally screwed.

But then, the truth is, we were always screwed.

Before the window well, before the virus made the leap, before Jasper's brain was eaten up with fire – you and me were already in trouble. So, if this is the end of the world, and I'm pretty sure it is, then for us, the end of the world began earlier than it did for other people, with our own private apocalypse . . .

| CHAPTER 0 = X + 62

In the letter, she tells Mac all of it.

How, throughout her childhood, there was a thin impermeable film between Dany and the rest of the world. How, before Mac, Dany lived life in a tiny bubble, one that only had room for her and Mom, but kept her a little bit apart from everyone and everything.

How all of that began to change with Mac.

When her baby sister was put into her arms – it was like a loose tumbler finally fell into place. Mac opened her tiny, silver-bright eyes, looked up at Dany, and in that moment, *everything* changed. Dany's love for Mac made it necessary to love Norah. Made it possible to love Eva. And weirdly, it made room for Faraday and Antoine, too.

Dany tells Mac everything. She even tells her about Darling-Holmes, about how that place slowly replaced her – the living, breathing girl – with a swath of terry cloth pegged to a wire frame.

And then the lights flicker and Dany looks up.

She suddenly knows that she's left it too late, waited too long. She should have said goodbye to Mac a long time ago. She should have said it at the dock. Before that, even.

But goodbye is very hard to say.

Still, she does it. She makes herself do it.

The fuel is running low, she writes. *So I guess this is it.*

The end. Sayonara. Do svidaniya. Shalom.

The lights are sputtering and the generator fuel is down to fumes . . . Soon, I'll be typing in the dark. In my own personal butterfly jar. But look, I've got no regrets. If I have to die in a stupid shoebox – it's not so bad if I'm doing it for you.

Love your sister, Dany

| CHAPTER 0 = X + 63

When the letter is done, Dany holds up the typewritten pages. But looking at the letter, she can't help but do the math. All of the words she's struggled over, in the end, they add up to just one word, really. And in a game of Scrabble, *goodbye* will only net you so much.

Fourteen stinking points. That's it.

Then, all at once, Dany looks past the letter and sees it for the first time. Really sees it.

The typewriter.

She sees the whole of it, sky blue and solid, and then she sees the whole of it broken down into parts, the parts as tools.

Dany goes at the thing.

Using the weight of her body, she breaks the first lever off by sheer will – holds up the key – it's marked with the letter *g*. And then she gets to work on the next one.

So what if the dark comes, what of it?

The dark never hurt anybody.

| CHAPTER ⊙ = X + 64

With the lights out, Dany does what she has to do to survive.

By feel, Dany strips the typewriter down to its last lever, setting each metal piece on the table in front of her. It takes time, to work the tip of the lever under the edge of the emergency panel. But eventually, the cover clatters to the floor at her feet.

Inside the hole, she finds an illegible jumble of parts.

Her fingers trace wires and metal parts, finds something that almost feels like the fail-secure of an electric strike.

Her eyes shift back and forth in darkness, trying to picture what her fingers touch. But all she can call up are fractured bits of mental schematics, ones she tried to memorize, back when she was planning to rescue her aunt. But the pictures are broken, and in the end, she just takes the electric strike to pieces with her typewriter key, turning first one and then a second screw.

And with that, somehow, the doors to her cell echo, click open and spring wide.

Still, even hearing that, it takes her a moment to understand that she's done it. That she's free.

| CHAPTER 0 = X + 65

For a long time, Dany wanders the lower hallways of what must be the Ministry of Disease Control.

Her right hand trails the wall, and her fingers seek doorways. She tries room after room, looking for the set of stairs she knows has to exist. Finally, she stumbles on a cell phone and uses it as a flashlight. With her eyes, the phone's dim light is more than enough for her to see clearly. And soon, she finds her way out.

CHAPTER 0 = X + 66

Dany isn't stupid.

Day after day, she's sat in a small concrete cell facing a mirror. So she's known, all along, about her eyes. After all, this last week, locked up in a box, she's had nowhere else to look.

Squinting at her own reflection, for long and empty hours, she's wondered what those kids feel, the ones they send out into the streets as living bombs. It's always a girl she pictures, a girl sent into a roadside market, an explosive vest wrapped around her little chest.

She imagines how it must feel to walk, heart fluttering in your ribs like a butterfly trapped in a drinking glass. What it's like to have no control over it, not when the button is pushed, not when the world flies to pieces, taking you and those you love with it.

Over the last week, her pupils have become huge black pools. And the little of the iris that remains has changed colour. A brilliant green.

She's read case studies.

She's knows how organs can become viral reservoirs.

She can guess what's happened to her. Figures that the only reason she's still alive is because – whether it's all the antivirals they pumped into her veins or that she was already infected with the old virus – somehow, the new strain has been confined to the orbs of her eyes.

What's more interesting though, is how the virus has changed her eyes. How it has lengthened her vision, while turning everything close to her into a soft, forgiving blur.

Maybe bright lights hurt her now, but the dark has changed too. Because the dark, like her past, is no longer a thing to fear, because it is no longer absolute.

| CHAPTER 0 = X + 67

Dany finds a decent pair of sunglasses in the pocket of one of the bodies in the lobby. But even with them on, the sun is sharp, painfully so. So, yes, it hurts a little, to step out into the sun, to feel it on her face.

But over the last days, Dany has become accustomed to pain.

The streets of the city around her have been transformed into the hospice grounds.

The air is thick with the muttering of those who have forgotten the old world. She sees them, dotting the car-strewn roads and grassy places, everywhere. Here and there, sprawled on the ground, are the ones who didn't survive the change. Dany surveys all of it, but most of all, she feels the sun on her face and the sun, which she never thought she'd see again, is good.

It's brighter than she remembers, this sun, and it sets things in greater relief.

Dany looks down at her socks. One of the first things they did – after blinding her with an evac hood and shooting her full of barbiturates – was take her boots.

Still, she hasn't missed her shit-kickers, not half so much as sunshine.

The sun is warm on her face, so warm and alive.

She looks up at the sky and sees the sun, a full and brilliant yellow. So bright, that even shaded by her glasses, the sun is galvanic, current-filled, dazzling. She looks at the luminous green of leaves on a tree – sees the electric blue sky – so bright and deep she feels like she is swimming in it.

All around her, the whole world trembles with light.

CHAPTER 0 = X + 68

Dany is so happy to be alive, so graced by the sun, that an hour passes before she thinks to look at the intersection. From a city block away, she can read the street names painted on the sign, can see the least flaw in the lines of paint.

She's never been here before, can't say what city she's in.

Still, glancing at the names on the street signs, she feels that familiar tickle of recollection – and yes, she knows she's seen those street names before – but instead of pulling up an image from the archive, a map, there is a long whirring moment that should be followed by a click, but isn't. In place of razor-sharp memory, there is déjà vu.

And then it's déjà done. The memory gone. Zeroed out.

It's as if a door has begun to close – on the vault of memory, taking who she is with it – and for the life of her, she can't remember if there is a key.

| CHAPTER X = 0

For the first time in her life, the girl isn't remembering. She's not remembering *what* she is. She's not remembering *who* she is. She's lost. She's standing there, lost, staring at lines on a street sign. And that's when she hears it.

The sound is distant at first, but grows louder.

The rickety wheels of a grocery cart on asphalt, a familiar rough rattle.

She's heard the cart over and over this last year. Soon, she knows, a woman with a familiar face will wheel her way around a blind corner. Maybe there will be a doll propped up in the child's seat of woman's cart – one with hair as wild as a little girl she once knew. And in the woman's cart, maybe there'll be photographs, little keepsakes, half-remembered from a lifetime ago, from childhood.

She'll see the cart, and in it, she'll see the history of two little girls, told in whatnots and bric-a-brac. A bauble-eyed bear won at a fair. A tiny house made out of Popsicle sticks. A tiny silver case that holds two locks of baby hair, and a handful of Tic Tac–sized teeth.

The woman will walk towards her, and to a stranger, it might look like the woman's spine is a fossil, as if she is a clockwork doll, like she's the Tin Woodman, joints weathered and rusted up. But the girl knows that isn't true.

The girl knows something else too.

When she sees the woman – this time, she won't run.

She looks up, and the sun on her face is good. The rattling draws close, and she tilts her head, listens. Then, all at once, she's crying. But these tears are different than any she has ever known. These are tears of a different kind, made of entirely different stuff. They even taste different. These tears are clean and wet and as warm on her face as the sun. She pictures an old bottle of pills, but she can't make out the letters, and she turns to face the woman with the shopping cart and –

"Hello," the girl says. "Hello."

ACKNOWLEDGEMENTS

Thank you to everyone at Buckrider Books: to Paul Vermeersch for *really* getting the book, for helping me see it through to its final form and creating the awesome space of possibility that is Buckrider Books; to Noelle Allen for being so incredibly supportive of Wolsak & Wynn authors and doing the hard work that allows books to be made and read. Thank you to Ashley Hisson for copy edits and all else; Michel Vrana for cover design; Jennifer Rawlinson for interior design; sales & marketing; and everyone at Wolsak & Wynn.

My immense gratitude to the Canada Council for the Arts and to the BC Arts Council – whose support of early drafts of this novel gave me the gift of time. Thank you to Banff, for offering me a self-directed residency (and a space in which I could really focus) and the Capilano University PD committee (for supporting that residency).

Threefold gratitude: to Wayde Compton (who read many drafts and parented as I wrote); to Senna Compton (for her huge heart and her inimitable art practice); and to Hiromi Goto (for the kind of brilliant editorial feedback that has made me a better writer). Gratitude to my families for love and stories. For child care, too, thank you to Ruth & Ross Stone, Alisha Hyrb, Pat & Levi Compton.

My heartfelt gratitude to Erin Soros, who did a sensitivity read of the book, and whose deep and thoughtful response helped me see the work anew (all flaws my own). Gratitude to Harry Karlinsky, whose advice and feedback on early drafts were not only empathetic and deeply informed, but so very generous. His insights made me ask the kinds of questions I could not have otherwise. Gratitude, too, to Harry's colleagues at the Lucid Book Club – members of UBC's psychiatric department – who spent their time and intelligence on an early draft, and Robin Evans, who shaped this session with great intelligence and care (once more, all flaws my own).

Many people have been generous over the years. Thank you to everyone who has read drafts, speculated on the world-building alongside me, loaned this novel an empathic eye, asked hard questions, shared knowledge with me about everything from brain chemistry to apocalyptic tropes to epidemiology to French idiom and grammar; who supported my writing, made space in the community, thought through titles with me; and of course, thank you to those who have been willing to get thoroughly drenched in cold rain while touring me around a real-life version of a book setting. Gratitude for the above and more to David Chariandy, Kevin Chong, Michelle Siobhan Cyca, Charles Demers, Daniel Demers, Ryan Knighton, Leanna McLennan, Mike O'Connor, Emily Pohl-Weary, Caroline Purchase, Melanie Fahlman Reid, Renee Rodin, my many colleagues at Capilano University and the larger writing community whose conversations about writing are a gift.

Books are born of reading, and I owe necessary debts to more books and writers than could ever be listed. In particular, I'd like to acknowledge the following borrowed words & phrases: Vincent Racaniello's virology blog describes viruses as "completely at the mercy of their environment" – a phrase I've loaned to Jasper Okello in this novel; the phrase "Character is destiny" appears in George Eliot's *The Mill on the Floss* and, as Alberto Moreiras points out, is likely derived from Heraclitus; Frank Baum authored the lines borrowed from *The Wizard of Oz*; Frantz

Fanon, in *The Wretched of the Earth,* wrote, "When we revolt it's not for a particular culture. We revolt simply because, for many reasons, we can no longer breathe"; Kara Roanhorse's ongoing work on the concept of the "Indigenous multiverse," gleaned only via a conference program, is the source of a too small to be legible quote on a T-shirt worn by a student at Dany's school; and finally, Diane Ackerman's *A Natural History of the Senses* is the book Dany's mom must have read to know about crickets. There are other nodes of intertextuality, of course, peppered throughout – tiny gestures to some of the books I love most.

Anne Stone is the author of three previous novels, *Delible* (2007), *Hush* (1999) and *jacks: a gothic gospel* (1998). She is currently at work on a collection of short fiction. She spent her childhood in Toronto, lived in Montreal and now makes her home in Vancouver, where she teaches Creative Writing and Literature at Capilano University.